# Perfect
# Match

# Books by Fern Michaels

Perfect Match
A Family Affair
Forget Me Not
The Blossom Sisters
Balancing Act
Tuesday's Child
Betrayal
Southern Comfort
To Taste the Wine
Sins of the Flesh
Sins of Omission
Return to Sender
Mr. and Miss Anonymous
Up Close and Personal
Fool Me Once
Picture Perfect
About Face
The Future Scrolls
Kentucky Sunrise
Kentucky Heat
Kentucky Rich
Plain Jane
Charming Lily
What You Wish For
The Guest List
Listen to Your Heart
Celebration
Yesterday

Finders Keepers
Annie's Rainbow
Sara's Song
Vegas Sunrise
Vegas Heat
Vegas Rich
Whitefire
Wish List
Dear Emily
Christmas at
   Timberwoods

## The Sisterhood Novels:

Eyes Only
Kiss and Tell
Blindsided
Gotcha!
Home Free
Déjà Vu
Cross Roads
Game Over
Deadly Deals
Vanishing Act
Razor Sharp
Under the Radar
Final Justice
Collateral Damage

Fast Track
Hokus Pokus
Hide and Seek
Free Fall
Lethal Justice
Sweet Revenge
The Jury
Vendetta
Payback
Weekend Warriors

**The Godmothers Series:**

Classified
Breaking News
Deadline
Late Edition
Exclusive
The Scoop

**E-Book Exclusives:**

Desperate Measures
Seasons of Her Life
To Have and to Hold
Take Down
Countdown
Upside Down
Serendipity
Captive Innocence

Captive Embraces
Captive Passions
Captive Secrets
Captive Splendors
Cinders to Satin
For All Their Lives
Fancy Dancer
Texas Heat
Texas Rich
Texas Fury
Texas Sunrise

**Anthologies:**

When the Snow Falls
Secret Santa
A Winter Wonderland
I'll Be Home for
   Christmas
Making Spirits Bright
Holiday Magic
Snow Angels
Silver Bells
Comfort and Joy
Sugar and Spice
Let It Snow
A Gift of Joy
Five Golden Rings
Deck the Halls
Jingle All the Way

**This Large Print Book carries the
Seal of Approval of N.A.V.H**

# FERN
# MICHAELS

*Perfect*
*Match*

KENSINGTON PUBLISHING CORP.

**Doubleday Large Print Home Library Edition**

I'd like to dedicate this book to Corinda Carfora, the composer of "What Was I Thinking," and to Henry Neunsinger, who really is the best hairstylist in the world as well as the best interior decorator. And to BFFs Terry Egger, Wayne Arnold, and Steve Wise. You're the best. Thank you all for being in my life and making it so enjoyable.

Fern

# Perfect Match

# Prologue

Beth Masters stood in her kitchen, staring out at her backyard, which was alive with flowers every color of the rainbow as well as beautiful fall foliage. Autumn had always been her favorite time of year.

She felt sad that she was going to be leaving her perfect little house on a tree-lined street in Garden Grove, a house that had been her home for the past five years, ever since the day she'd graduated from Clemson University, actually. The house was a gift from her brother, older by two years, for her outstanding academic achievement during her four-year stint at college.

Her beloved older brother, Jake Masters, had been an NFL superstar. But not now. These days, Jake Masters was in a wheelchair thanks to an injury sustained during the fourth quarter of the Super Bowl, three years ago.

Beth, known as Beezer to her older

brother, was even sadder that she would be leaving Jake. Not that Jake needed her—he didn't. And that was part of the problem. He had his longtime trainer, Moose, to see to his every need. Maybe that was what was bothering her. Jake didn't need her; that was the bottom line. He'd done so much for her over the years, and just when she needed…no, wanted to try to pay him back, he closed up shop and pretty much told her to stay out of his crippled life. The really awful part of all that was she'd actually listened to him and stayed away.

Beth swiped at the tears that were puddling in her eyes. She should have told Jake months ago that she was leaving. If not in person, then either by e-mail or a letter. She'd kept putting it off, and now she was out of time.

Beth walked around, looking at everything in her house. Her life, all thanks to Jake. She picked up a sorry-looking piece of pottery in her family room. Jake had backed her when she thought she would be the world's next stellar potter. It hadn't happened. Money, Jake's money, down the drain. She moved on and picked up a beer stein. That hadn't exactly worked out either. The world wasn't ready for a female brew-meister. More of Jake's money down the drain.

And on and on it went, the evidence of all of her failures, all of Jake's wasted money as she made her last, lonely walk through the house, which brought her to the foyer and the front door. But today she had a check for Jake, for all his wasted dollars.

Beth started to cry again when she thought about how successful she was now, and she'd done it on her own, with just her computer and a lot of guts. No real money invested, either. She'd done it as a lark, but before she knew what was happening, she was making so much money she couldn't count it fast enough. So many times she'd wanted to share it all with Jake, but he always sloughed her off because he had his own pity party going on.

The greatest NFL player of all time wouldn't be blowing her off today. Not today. In just a little while, she was going to drive the ten miles to where Jake lived in a fortress of his own making, or, as she thought of it, where he hid out from the world, and that included her. Not today, buddy. More tears leaked out of her eyes.

Beth looked at her watch. A frown started to build on her face just as she heard the key in the lock. Okaaayyy. She ran to the door and fell into Gracie Sweet's arms. Gracie was her best friend in the whole world and her business partner. Gracie was so smart, it was sinful. Unlike Beth, who was dumb as dirt according to Jake Masters.

And yet here she was, a multimillionaire, as was Gracie. And they'd done it on their own, with no help from anyone.

Gracie Sweet was a ball of fire. She had a Shirley Temple mop of russet-colored curls and a face full of freckles. She had a reckless smile that showed off teeth that were more beautiful than rare pearls. She had summer blue eyes that Beth swore could see into a person's soul. She was tall, and not exactly lanky but close to it. And yet she looked good in anything she wore, which was mostly jeans and T-shirts with clever sayings emblazoned on the backs.

"I see you've been crying, Beth. What's up with that? You know it's okay to change your mind if that's what you want to do." Gracie's voice was gentle yet firm.

"Are you out of your mind, Gracie? I can't deprive the world of the next greatest country-western singer to hit the billboards. Read my lips. I-am-going-to-Nashville!"

"One more time, Beth. You can't sing. You can't even carry a tune."

"That doesn't matter. The machines do it all for you. I've got the looks, the personality, the body, and the stamina to make it work. They won't even notice I can't sing. Besides, I'm going to take lessons. I have it all worked out. John is going to join me in two weeks. By the time he gets there, we'll be ready to take on Nashville like it's never been taken on. By storm. You watch!"

"You can't sing."

"I do wish you'd stop saying that. I'm working on that end of it. You need to be more optimistic, Gracie."

"And you need to be more realistic, Beth," Gracie snapped.

"I was meant to do this. It's in me. I just have to make it happen. I promise you, I am going to make it happen."

For some strange, ungodly reason that she couldn't define, Gracie believed her friend implicitly.

"Okay, now that we've settled all of that, do you have the plan down pat?"

Gracie grimaced. "I do. I can recite it in my sleep. I know exactly what to do, when to do it, and how to do it. I start the wheels in motion one month from today."

"Good. That's good. In a month's time, Jake will be pulling his hair out by the roots and begging you to help him when you show up on his doorstep. From there on in, it's your gig. I know that if anyone can make it happen, it's you.

"I guess we should say our good-byes here, okay? Let's not cry." Beth sobbed as she gathered Gracie in her arms, who was sobbing harder than she was.

Ten minutes later, both young women

were dry eyed, with Beth shouting over her shoulder about watering the flowers and to only use Old English on the furniture and a host of other things. She stopped in midsentence when Gracie slammed the door shut.

Gracie would take care of her house, she had no doubt. That worry was behind her now. Now she had to beard the lion. Maybe **wolf** was a better word. On the other hand, maybe Jake would act like her big brother, the brother she loved heart and soul. This time, her gut told her hope would **not** spring eternal.

Beth climbed behind the wheel of her Jeep Cherokee and started the engine. The Jeep was packed to the max with all her personal possessions, things she couldn't bear to leave behind. She wished she felt light of heart as she started the ten-mile drive to her brother's hidden fortress. That would come later, she thought, after she had left Jake behind.

The drive to the outskirts of Garden Grove, a small, private community between Charleston and Columbia, South Carolina, was uneventful. Beth arrived and parked in the driveway. She got out her cell and sent off a text to Moose since Jake never responded to her. It was simple. **I'm in the driveway. I need to see Jake**.

The returning text was almost instantaneous. **Jake isn't up to seeing anyone today, Beezer.**

Beth returned the text. **Then I will climb the fence. You know I will, so open the damn gate and let me in. Or I might decide to smash it and drive straight through. Make it easy on yourself. I'm not going away.**

There was no return text. Instead, the gate swung open. Beth was through it in a nanosecond. When she arrived at the front of the house, Moose was already on the steps of the veranda, waiting for her.

Beth hopped out of the car.

Moose looked at the loaded Cherokee. "You going somewhere, Beezer?"

"Yeah. I came to say good-bye to that no-account brother of mine. Don't try to stop me, Moose. Where is he?"

"Where you going?"

"None of your damn business. Now where is he?"

"Out on the back deck."

Beth took off, sprinting around the side of the house to the deck, which was half in the shade and half in the sun. She stopped short and stared at her handsome brother until a giant lump formed in her throat.

"Hey!"

Jake Masters turned around and stared at his beautiful sister. "Hey!"

Beth walked around Jake's chair and perched on a wooden coffee table littered with sports magazines.

"I'm not in the mood for visitors, Beezer. You should have called ahead."

"I'm not exactly in the mood for visitors either, Jake. I've been calling ahead for three years now, and you never call me back, so what's the point?" Beth said, noticing Moose hovering by the French doors, listening to everything they said. Ever the protector.

"Then what the hell are you doing here?" Jake snapped.

Beth almost lost it then and screamed

at him, but she remembered the promise she made to herself not to lose her cool and not to cry. She sucked in a deep breath. "I came here for three reasons. One, to thank you for all you've done for me. Two, to pay you back. Three, to say good-bye."

The good-bye was what got his interest. She could tell.

"You going somewhere?" Did she sense anxiety suddenly in his voice?

"Yeah. Yeah, I am. The Jeep is all packed up and parked in front. Couldn't leave without telling my big brother good-bye even if he is an ass. Here," she said, holding out a small manila envelope to him. He reached for it.

Jake slit the envelope and pulled out a check made out to him in the amount of $887,433.11. His eyes popped wide. "What's this for, and where did you get this kind of money?"

"I told you, it's payback for all you did for me." Beth tossed a black-and-white marble notebook onto the table. "It's all in there, right to the penny. I kept track, Jake. We're square now unless you want the house back. I can deed it back to you. I wasn't sure what you would want to do about it."

Jake felt his insides start to crumble. This all sounded so serious, so...so **final**.

"The house was a gift. Why would I want it back?" he asked gruffly.

"I don't know why, Jake. I don't know anything about you anymore. You cut me off."

"This hasn't been easy for me, Beezer. In case you haven't noticed, I'm crippled and in a wheelchair."

"Oh, I noticed. I want you to stop calling me Beezer. I also know that your surgeons told you that another operation could do the trick, but you said no and took your marbles and went home and settled into that chair. You're a quitter, Jake. I never thought I'd say that to you, but you are, you...Oh, what's the point? You never listened to me in your life, and you aren't going to start now." In preparation for leaving, Beth got up and slung her purse, which was so large that it could have doubled as a weekend bag, over her slim shoulder.

"Wait just a damn minute here. I've called you Beezer from the day you were born because Mom said I couldn't say Bethany. If you went through what I went through, you'd quit, too. Fifty-fifty isn't good enough—that's what the surgeons said. Where the hell are you going and where did you get this money?" Jake barked, his stomach churning like a windmill.

"I should have said I came here for four things instead of three. I'm turning over my business to you, and God help you if you run it into the ground. If you do, I will come back here and cut your balls off. I started a matchmaking service three years ago, and it is now a multimilliondollar business. I did it on my own, with no backing. Me. I did it. This," she said, pulling a thick padded envelope out of her bag, "is all you need, plus your computer, to keep the company running. And guess what, big brother? You can do it in a wheelchair. I am going to Nashville to become the world's next country-western singer, to answer your last question."

Whatever Jake was expecting to hear, this wasn't it. He felt like he had just dropped through the rabbit hole. "Beezer, you can't sing," he blurted, his eyes on the check in his hands.

"I'm getting a little sick and tired of hearing what I can and can't do. Did you know you could play football back in the day? You had to jump through hoops, tryouts, the whole nine yards. Yeah, yeah, I've heard you say a thousand times you were born to play football. How's that working for you now, Jake? Where's your backup? You tried, why can't I?"

Beth could feel her eyes start to burn. **I will not cry. I will not. I absolutely will not cry.** "Yes, I failed at all those things you helped me with. I admit that. I was trying to find my way. Do I have regrets? Hell, yes, a ton of them, but that isn't going to stop me from doing what I know I was meant to do, what I was afraid to do until now. That's the best defense I'm prepared to offer at this time. And, I just paid you back, so we're square. Plus I gave you a bonus. My business. See ya, Jake."

"Beezer, wait!" Jake said through clenched teeth. "I wasn't judging you."

"Yeah, you were, you always judged me, and I always came up short in your eyes. Enough with the bullshit, Jake. I've had it with you and your poor-me attitude. You should be glad you're alive. And all that money you won in the court case, what was it I read, seventy-five million? Not too shabby, big brother. I guess the next question should be What's a cripple like you going to do with seventy-five million plus all those other megamillions you earned along the way, with your salary and those endorsements? Figure it out, Jake. Go for the operation and stop being such a pussy." Beth hated the words she'd just spewed, but she had to say them in the hopes she'd make her brother mad enough to do **something** besides vegetate in the wheelchair he was sitting in.

Beth moved then, past the chair, and was off the deck, calling over her shoulder, "I always looked up to you, Jake. Always. Not anymore. And that goes for you too, Moose. You suck, both of you," she bellowed as she sprinted around the side of the house and out to the Cherokee. She held the tears in check until she was inside the Jeep and down the long driveway that led to the main road. And then they spilled from her eyes like a waterfall. She turned on the windshield wipers, but they didn't help. Not one little bit. As she sobbed her heart out, she knew she'd just left part of herself back on her brother's deck.

Back on the deck, Jake looked up at Moose Dennison, who was holding out a cup of coffee to his boss. Jake's eyes were suspiciously moist. He had to clear his throat twice before he could get the words out. "She can't sing, Moose."

"You didn't know your ass from your elbow the first time you hit the football field either, Jake." With that, Moose marched back in the house. When he was certain he was out of his boss's line of sight, his fist shot in the air. **Atta girl, Beezer. Go for it!**

# Chapter One

**One month later**

Gracie Sweet looked around at what she and Beth Masters had called their lair, their working environment. Or the professional, politically correct phrase—their office. It looked like an office, and yet it didn't look like an office at all. Together, she and Beth, along with a young architect, had worked overtime to make the long room that ran the entire length of the house work friendly. Both of them always looked forward to starting work at eight each morning.

One entire wall was a row of French doors that led out onto a tiered deck that was full of pots of flowers and hanging ferns. It also offered a view of the backyard, awash with flowers and healthy shrubs. The opposite wall held an exotic fish tank with one-of-a-kind tropical fish that both of them doted on. They'd named them Larry, Moe, and Curly after the Three

Stooges. In truth, they had no idea whether the fish were male or female.

The two end walls were covered with paintings by local artists, and each painting had its own story. In the middle of the room, two long, custom-made desks sat back-toback so that the two women could converse with each other while they worked. Each desk contained five computers. At the end of each desk were four printers, which had each been replaced three times because of the heavy usage.

Because they both liked music, surround sound had been one of the first things both women had insisted on when they began making the conversion from household living space to work space.

The long, spacious room had two alcoves that allowed for a tiny kitchen with a table, two chairs, a microwave, a toaster oven, and a refrigerator. The opposite alcove was a small lavatory.

Gracie sat down at her workstation and turned on all the computers. She looked around as they booted up. She felt sad, just as sad as she'd been every day since Beth had left a month ago. She dreaded what was to come and didn't know if she could really pull it off or not, but she'd promised Beth she'd do her best. If her best turned out not to be good enough, she would simply fall back and regroup. Beth was just a phone call away.

Gracie reached down into one of the deep drawers and pulled out a bright yellow folder that said **Jake Masters** on the cover. Beth's dossier on her brother. She'd read it before. In fact, she had pretty much memorized the contents. The pictures of the virile Jake burned into her brain. Before pictures. There were no after pictures, of Jake in his wheelchair. There were even some pictures of Moose Dennison, Jake's old trainer, who was also his mentor, his best friend, and his houseman. Beth had said earlier to make a friend of Moose, and she would be in like Flynn. Whatever the hell that meant.

Gracie smiled when she saw the home page on the computer. Perfect Match. And then a picture of a man's hand clasping a woman's hand. She hit the key that would

take her to the in-box to check the overnight mail. As always, there were hundreds
of e-mails that required a response. She'd
get to them before bedtime even if it took
her till the middle of the night. It was
Beth's Rule Number One. All e-mails were
answered the day they came in. That alone,
Gracie knew, was the main reason Perfect
Match was so successful.

Gracie moved then from the e-mails to
the satellite offices and checked in one
by one. As was her daily custom, she
hit New York first since they were in the
same time zone, then Chicago, Texas,
and lastly, California. She quickly scanned
the overnight reports and was satisfied
that there were no blips that required her
attention.

Gracie bit down on her lower lip and
dreaded hitting the key that would take
her to the site that Jake Masters was
supposed to be working on. No activity.
She hadn't expected anything less. Well,
today was the day she was going to shake
up Mr. Jake Masters's world. If she hadn't
been working behind the scenes here at

Beth's house and taking care of business unbeknownst to Jake Masters, the thriving matchmaking service they'd slaved over would be halfway down the drain.

She played back the conversation she'd had with Beth last night and winced at her partner's tirade against her brother. If it were up to Gracie, she would have told Jake Masters where to get off from the git-go. If there was one thing Gracie Sweet couldn't stand, it was a person who wasn't motivated by at least **something.** Otherwise, why bother getting up in the morning?

Gracie stood up and walked over to the printer, where a copy of an ad she'd run on the Internet for all of ninety seconds was sitting. Just long enough for her to print it out so she had a bona fide reason to show up at Jake Masters's door. She stuck it in her briefcase, along with a doctored up résumé that said she'd worked as an assistant to the owner of another matchmaking company and had oodles of experience. The reason for leaving was because the company was being sold, and the new manager was going to do her job himself with the help of his girlfriend, and thus eliminate her robust $210,000 annual salary plus health benefits, sick pay, and vacation pay that added another $25,000 to her total compensation package.

If Jake Masters decided to verify her résumé—which Beth said he would not do—but if he did, it would all check out, thanks to having friends in high places.

Gracie didn't bother turning anything off because she knew she would be back in a few hours. Today's mission was, as Beth put it, to get Jake riled up enough that he would join the land of the living. Gracie wasn't so sure, but she was game if it would help Beth.

Gracie took a last look at herself in the mirror hanging on the bathroom door. She looked good, just the way the magazines said a woman who was applying for a job should look. Her hair was neat, her makeup perfect, she smelled good, and her Armani suit fit like it was made for her tall, lanky form. The clear-lens glasses she would put on to complete her professional look were in her pocket.

Time to go. She looked over at the massive dog that was her constant companion. "You have to stay behind, Giz. I won't be long." The big dog looked up at her and barked. Then he lowered himself and wiggled under her desk. "You know what to do if anyone breaks in. You go for the **jools,** and you hold on till I get home." Gizmo barked again, and Gracie giggled.

Muttering to herself, Gracie marched out of the house to the driveway, where her bright red Jeep Cherokee waited. She and Beth had bought the Jeeps at the same time so they would get a good deal. Beth was frugal, but then so was Gracie. They both loved bargains. They were so much alike it was almost scary.

As she drove to Jake Masters's house, she recalled the conversation she'd had last night with Beth. Beth had told her she'd called Moose and left a message saying that Gracie would be arriving at ten o'clock and to have the gate open, at which point she'd turned off her phone so that neither Moose nor her brother could say no to the meeting.

Gracie knew she was going in cold. Would she get tossed out on her ear? She had no clue. If so, it wouldn't be for lack of trying. The part she hated about all of this was that her life was changing, and if there was one thing in life Gracie Sweet hated, it was change of any kind. Beth was just the opposite, and that was why they got on so well and made the business work. Jake Masters was a whole other story. And yet Beth had such faith in her, Gracie simply could not let her down.

She looked at the speedometer. She was only going forty-five miles an hour, and the speed limit was fifty-five. She pressed the gas pedal, hating herself for doing it. Still, a professional such as herself would arrive on time for an interview. She started talking to herself the way she always did when she was stressed, and today, she was stressed to the max.

No one was more surprised than Gracie when she pulled into Jake Masters's driveway to find the gates standing wide open. She sailed through and parked right in front of the house. There were three steps that led up to what she supposed was a porch of sorts. She looked around before she rang the doorbell. Nice digs. Some heavy-duty money went into this place, she decided. The gardener alone probably cost a fortune. She recalled Beth saying the house sat on five acres, and all of it was manicured. She tried to remember what else Beth had told her. Twelve thousand square feet. Pool, tennis court, a home football field where Jake and his buddies used to wrestle up games on the weekends. A home theater, where he had an extensive library of thousands of videotaped football games.

Gracie rang the bell and took a deep breath.

The solid mahogany door opened. A skinny, squirrelylooking man wearing a baseball cap looked at her like she was a bug on a stick.

"I'm Grace Sweet. My friends call me Gracie. I'm here to...I'm not sure, report for work or be interviewed by someone named Jake Masters. Miss Beth Masters hired me to manage a matchmaking service that supposedly is being operated on these premises." She waited. When the scraggly-looking man just stared at her, she snapped. "Well, do I come in or do I leave? Good manners dictate you make some kind of comment about now."

Moose stepped aside and said out of the corner of his mouth, "Well, you're here, so you might as well come in."

**This was not going to be a walk in the park,** Gracie decided as she followed Moose Dennison down a hall, through a trophy room, and into another room that looked like a rat's nest of an office. Jake Masters sat behind a glasstopped desk that was littered with what looked like nothing other than junk. She recognized him immediately, and decided that Beth was right—he was one good-looking hunk. Dark, curly hair, eyes the color of a summer sky, and he was tanned—in November, which told her he must have a tanning bed someplace in this monstrosity of a house.

Moose cleared his throat. "Lady to see you, boss. Says your sister hired her, and she is your new assistant."

"Here's my résumé in case you don't already have it. Also a copy of the ad I responded to. I interviewed twice with Miss Masters, and she hired me after the second interview. She said the salary is two hundred and fifty thousand a year plus a generous health-care package."

"I really don't need an assistant, Miss... Sweet, is it?"

**Definitely not a walk in the park.** "Well, your sister, Miss Masters, said you did. She also said in the month since she turned over her business to you that you have not followed through. Ergo, here I am to do what you were supposed to do. How could you allow a multimillion-dollar business to stagnate like that?"

"I'm...I'm trying to get a feel for it," Jake blustered.

"And...how's that working for you?" Gracie snapped.

"There is no...**and**. My sister just dumped this on me and left. I don't know the first thing about matchmaking. I'm a football player. **Was** a football player," he corrected his statement.

"And…" Gracie said again.

"I'm working on it. Rome wasn't built in a day. I do not need an assistant."

"No, but fortunes are. Built in a day, that is. Just check out Wall Street on any given day, Mr. Masters. Miss Masters told me how hard she worked to make her company the thriving business it is today. A month of…of…nothing does not bode well. I worked for another matchmaking service," Gracie said, pointing to her résumé on the desk, "and I know what a dormant month can do. Your sister said you would do this."

"My sister said that?" Jake asked, his eyes spewing sparks.

"Among other things," Gracie shot back. **Very definitely not a walk in the park.**

"What other things?" Masters demanded.

Gracie squared her shoulders. "Look, Mr. Masters, I didn't come here to get involved in a situation between a brother and a sister. You two need to work that out between yourselves. I came here to do a job. I answered an ad on the Internet, your sister hired me, everything is in place, but now it doesn't look like that's all going to work out. Jobs that pay the kind of money I earn are not all that easy to come by. So, having said that, I guess I will have to sue you."

"Sue me! For what?" Jake bellowed.

"Discrimination, that's what. I'm a woman. You had a whole month to keep the company running, and all you can tell me is Rome wasn't built in a day. That doesn't work for me." Now Gracie's dander was up. She sucked in her breath and narrowed her eyes.

Moose wiggled his eyebrows at his boss, who didn't seem to notice, a signal to back off and leave well enough alone.

"What else did my sister tell you?"

"Probably nothing she didn't say to you herself. Miss Masters seemed pretty open and aboveboard to me, very much unlike you. But if you really want to know, she said you were a king-sized pain in the ass and not to pay any attention to what you say because you are so full of yourself it is a sin. She said you're a lazy laggard who has daily pity parties and in general you are a whiny puke. Now, those are her words, not mine. But I can see how they could turn into my own thoughts over time.

"She also said this room was depressing, smelly, and ugly. She's right. You need curtains in here. You need color on the walls. You need to get rid of this ugly carpet, which smells, and get a desk that has some spit to it. You need some plants to suck up that negative oxygen you expel. And some fresh flowers. Soothing music and maybe a fish tank."

Jake Masters was so speechless with indignation his face turned red under his tan. Moose Dennison excused himself so he could laugh out loud without being heard.

Jake finally found his tongue. "You can't sue me. I don't own this company. I am not in the matchmaking business."

"You wanna bet!" Gracie said, stuffing her résumé and the copy of the Internet ad into her shoulder bag. "And you just lied to me, Mr. Masters. Miss Masters, your sister, told me she did it all legally, and the company is yours until she says otherwise.

I took that to mean until she finishes whatever it is she's doing in Nashville. You have a nice day now."

If Gracie Sweet had a fault, it was that she always wanted to have the last word. She leaned across the desk and said, "Your sister is such a nice professional person, considerate, hardworking, and courteous. You are nothing like her. Nothing!" she said, raising her voice. "You must really hate your sister to let a whole month go by doing nothing to help her. What an ungrateful person you are. Actually, I think you are a **hateful** ungrateful person to do what you're doing. Look forward to hearing from my attorney, Mr. Masters."

Moose Dennison knew when to step in. "Coffee anyone?" he said cheerfully. He swept a pile of junk off the corner of the desk and set down a plastic tray with three cups of black coffee on it.

"Now, why don't you two make nice and start all over? I'll moderate the conversation, so things don't get out of hand. Jake here has a problem when it comes to his...domain. He doesn't like change. He's new to the matchmaking business, but he is trying to learn. And he's the first to admit he needs help. He just doesn't know how to ask for it. How am I doing so far, young lady? You willing to listen to this lout's apology and start over? I mean, you are here and all."

"Well..." **This is so not a walk in the park.** The word **lout** worked for her. Beth was going to go nuclear when she reported in. "I have no interest in continuing this... I don't even know if we can call it an inter-view unless Mr. Masters agrees that I have the job. So, do I or don't I?" Gracie said, leaning so close over the desk she could smell Jake's minty breath.

Jake clenched his teeth. "It would appear that you and my sister have me over a barrel. Okay, but no curtains," he said, looking at the heavy velvet draperies, which were closed.

"Now you see, Mr. Masters, that's a game changer for me. I happen to love curtains. They so make a room. I like to work in a cheerful atmosphere, and there is nothing cheerful about this ugly room. All it needs is a suit of armor, and you could call it a dungeon. Or it could easily double as a funeral home if you haul in a dead body. Are we clear on the curtains? Dotted Swiss."

"We're clear on the curtains," Moose said. Damn, he had to get out of there before he split a gut.

It was all Jake could do to nod. Then he wheeled himself as fast as he could out of the room.

Gracie set her coffee cup back on the tray and winked at Moose, who got so flustered he dropped his cup, spilling coffee all over the floor. "Not to worry; this carpet is going," she said. "Since you seem to be...um...in charge, I can have someone here later this morning, noonish, and  this room will be good to go in forty-eight hours. Today is Monday. I will report for work Friday morning at nine o'clock. I leave at six. I do not punch a time clock. My hours are my own. I often work at home at night. I expect a nutritious lunch that your boss is to provide. I will handle all the banking. That's part of my job. I believe in transparency all the way around.

Are we clear on that, Mr. Moose?"

Moose nodded, thinking, **What planet is this woman from?**

"Oh, there is one other little, teeny-weeny thing I forgot to mention," Gracie said as she screwed her face up into a grimace.

"And what would that other little, teeny-weeny thing you forgot to mention be?"

"My dog. Where I go, he goes. He's fully trained. In many ways. Gizmo will rip your throat out if you raise your voice to me. He will kill you if you lay a hand on me. That's why we will be putting surround sound in this room. He likes soothing music. He's really an angel. I guess you could say he's protective. I just love him to death. Oh, and he doesn't like people sneaking up on him, so you and Mr. Masters are going to have to wear a bell or have a bell on your person so he knows you're coming. Once you get to know him, you will love him as I do. I guess we should say good-bye for now, Mr. Moose. I also want to thank you for your timely intervention. I so do not want to disappoint Miss Masters. She's been most kind to me. Such a lovely person. You just stay right where you are, Mr. Moose. I can see myself out. My people will be here shortly to take measurements and will be back at seven tomorrow morning, so be sure the gate is open. Nice meeting you," Gracie called over her shoulder.

When the door closed behind Gracie Sweet, Moose let himself drop to the floor. He could hardly wait to tell Jake he was going to have to wear a bell around his neck. He guessed he'd have to go on eBay and order them. He cackled so loud he went into a spasm of coughing as he fought to get his breath. Things were certainly looking up around here. Then he rolled across the floor as another wave of laughter overtook him.

"Nice going, Beezer," he gurgled.

## Chapter Two

Jake Masters's doorbell rang ninety minutes after Gracie Sweet left the house.

Jake looked up at Moose, who was slapping chunks of pastrami on rye bread, then lathering it with eye-watering horseradish —Jake's favorite sandwich.

"Better get that, Moose. Must be that person's work detail. I can't wait to see how this goes. I've already sent Beezer nine texts, and she's ignoring me. Maybe you should try, since she's so pissed at me. The first thing you tell her is I am not wearing any goddamn bell around my neck. If you want to wear one, be my guest."

"Do your own dirty work, Jake. Besides, it's too late; I already ordered two pure silver bells whose tone is also pure, the sound crystal clear. I'm not about to cross that young woman. Remember her dog. If she says we wear bells, then we wear bells," Moose growled as he stomped through the house to the front door.

Moose took in a big gulp of air and swung the door wide to see a big man staring down at him.

"Henry Neunsinger," the big man in the ball cap and ponytail said, holding out a business card. "My two associates, Terry Egger and Wayne Arnold."

Moose gaped at the colorful business card, and commented, "It says you are a hairstylist." With a perplexed expression on his face, he looked at the big man.

Neunsinger sighed. "Turn the card over."

"It says you are also an interior decorator. You have two jobs!"

"I don't consider them jobs, I consider them professions. I style hair three days a week and I design and decorate three days a week. My client, Grace Sweet, hired me. We need to be clear on something right from the start. Even though Miss Sweet hired me, she said Mr. Jake Masters would be paying the bill. I require half of my fee up front when the contract is signed and the balance on completion. It's my understanding that the job has to be completed in forty-eight hours. Is that your understanding? And you are...?"

"Moose Dennison. Well, Mr. Neunsinger, I just work here. You need to speak with my employer to confirm the arrangement you made with Miss Sweet."

Jake appeared from around the corner. His hand shot out. "Jake Masters."

Neunsinger gripped Jake's hand and introduced himself and his associates.

Moose handed the business card to Jake, who looked at it and turned it over. "A man of many talents," he said quietly. He looked the big man over, noted the ponytail and the red ball cap, the flowing Polo T-shirt and the cargo pants. Work attire. "You're from Summerville?"

"Yes," Neunsinger said, his voice and tone matching Jake's. "Been there for a good long time, 117 West 7th North Street, but these days I'm so busy I only take a few select clients. If you're thinking of calling for an appointment, I'm booked through the end of December. Miss Sweet is a client. I'd like to get started. If you have any other questions, we can talk as I work. 'Time is money' is my motto. Just so you know, I do not like to waste my client's money or waste my time. Let's not be so formal— call me Henry." He looked pointedly at Jake's mop of dark curls and itched to take a scissor to them. His gaze traveled to Moose's wild mane of straggly gray hair. which was down to his shoulders, and winced. **That** would take a lot of work.

Jake nodded. Whatever he had expected in the way of fast tracking Sweet's renovations, this was not it. He did understand the "time is money" concept, however. He led the way, the motorized wheelchair whirring softly over the polished floor.

Moose opened the door, and Henry gasped. The two assistants groaned.

"Lights, please," Henry said. Moose obliged. This time there were no gasps, just stupefied expressions on the trio's faces. For the first time in his life, Henry Neunsinger was literally speechless. He walked over to the bank of windows covered with thick burgundy velvet drapes and pulled them aside. A cloud of dust enveloped the room. Everyone started to sneeze and cough, even Jake.

"The last time I saw drapes like this was in a funeral home, and that was twenty years ago," Henry said as he covered a robust sneeze.

"They came with the house," Jake said defensively.

"What about the rest of this...stuff? Do you want to save it or sell it or have it taken to the dump?"

Jake thought about it. He knew when he was beaten. Finally, he just said, "Get rid of it."

The trio walked around, taking notes and mumbling to each other. The one word that both Jake and Moose heard over and over was **disaster.**

Henry, with years of expertise under his belt, sized up the situation in a minute. "Since we are on a tight schedule here, that means we're going to be working around the clock to meet Gracie's deadline. That means we'll be working through the night. You do understand this, right?" Henry said. His tone of voice clearly said he didn't care one way or the other if Jake agreed or not.

"Price," Jake said through clenched teeth. "You said something about half up front and the other half when the job was completed. So how much?"

Henry looked at Terry, who was busy scribbling on her clipboard. She fished a mini calculator out of her pocket and tapped at the keys. She showed the readout to Wayne, who then pulled a contract out of his backpack. Henry was the last to view the readout. "You forgot the travel time to and from." He looked at Jake and Moose and said, "It's customary to feed the crew. If you don't, that means we have to order in, and that takes time and money. That means your total would go from sixty-seven to sixty-eight thousand dollars. Just so you know, I do not negotiate. One other thing—it's entirely possible we will go over the figure I just quoted you. If so, are you okay with that? It's already written into the contract. What that means is I might have to bring in other people to help us finish on schedule."

Jake looked like he was going to pitch

a fit, but Moose clamped his hands firmly on his big shoulders, and said, "We have no problem with that. I'll prepare your food. Am I to assume you want breakfast, lunch, and dinner?"

"You assume correctly." Henry looked down at Jake Masters, who finally got the point and nodded to Moose to write out the check.

Moose was back within minutes with a check he handed over to Henry, who in turn handed it to Terry to put in her briefcase.

Everyone looked at everyone else, until Henry said, "We need to get to work. You can leave now." He was already tapping out a text on his phone, as were Terry and Wayne. There was nothing left for Jake and Moose to do but leave.

When the door closed behind the two men, Henry sat down on the desk chair and looked at his colleagues. "This is a challenge. The only thing this room has going for it is the size and the view out these windows. I know what Gracie likes; I just don't know if we can deliver in forty-eight hours. We may end up going over the price I quoted. I hate when that happens, but the bottom line is I want a pleased client. I don't want her saying 'It's okay, Henry.' I want her to say '**I love this, Henry**!'

"Wayne, this...this ugly carpet has to go. God knows what's under it. Make it work. Call Steve Wise and anyone else you know who can help with the floor. Terry, call Cheryl, tell her the measurements on the windows and to go to the fabric store and get the dotted Swiss and get out here with her sewing machine. Get rid of these drapes ASAP. We'll have to take all the discards ourselves since we can't get a Dumpster here in the time allotted. Donovan has a big pickup—call him. Gracie wants a fish tank, so, Terry, you're in charge of that. Call Handyman Mike to do the painting. Misty Mountain Green is the color I want on the two walls. Gracie is ordering the computers, printers, and faxes. The desk is going to be a problem, but I have some ideas. Wayne, aside from the floor, you are in charge of the plants since you owned your own nursery at one time. I'm going shopping now, so let's get this show on the road and make Gracie happy."

In the kitchen, Moose looked at the sandwiches that were now dried out. He tossed them and started new ones.

"This is a nightmare. I hate this, Moose."

"Yeah, well, suck it up, boss. Of course, you could call Beezer and bail out if you're that upset over the whole thing. Or is it that you're put out that Beezer made it on her own, then walked away from it to follow her dream?"

"She's ignoring me. I didn't know a thing about all she's been doing these past couple of years. I want to strangle her for putting me in this mess. I do not want to be a matchmaker. How could she be so stupid to think I could do this?"

"Don't you have that all ass backward, Jake? You chopped her off at the knees. You just shoved her to the curb and gave up. What was she supposed to do, go crawling to you? She tried that, I have to give her credit. And then that didn't even work, so she finally got wise and said screw it all. You have no one to blame for all of this but yourself, so give it up already."

"Look, you aren't walking in my shoes. Neither is she. Do you have any idea what—"

"Oh, spare me, Jake. I've heard it so many times, I know it all by heart. What's sticking in your craw is your sister called you a whiny puke among other things. She doesn't respect you anymore. That's all gone—you need to realize that. If you want to ever see your sister again, you, my friend, are going to have to do some serious groveling. Read my lips. She-does-not-need-you, Jake! How does it feel?"

"Shut up, Moose," Jake said, taking a bite out of his sandwich. His eyes started to water immediately at the fire-hot horseradish. "I'm sorry, Moose. I didn't mean that. I'm just upset right now."

"Well, as long as you're upset, I might as well tell you that Gracie Sweet forgot to tell you something. She's bringing her dog with her. When she first told me about the dog, I felt like I knew about it somehow, so I Googled the dog. Don't look at me like that. How many dogs do you think there are out there named Gizmo? I only found two. One is deceased, and this one belonged to a soldier. The dog is a combat veteran. His handler was killed in Afghanistan. Gizmo made it home. He even got medals. The only dog in the entire world to get the Medal of Honor. The only dog in the whole world, Jake, and he's going to be here in this house. The handler, a soldier named Alex Samson, was a friend of Gracie Sweet's, and that's how she got the dog. She said the dog was a killer. I thought she was blowing smoke until I read the Google report. Anyway, she's bringing him with her to work. Like every single day."

Jake wondered how many more surprises were coming his way. He wiped at the tears in his eyes, finished chewing what was in his mouth, and looked up at Moose. "It's okay. I like dogs. Off and on, I've thought about getting one but realize the bulk of his care would fall on you, so I just never followed through."

"You could take another crack at surgery, Jake. The docs say there's a good chance you can get out of that chair if you do." He must have said those same words over a thousand times these past few years. Then he wondered why he even bothered. Jake was deaf, dumb, and blind when it came to his physical condition.

"Don't go there, Moose. I've had enough."

"Yeah, me too. Beezer is right—you are a whiny puke." Long years of mentoring and training Jake, plus the fact that he had been Jake's father's best friend, allowed Moose to talk that way to the kid he loved like a son.

Moose blinked at the moisture in his eyes as he started to clean up the mess he'd made. Now he had to think about making dinner. Making dinner. That would be an event. For the past few years, he and Jake ate on the fly, takeout, fast food, a sandwich here or there, maybe some soup. While he considered himself an excellent cook, these past years he hadn't worked at it. Obviously, he needed to resurrect his cookbooks. This now required thought. His first thought was Crock-Pot. Yeah, yeah, just dump everything in it and hope for the best. Somehow or other, he knew the big guy Henry, the boss of the outfit, was a meat loaf and mashed potatoes kind of guy. He decided at that moment that he liked Henry and was going to give some serious thought to getting his hair in shape. Ooops, **styled** was the operative word here. Maybe if he spruced up a bit, he might catch a few looks from Birdie Openhimer the next time he went to play bingo at St. Ann's. Bingo, his one vice. And he always won at least once during the evening. And every time he left his winnings in the poor box before he left the church auditorium. If nothing else, it was a plan. He liked plans, even when they didn't work.

He gave a moment's thought to sending a text to Beezer but decided against it. Beezer had her own plan, and for whatever it was worth, he hoped it would work.

# Chapter Three

Gracie Sweet could barely keep her eyes open. It was well past midnight, and Beth had yet to call. It was unlike her, as she was usually prompt and called at the same time each night, at ten o'clock, to get a business update and bring Gracie up to speed on what was going on in Nashville. Wherever she was, and whatever she was doing, Gracie hoped she was having a good time. Maybe another cup of coffee. She looked at the pot and decided she was too tired to even bother. Gizmo nudged her leg. He knew it was past their bedtime. "We'll give it five more minutes, then we'll hit the sack, Giz."

The 140-pound shepherd looked up at his mistress and tilted his head to the side as though to say "I'm holding you to the five minutes" before he lay down by her feet. She loved the dog almost as much as she had loved his previous owner. Tears pooled in her eyes. **Don't go there,**

**Gracie.** Her cell phone peeled at just that moment. She jacked her voice up a couple of notches, so Beth wouldn't pick up on how tired she was.

"Gracie, I'm so sorry. I was out, and my cell died. I didn't wake you, did I?"

"No. No. I'm wide awake. Well, almost."

"How'd it go? Tell me everything. But first, does Giz miss me? God, I miss that dog!"

"He does miss you. When we're at your house, he looks everywhere for you. Talk to him; I'll put the phone by his ear."

Gracie smiled as she listened to Beth purr sweet ditties into Gizmo's ear. She swore the huge dog grinned at her. He whimpered, then barked his own greeting before Gracie put the phone back to her own ear. "Well, I did it. Your brother was barely hospitable. That guy Moose doesn't say much, but he does a lot of hovering. I sent Henry and his people over to renovate that...that...space. God, Beth, I could never ever work in such a dungeonlike atmosphere. They're still there and will work around the clock.

Henry said it could be done, and you know when Henry says something, you can take it to the bank. He did call to tell me it was the ultimate challenge. Your brother ponied up the deposit and, as far as I know, was okay with it.

"Listen, Beth, if I didn't love you like a sister, I would not be doing this. Your brother resents me. I'm interrupting his life. He does not want to run your company. That is the only thing I'm certain of. When I told him what you called him, I thought he was going to go into orbit. I gave it to him verbatim. I think the **whiny puke** was what got to him. Yeah, yeah, before you can ask, I can make it work."

Beth Masters laughed, a really nice sound to Gracie's ears. "Give Henry my best and remind him he is to do my hair when I hit the Country Music Awards. Notice I did not say **if,** I said **when.**" Beth laughed again.

"Will do. So, any news? What's going on in Nashville?"

"You know, Gracie, I finally found the rhythm and the beat of the city. I know what makes it tick. I've walked hundreds of miles getting the feel of it. I'm comfortable here now. I found a singing teacher. I auditioned for him.

He said I can't sing worth a darn, but we all know that. He said I show promise. He's a has-been here, but he knows everything and everyone worth knowing, and he agreed to take me on. One two-hour lesson every day. I started today, and I really like him. He's a good coach. His wife is sweet, too. He has a studio on his property, all the equipment, blah-blah-blah, and he's not expensive, either. John likes him, too." John Rossmon was Beth's significant other and a kick-ass guitar player with a singing voice that would make Tim McGraw turn green with jealousy, according to Beth, but on that point, Gracie agreed.

"We're finally settled in. The last piece of furniture was delivered today, so we're comfortable now. We almost belong. We're making friends, networking. The bottom line is, Gracie, I'm happy. John is happy. It's going to all work out. I'll still keep checking in nightly and e-mailing if I can't make the call. I meant it when I said if you need me, I'll come back, but only on a temporary basis. We're still okay with that?"

"We're still okay." Gracie loved it that Beth sounded so happy. She wished she could be that happy, to have that lilt in her voice again. Someday. Maybe. Then again, maybe not.

"Did you hear from Fred?" Beth asked.

"I did, and I responded just the way we always do." Fred Fineberg was Beth's first client. A seventy-two-yearold widower who had been lost when his wife passed away. A year after her passing, he turned to the Internet and Beth to find him a companion. It took both Beth and Gracie five months to figure out that Fred wasn't exactly looking for a companion but a lady who could make noodle pudding and potato latkes the way his wife had made them. These days, he and the plump Sophie Gold were for all intents and purposes a couple with no fringe benefits. Fred checked in every day to report on Sophie's culinary endeavors.

Fred and Sophie were the reason Beth and Gracie started up a division that provided matchmaking services for the over-sixty-five crowd. Even they were amazed at the success and how it had taken off. With all the friends in various organizations Fred and Sophie belonged to, it didn't take long before Gracie and Beth were so swamped, they had to hire additional help just to oversee the matchmaking needs of those over sixty-five. Flowers and fruit baskets arrived by the hundreds in thanks for making all their lives more interesting. Gracie and Beth donated it all to the hospitals and nursing homes in the area.

"I miss hearing from him. Do you believe I've been here a whole month?"

"Hard to believe," Gracie said, yawning. Gizmo was on his feet in a second.

"John and I have been going every night to all these local hot spots, where they allow all the wannabes to get up and do their thing. They call it improv. They're awful, but we all clap and stomp our feet. You never know, one of them might turn out to be the next Nashville star. I'm gonna do it when I'm ready. I know I will be just as awful, but they tell me it's a lesson in humility every wannabe has to go through. Okay, I kept you up long enough, so I'll say good night. John says hi. Give Giz a smooch for me. Tell him I think about him every day."

"Will do." Gracie yawned again and got up. She put her phone in the charger. To Gizmo, that was the ultimate clue that they were finally going to bed. "Okay, get your baby, and let's hit the sack."

Gizmo poked through his basket of toys and picked up a ten-tentacle purple octopus with a squeak and headed for the second floor.

Already dressed in her pajamas, her face creamed, her teeth brushed, Gracie slid under the covers as Gizmo stretched out on the king-sized dog bed that he slept on for ten minutes before he hopped onto Gracie's bed, thinking she didn't know he was there. He let loose with a soft **woof** of sound, his signal that all was well in the Sweet household.

As tired as she was, sleep eluded Gracie.

She tossed and turned, almost strangling herself in the bedcovers. Gizmo was on his feet, sensing things were not right. He hopped up on the bed and nuzzled Gracie's neck. She stroked the dog's big head and started to talk. "I talk a good game, Giz, but I don't think I can make this all work. Beth has such faith in me, but...we always worked as a team, and that's how we made it all happen. The brother...my gut is telling me it's all going to be one giant headache, with me doing all the work and him doing nothing." Gizmo whimpered as she stroked his head and kept on talking.

"Just because he let me get a bead on him with the renovations doesn't mean anything in the scheme of things. Even I could see that guy is in a dark place. Matchmaking is not something he is even remotely interested in. He might be smarting a bit that his little sister kicked him to the curb, sort of, the way he did her. What goes around comes around, as they say. He just thought Beth would always be there for him. He can't come to terms with her turning the tables on him. I don't know, maybe it's a guy thing, or maybe it's that wheelchair thing." Gizmo whimpered again.

Gracie could feel her eyes starting to burn, meaning tears weren't far off. She stretched out her legs, then let out a yelp as the calf of her leg cramped up. She struggled to get out from under Gizmo and get her feet on the floor. She'd forgotten to take her magnesium tablet. Again. Come to think of it, she'd not taken the tablets for a few days now. She hopped around, the pain unbearable, as Gizmo followed her, barking and growling. He hated her crazy dance and the strange, pitiful sounds he was hearing.

"It's okay, Giz, it's okay. Just a cramp in my leg. C'mon, let's go downstairs so I can drink some water and eat a banana. It might help."

Back downstairs in the kitchen, Gracie uncapped a bottle of water and gulped it down in three long swigs along with the magnesium capsule. She looked at a bunch of overripe bananas on the counter and peeled one. She should have thrown them out days ago, but she managed to swallow the banana as she hobbled around, Gizmo right on her heels. Nothing was working. She wanted to cry but bit down on her lower lip to hold the tears in check. Only sissies cried.

Beth once said that was bullshit, and it was cathartic to cry. Beth had gone on to say she had shed buckets of tears over her brother, and it did help to cry. Otherwise, how else could she have survived? Who was she, Gracie Sweet, to argue with such logic?

Gracie limped into her studio and turned on the gas starter on her fireplace. She was glad now that she'd cleaned out the ashes and laid in fresh wood. She dragged a pile of cushions from the sofa and lined them up on the floor. Maybe the warmth from the fireplace would ease the cramping. She lowered herself to the cushions and let out a loud sigh. The cramping was abating. She made a mental promise to herself that no matter what, she would faithfully eat a banana every day, never again fail to take her magnesium pill, and drink at least six glasses of water daily. She finally slept, then, with Gizmo's big head cradled in the crook of her arm.

Gracie woke to soft licks on her cheek and the shrill ringing of the house phone and her cell phone. She cracked one eyelid to stare into the smoldering remains of the fire she'd built the night before. Her first thought was the pain in her leg was gone, with only a dull muscle ache remaining. Well, she could live with that. What she couldn't live with was the 140 pounds of pure dog sprawled across her chest and the two ringing phones.

Gracie managed to get to her feet without falling over. The horrible cramp was gone, but her leg ached. She made her way to the kitchen to let Gizmo out. She shivered at the blast of cold air that greeted her. She shook her head; it was November after all. Even in the South, it got cold during the winter months.

Gracie looked at the clock on the microwave and did a double take—9:05.

Impossible. Then she looked at the clock on the stove—9:05. She never, as in never, slept past six-thirty. Now her whole day was ruined, and she was down two and a half hours. If nothing else, she orchestrated her daily life and lived it to the minute. Damn. Now she was all screwed up.

Gizmo rang the doorbell and she went to let him in, muttering and not for the first time that she had to teach him how to open the door. The big dog looked at her as much as to say, "Yeah, right, whatever... and where is breakfast?"

"Okay, okay, we're all screwed up, so let's screw it up some more. How about scrambled eggs and bacon?" Gizmo let loose with his approval bark and sat back on his haunches to wait.

As Gracie prepared the food, her thoughts took her to Alex and the e-mails he used to send from the other side of the world. He said when he and Giz got back, he was going to feed him porterhouse steaks every day for the rest of his life. And other table food, too. No more of those dog rations for Giz, the bravest dog he'd ever known. And that's what Gracie did; she grilled Giz steaks until he didn't want them anymore. From that point on, she just fed the dog whatever she ate. She gave him vitamins and some other junk the vet recommended, and the dog was healthy and happy.

Gracie set the plate down, and the dog waited. "Right, right! Sorry, Giz. See what sleeping late does to me! I forgot the vitamins. She shook out two of what she called horse pills because they were so big and set them down near his dish. Giz knew he had to take the pills before he could eat. He gulped them down and literally inhaled the six scrambled eggs and four slices of bacon.

Gracie tackled her own breakfast, but she wasn't really hungry. She nibbled on the slice of bacon, took a bite out of the slice of six-grain toast, her concession to good eating habits, and stirred the egg on her plate. Her thoughts were everywhere, on Alex and what might have been, on the whiny puke Jake Masters, and on

Beth and the fact that she'd slept so late. That had to mean something, and it had nothing to do with the cramp in her leg. She'd had cramps in the middle of the night before, and she'd never overslept.

Looking around her kitchen for answers provided no insight into her immediate problem. Screw it, she thought as she got up to fill her coffee cup. The landline rang just as she set the cup down on the table.

"Mandy!" Gracie said, grateful to hear a human voice. "Please don't tell me you're calling with a problem. If it is a problem, can you call me back this afternoon?"

Mandy Franklin managed the New York satellite office and had been hired by Beth and Gracie the day they'd decided to expand the company. Mandy was a business whiz and ran the office just the way Gracie and Beth ran theirs.

"Whoa! Whoa! Calm down and take it slow and repeat everything you just said." The fine hairs on the back of Gracie's neck moved. She could hear Mandy draw a deep breath.

"Okay, okay, here's what happened.

Sometime between eleven o'clock, when I shut down for the night, and this morning, all hell broke loose. We were hacked. Someone is posting ugly trash stuff on social media. I called the Web people, and they're on it. The first thing they did was to shut down the Web site. I called Callie in Chicago and she was just about to call me, but I got to her first. The same thing happened to her. Someone is gunning for us, Gracie. I've been trying to call Lily Wexler in California, but it's just six in the morning out there, so I'll keep trying. I wanted to know if the same thing happened to the home site. Did you check this morning?" Gracie hated how jittery Mandy sounded.

"Not yet, I'm running late today. I'll do it now and call you back. I don't understand how that could happen with all the security and firewalls we have in place. Please tell me your backup is current. Please tell me that. I'll call you back."

"Absolutely it is in place. Beth drummed it into my head from day one. Before I shut down for the day, I make sure the books are updated." By updated, Mandy meant the pen to paper backup because Beth didn't trust computers a hundred percent. "My client list is safe and sound."

Gracie's relieved sigh could be heard all the way to New York. She leaned back in her chair, in no hurry to go to her home office. She knew what she would find. This had always been hers and Beth's biggest worry. That someone would find a way to hack into their system and steal their clients, and that's why Beth had decided to keep that particular list in actual ledgers. What they hadn't worried about too much was the trash talk that could and would be posted on social media. Their big mistake. Industrial espionage.

If not brought under control, it would be the kiss of death for Perfect Match. Gracie debated with herself for one whole minute as to whether she should call Beth or not. That was a no-brainer, she thought as she punched in the numbers to Beth's cell phone. The minute she heard a sleepy hello, she went at it full bore.

The sleepy voice in Nashville was instantly

alert. "Our worst nightmare, and wouldn't you know it's happened now, after I left. Makes me wonder. Are you wondering, too, Gracie? I'll get dressed and be home in a few hours. You can hold on till I get there, right? Thank God we didn't computerize our client list."

"Hold on, Beth. I can handle things here. Stay where you are and do what you're doing. If I run into something I can't handle, I'll call. For now, let's take it slow and easy. We might be able to nip this in the bud. People aren't stupid....Let me back that up a little. Most people are not stupid, and they'll see right through this attack. We've always had a stellar reputation. Our testimonials from our clients are heartfelt and not just photo ops.

"I really debated about calling you, but you and I have always been on the same wavelength. Let's see how all this plays out in the next day or so. Do you want me to alert your brother or handle it on my own for now?"

"He'd be useless is my first thought. Play it by ear. Are you sure you don't want me to come home?"

"Beth, I am absolutely sure. I can send you hourly texts if you want."

"I want," Beth said, relieved and yet somehow disappointed that she didn't have to make the trip back to Garden Grove. "Call me after you check our site and speak with Lily in California."

"I will. Give me a couple of hours to sort through all this. Are you really sure you don't want me to mention this to your brother?"

"Gracie, think about what you just said. You met my brother. What kind of help do you think he could offer you? Moose is no better. But if you think he should know, then by all means tell him. You're in charge here. Do whatever you think is best."

Gracie ended the call and stared down at Gizmo, who was sleeping on the small carpet in front of the sink. He looked so peaceful.

Gracie sipped at her coffee, which was now cold. She barely noticed because her brain was racing at warp speed.

She needed a plan.

# Chapter Four

While Gracie was stewing and fretting about a plan, Jake Masters was, as he put it, sweating his ass off with his physical therapist. "Three hours is enough, goddamn it! I need some fresh air. And something to eat."

Calvin Winters, the therapist, looked at Jake and said very quietly, "No pain, no gain. I am simply following your doctor's orders. You want to wuss out, it goes on the chart. It's your call, Jake, not to mention you have to pay me for the full time I'm here even if I just sit here drinking herbal tea." Three long years of therapy and familiarity allowed Calvin to take verbal liberties where Jake was concerned. "If you'd just go for the operation, we could be done with this in six months. You're fast approaching the point of no return, buddy. Either do it, or reconcile yourself to the fact that you're going to be in that chair for the rest of your life."

"He's right, Jake," Moose bellowed from the other end of the home gym Jake had had installed at the beginning of his career in the NFL.

Jake clenched his teeth, and bellowed back, "Help me into the chair."

"Get in it yourself. You've done it before. I'm not here to coddle you. I'm here to work your ass to the bone. But here's a thought for you today, Jake. What if Moose and I walk out on you and you're left on your own? How are you going to manage? That's another way of my telling you I'm getting sick and tired of your verbal abuse when all I'm trying to do is help you. Just so you know, I'm on my last nerve where you're concerned," Calvin said in his best pretend-fed-up voice.

Moose walked across the room and stared down at Jake. He wanted to say something warm and fuzzy, something kind and encouraging, but the words wouldn't come. He loved Jake like the son he never had, but he, too, was on his last nerve where the young man was concerned. And now with Gracie Sweet and Beezer's business, he wasn't sure he could hang on if Jake didn't man up. "I'm with him," he said gruffly. "I've had it, Jake. I might love you like a son, but even I have my limits. And if you think that young woman, and I am referring to Miz Sweet, is going to cut you any slack, you're way off base. She's going to chew you up and spit you out, and you are going to have to take it, because like Calvin said, you've turned into a wuss. It pains me right here," Moose said, thumping his scrawny chest, "but Beezer was right. You **are** a whiny puke."

Moose turned on his heel, and added, "I'm going to make some lunch, Calvin. Come talk to me and let this poor excuse for a man find his own way."

"I thought you'd never ask," Calvin said, trotting behind Moose. They could both hear Jake cursing a blue streak, some of the curses actually so laughable that both men ignored them entirely.

While Moose busied himself at the refrigerator and stove, Calvin sat down on one of the stools at the counter and let loose with a long sigh. "I can't believe I said what I said. Just so you know, Moose, what I said was the truth and way overdue. Jake is almost to the point of no return. There's just so much therapy he can do. The surgeons I spoke with are almost one hundred percent certain Jake can walk again. No foolproof guarantees, but what they're offering sounds pretty damn good to me. Do you know something I don't know, Moose? Why is he so adamant about not going for this final surgery?"

Moose dumped some pasta into a pot of boiling water. He gave it a quick stir. "The pain. The drugs they gave him. He was the next thing to a junkie after the third operation. Then it was the withdrawal from the drugs, more pain. The next two operations didn't help, more drugs, more withdrawal. He'd had enough."

"He's drug free now. He's as healthy as an ox. His upper-body strength is phenomenal. I'm worried about his mental health, almost as worried as I am about his physical health. When you told me about his...ah...new business, I sensed a change in him, a spark of something. I'm not going to give up on him, but he doesn't have to know that. I say we unite, Moose, and really sock it to him."

"You got my vote, young man." Moose cackled. "Wait till you meet Miz Gracie Sweet. If anyone can give Jake a run for his money, it's that young woman. And now he's got Beezer on his mind and is trying to come to terms with her opinion of him. To hear that young woman tell him that Beezer called him a lazy laggard, a king-sized pain in the ass, and a whiny puke didn't do anything for his ego, nor did her reference to the fact that he was full of himself and had daily pity parties. Believe it or not, Jake loves and adores his little sister.

"I'm not defending him, but truth is truth. He lost sight of all of that for a while, and when it reared up and hit him in the face, he didn't—Strike that, **doesn't** know how to deal with it. Beezer is all he has aside from me. He never had a lot of friends, but the few he did have got fed up with him and went on their way. They tried;

it was Jake. He said he didn't need their pity. It wasn't pity; they just wanted to be there for him, but he wasn't buying that. So he shut himself up here. Days, weeks, months go by, and you and I are the only people he talks to."

"What the hell kind of life is that?" Calvin exploded.

"You're preaching to the choir here, Calvin," Moose said, draining the pasta into a huge red colander.

"So what's our next move?" Calvin asked, his voice teetering on the nervous side.

"We, as in you and I, don't have a next move. The next move is up to Jake."

Calvin walked over to the refrigerator and popped a Gatorade and swigged it down. He gave Moose a pat on the back, and said, "If you say so. Whatever you're making smells good. So, tell me about Miz Gracie Sweet."

While Moose proceeded to give Calvin what he himself perceived to be the low-down on one Gracie Sweet, Jake Masters was rolling across the floor to where his wheelchair was parked. His body screamed with pain so bad, he felt his own sweat drip into his eyes. He cursed some more as he gritted his teeth. What the hell was wrong with him? He'd done this exact same thing hundreds of times, and while the pain was bearable, it was nothing like this. He struggled to take deep breaths. **Mind over matter, Jake. Shift into neutral and realize it isn't physical pain you're experiencing, but mental pain. Admit it. You're a mess. A real, hard mess.** Something was burning his eyes, something alien, something he hadn't experienced since that long-ago day when he'd stood at the cemetery holding his sister's hand and mumbling he'd take care of her because he was her big brother, and that's what big brothers did. "Well, you screwed that up, Jake Masters," he muttered as he rubbed at his burning eyes.

Time to get this show on the road. He inched his body closer to the wheelchair, swiveled around on his butt, grabbed the arms, and hoisted himself into the seat. He sat there for a few minutes as he tried to figure out what his next move should be. Pretend nothing was wrong? Well, that was a stupid thought. Go with a temporary meltdown? Just as stupid. Apologize and say let's forget this ever happened? Really stupid, except for the apology part. Go with a straight apology and say he was out of line? That made sense because it was the truth. Still, could he actually do it? He couldn't remember the last time he'd apologized to anyone for anything. A really sad state of affairs.

**Whiny puke**. How could his sister say that about him? How? Every time he thought of the offensive words, he got livid. He yanked at his cell phone and sent off another text to his sister. What number was it? Maybe thirty-three. No, thirty-four. Had he really sent her thirty-four texts that she'd ignored? Beloved sister my ass. Now he was mad all over again. **Let it go, let it go,** his mind screamed. **Beezer is done with you. As in** done. **She wants nothing more to do with you because you're a whiny puke, and there's no room in her life for whiny pukes. She's going to be this famous country-western music**

**sensation, and there's no room for a whiny puke like you in her new life. Get it through your head and own it, Jake.** Like that was going to happen.

He tapped out number thirty-five. Two simple words. **I'm sorry.** Then he tapped out number thirty-six. Four words this time. **I love you, Beezer.**

Jake hit the control on his motorized chair, whirled around, and headed for the kitchen. On the way, he decided to go with "pretend nothing was wrong." If that didn't work, he'd switch to Plan B, as soon as he could figure out what Plan B was.

No one said a word when Jake appeared in the kitchen and took his place at the table. Moose and Calvin were discussing Thanksgiving menus since the holiday was a little more than a week away. They didn't stop talking, and in fact made it a point to ignore Jake, who helped himself to the bowl of pasta sitting in the middle of the table. He responded agreeably when Calvin asked him if he was a leg or breast man, referring, of course, to a turkey.

"I like the thigh, actually," Jake said.

"How big a bird are you cooking this Thanksgiving, Moose?" **So, in the end,** he thought, **I'm going with business as usual.** He waited to hear what if anything Moose was going to say.

"Who said I was cooking anything this year? I've been meaning to talk to you about that, Jake. My brother invited me to Montana for Thanksgiving. My niece is getting married the Saturday after Thanksgiving. I already bought my ticket." It was all a big lie, but Jake didn't have to know that.

"And you're just telling me this **now**? What about me?"

"What about you, Jake? It's always about you, isn't it? I can call in a temp for the few days I'm gone. I **said** I needed to talk to you about something. This is the something."

"Glad you brought that up, Moose. I keep losing track of time and forgot how close we actually are to Thanksgiving. I'm going to New York to my folks' for Thanksgiving. I can send a substitute. We should discuss this, so I can schedule my replacement.

You want to do it now or later?" Calvin asked.

"Later's fine," Jake said coolly. He hated coincidences. And this sure smelled and felt like a coincidence. He reached for a pickle and jammed it into his mouth. He looked down at his plate, then up at Moose, and in the same cool voice, said, "Something's missing in this pasta. It's not up to your usual, but it's still good. I only mention it because you always want to know if something can be improved on. This could definitely be improved upon," he said, pointing to the bowl of pasta.

Moose got up from the table. It was clear to Calvin and Jake as well that he was ticked off. Moose knew damn well there was nothing different about his pasta dish with the sun-dried tomatoes, crumpled shrimp, and a medley of his own special herbs that he never deviated from.

Not wanting to get further embroiled in Jake Masters's affairs, Calvin looked over at his client, and said, "I'll be in the gym. We pick up in an hour. I need to bring your chart up to snuff. One hour, and don't be late."

"Don't be late," Jake said in a snarky voice as he mimicked Calvin.

"You need to grow up, son," Moose said as he placed dishes in the dishwasher. "You need to get out of my kitchen now so I can make lunch for Miz Sweet's people. Why don't you spend the next hour trying to make peace with your sister."

"I just sent her two texts. All told I've sent thirty-six. She's ignored them all. I'm not sending any more. If that's how she wants to be, then that's okay with me. I don't give a good fiddler's fart about her anymore."

"Well, that's a bald-faced lie if I ever heard one," Moose snarled. "Maybe you should give some thought to getting in that specially equipped van you spent a fortune on and have never driven and drive up to Nashville to see your sister in person."

"Maybe you should mind your own business, Moose. I'll drive that van when I'm damn good and ready and not one minute before. I haven't had it all that long," he said defensively.

"You've had that van for almost a year.

A year is not all that long. It's a whole year."

"What are you cooking now?"

"Shrimp scampi with lots of garlic and wine. Why?"

"Is that what we're having for dinner this evening—the leftovers, that is?"

"Nope. Tonight you're on your own. Tonight is my bingo night at St. Ann's. It's right there on the calendar. Don't go all huffy on me now, Jake, or I'll walk out of this house, and I won't come back. Get your own house in order. I'd do it quickly if I were you, before you implode."

Moose talked to him like this all the time, and he just shrugged it off, but today he heard a new tone in his old friend's voice that clearly said he was fed up and on his last nerve. For a moment, Jake panicked. He'd been having these moments a lot lately. He quickly backtracked and said, "I forgot. Don't worry about me. I can make a sandwich."

"At least you got that part right, the part about me worrying about you. I quit doing that a long time ago. I'm kind of hoping that Beezer asks me to be her road manager.

If she does, I'm taking the job. So consider this my notice in case that happens."

"What the hell! Where's all this coming from all of a sudden? Things were going along just fine until my crazyass sister decided to take it on the lam and do something that is only going to give her heartache, and suddenly our world as we know it is falling apart. Like I said, what the hell is going on here?"

"If you're looking for answers, Jake, look in the mirror," Moose said, banging two pots together just to hear the noise. "Now I'd be happy if you'd leave my kitchen so I can get to work. I don't like it when that big guy Henry comes in to see what the holdup is on lunch. He scares me. Now, git!"

Jake thought about a snappy comeback but realized he was fresh out. He turned his chair around and headed to his private lair or, as Beezer used to call it, his man cave, where he went to lick his wounds in private. He had an hour to fill. A whole lousy stinking hour. To do nothing but feel sorry for himself.

A whole hour.

Sixty minutes.

Thirty-six hundred seconds.

Jake gave up when he tried to compute the nanoseconds.

Sometimes, like today, and most of his days, life just out and out sucked.

# Chapter Five

John Rossmon, Beth Masters's longtime significant other and the love of her life, watched his ladylove with clinical interest as she tossed clothing and cosmetics into a designer duffel bag at the speed of light. He tilted his head to the side, and asked, "Are you sure you want to do this, Beth? Think about it. What kind of signal will you be sending to Gracie if you bolt home? That you don't trust her to handle the business? Since you had her on speakerphone, I can't pretend I didn't hear her end of the conversation. She's more than capable of handling anything that comes her way, except for maybe your brother, and if I were a betting man in that instance, my money would be on Gracie. She's got Mandy, Callie, and Lily. The four of them can kick some serious ass, as you well know. Why are you going off the rails like this?"

Beth sat down on the edge of the bed.

She looked at John and smiled ruefully. "I do trust her. More than you could ever know. She's the sister I never had. We always worked well together—that's why I made her a full partner in the business. I'm just worried that I dumped too much on her. I'm worried about Jake and her going at it, and yeah, Gracie will give him a run for his money. Couple that with what's going on now, and it's a double whammy. It would just kill me if she ever came back to me and said I took advantage of her for my own selfish reasons. And, John, I did say if there was trouble, I would be there. This **is** trouble. I can smell it all the way here in Nashville. I need to go."

"No, Beth, you do **not** need to go. I heard Gracie clearly. She said she does not need you to come home, and if she did, she would call you. Gracie can handle anything that comes her way, and we both know it. Now, having said that, if you're having second thoughts about us and Nash-ville, that's something totally different. Don't confuse the two, and be honest. If you want to back out, that's okay. I'm staying because I like it here, and we've made some inroads already. I am not prepared to give that up. I'm starting to think you're having second thoughts. If you are, now is the time to tell me, so we can sort it out and make realistic decisions."

Beth reached for John's hand and squeezed it. "I'm not having second thoughts. If anything, I'm more convinced than ever that I was meant to do this. It's guilt. I feel guilty. About Jake and how I handled it. About dumping it all on Gracie. For some reason, I thought this was going to be easy, and by that, I mean the leaving part. It's killing me, John. I feel so guilty that I love what I'm doing. I feel guilty that I have you, and you know how much I love you. Gracie has no one but Gizmo and Jake....Well, Jake has no one either, except Moose. I've got it all. I should be happy, but I'm not. I am, but I'm not. Does that make sense, John? I'm frazzled, and I know it."

"Of course it makes sense," John lied with a straight face.

Beth squeezed John's hand harder. "You have always been my voice of reason. And

you're right, you're always right. Okay,
I won't go. By the way, Jake has sent
me thirty-six texts since I left. I haven't
answered any of them. He said he was
sorry. He's not sorry. He doesn't know the
meaning of the word."

"So you're just going to let him stew?"
John grinned.

Beth laughed out loud. "What's that saying? What's sauce for the goose is sauce
for the gander. He hung me out to dry for
over three years. He needs to see how it
feels."

"Oooh, you are a coldhearted woman,
Beth Masters," John said, hugging her close.

"We're good then, right?" Beth cooed.

"Yes, ma'am, we're good. You want me
to drive you to your lesson? It's on my way
to that interview I told you about."

"Oh, John, I am so sorry. Here I am
rambling on and on and taking away from
your big moment. Of course you can drive
me. Come by the studio and let me know
how you make out. I know you'll ace it. I
have that feeling."

"I don't think either one of us should

get too excited. Even if I get it, it is just temporary until the other band member recovers from his surfing accident. Plus, I heard that over forty other guitar players are auditioning."

"But there's only one John Rossmon. That gig could open so many doors for you."

"I'm thinking more along the lines of helping me pay the rent. We have a deal, Beth. We split everything down the middle. You do **not** pay my way. If I run out of money, I'm heading home. I got a lead on a waiter job. I'm going to give that a shot. It's just at a café that serves breakfast and lunch. If I get that, I'll be okay."

"Why don't we get married? That way you could stop worrying about paying your way."

John was so outraged at Beth's words, he literally dumped her on the floor. "Tell me you didn't just say what you said! I'm ready to get married anytime you want, but I am not living off your money. I thought we had an understanding," he growled. "What about that part where you won't marry me till Jake can walk you down the aisle? Huh? Huh?"

"Okay, okay. Yes, I understand. Damn, you're touchy today. You're nervous about the audition, aren't you?"

John reached down and pulled Beth to her feet and drew her close. "Yeah, yeah, I am," he murmured. "Talk me down."

"I have a better idea. Let's go for a walk and hold hands. It's really cold out, so we can get your adrenaline pumping. I'll even let you buy me a hot pretzel with mustard."

"Deal," John said as he reached for his jacket.

"Hold on, hold on. Here comes another text from Jake. I don't believe this." Then Beth started to laugh and couldn't stop. She finally held out her phone so John could read Jake's text: **I'm going to drive up there and bang some sense into your head.**

"Like that's really going to happen. Moose told me that about a year ago, Jake bought this specially outfitted van with hydraulics so he could drive. As far as I know, he's never even set foot in it, and yet he's going to come here and bang some sense into my head." Beth went off on another peal of laughter as John helped her into her coat.

"If nothing else, honey, you roused him from his stupor. You know what they say about waking up sleeping tigers."

"No, tell me about that," Beth purred as she linked her arm with John's. "And anything else you might want to tell me."

"You're so bad." John chuckled.

While Beth and John were billing and cooing with each other and holding hands, Jake Masters was stewing and fretting and cursing up a storm that Moose tuned out as he fried bacon and eggs for Jake's breakfast.

"You need to give it up, Jake," Moose thundered so loud Jake winced. "You own what you did, and your sister is not about to forgive you. Put that in your pipe and smoke it, pal. She's done with you. I can't say as how I blame her, either. You trampled all over her. She used to show up here at the gate and cry her eyes out. Did you care? Hell no, you didn't. All you cared about was your own sorry ass, and don't you dare tell me differently. If you think for one minute your going to Nashville will turn Beezer around, you are living in a world of total fantasy. She'll kick that sorry ass of yours to the curb so fast, you won't know what happened, and if she has trouble doing it, John Rossmon will be right at her side. He might have been your best bud there for a while, but when you turned on Beezer, that was the end for him. Are you getting this all through that thick head of yours, Jake?"

Jake looked down at the plate of fluffy yellow scrambled eggs with six slices of extra-crisp bacon that looked so perfect it could have been a picture in a food magazine. He looked up at Moose, a pitiful expression on his face. "Yeah, Moose, I'm finally getting it. I'm just someone she used to know, and she no longer wants to know me. End of story. Period. I get it. I get it! So, in your opinion, and you know how I value your opinion, what should I do?"

"What Beezer asked you to do. Take over her business and run it the way she did. You've had a month, and you've done squat. We wouldn't even be having this conversation if Miz Gracie Sweet hadn't showed up. That's just one more tick Beezer has against you. Even though she turned over her business to you, she knew she couldn't trust you, so that's why Miz Gracie Sweet is now in our lives. When a person loses trust in a person they love and adore, like Beezer used to love and adore you, it's a major calamity. To be honest, Jake, I do not know how you can recover from this. Because...you are so wrapped up in yourself, you can't see the forest for the trees," Moose said, deliberately laying it on as thick as he could to try to shake some sense into Jake's head.

Jake jammed his fork into the mound of eggs on his plate. "Who the hell's side are you on, anyway?"

Moose finished loading up the food tray and set it on a rolling cart that he would take in to Henry and his workers. "I wish you hadn't asked me that, Jake. I really do. I'm on Beezer's side. I can see that's going against your grain here, so after I take this food into the office, I can pack my gear and be out of here in thirty minutes. Think about it and give me your decision when I get back. We have finally reached a point where the rubber is meeting the road. I'm too old for this kind of shit. Like I said, think long and hard before I get back."

Guy talk. Down-and-dirty talk. Moose would never talk or say things like he'd just said in front of anyone else. That alone told Jake that Moose was more serious than he'd ever seen him. Rubber meeting the road, fish or cut bait time. Crap!

Jake pushed his plate to the middle of the table. He turned his chair around and headed for the back door. On a hook was a plaid car robe that he threw over his shoulders. He was seething as he opened the door, pushed it aside, and propelled his chair out onto the deck and the ramp he'd had installed, which would take him down to the yard, where he could sit closer to Mother Nature than up on the deck. He needed to calm down, and he needed to calm down **now,** before things got so far out of control there would be no hope of recovery.

His sister was right. Moose was right. He was wrong. Dead wrong. There was no halfway mark, no wiggle room. This was look-it-in-the-face-and-deal-with-it. When you're wrong, you're wrong. End of story.

He was an unmitigated bastard. No doubt about it. Who wouldn't be if they were in his position? Jake knew that kind of thinking was a cop-out, so he back-tracked. The doctors, the surgeons, the therapists said it was okay for him to feel sorry for himself. For a little while. He knew in his gut a little while didn't mean three years. They'd all told him he had to face his demons and get on with his life. That he had years and years ahead of him. Yeah, yeah, what they didn't say was how bleak-looking those years were going to be. They weren't sitting in this goddamn chair like he was. Excuses! Excuses!

Throw caution to the winds, go for the operation, forgo the drugs afterward, go with Tylenol or Aleve. They'd tried to tell him that, but he'd refused their advice and asked for the painkillers until he got addicted. Never mind that he slept eighteen hours out of twenty-four. Stupid is as stupid does. And now it was front and center and biting his butt.

What did he know about the match-making game? Not a damn thing. Beezer knew that, and yet she'd turned her business, a very lucrative business, over to him. She'd even taken an extra step and hired someone to help him. How much more fair and responsible could a person be? And she'd paid him back for all the times he'd invested in job opportunities for her. Plus interest. **Don't forget the interest she paid you,** Jake, he again cautioned himself in his thoughts. Fair-minded, responsible Beezer.

Jake felt his throat start to close up, and his eyes began burning. Was this the end of his and Beezer's relationship? Obviously, and he was just holding out for the impossible. Thirty-six unanswered texts told him all he needed to know. He blew it, and he knew it. He also knew no matter what he did, even if he groveled, that Beezer was done with him. His little sister was done with him. It hurt. God, how it hurt. And he had no one to blame but himself.

"Okay, I own it all," he bellowed, as his words were carried away on the wind.

Jake heard the kitchen door open. He didn't turn around because in his mind he knew he'd see Moose with his suitcase in hand. He raised a hand and waved as he stared across the yard at a row of privet hedges that were thicker and more secure than a chain-link or wooden fence. It was all about his privacy.

"Well!" the single word was like a thunderclap. Jake turned his chair around, steeling himself for the sight of Moose and his suitcase. He blinked when he didn't see it. He felt so light-headed he almost blacked out.

"Okay. You win! I was wrong all the way down the line. Call Dr. Frey and schedule an appointment for me. And while you're at it, schedule an appointment with the shrink, what's her name...Ardeth...Ardeth Ames. Did Calvin get here yet?"

"Calvin is in the gym waiting for you. I think you need to make those appointments yourself, Jake. That way, when you cancel them like you've done dozens of times before, you can't blame me for it." Moose turned on his heel and entered the house. His fist shot high in the air. Maybe this time. Maybe this time Jake would actually go through with it all. Maybe there was something to this tough-love business everyone talked about after all. Maybe, maybe, maybe.

"Just a damn minute, Moose!" Jake shrilled, but Moose was already in the house. He heard the door slam shut. Moose was probably hiding out somewhere, which meant Jake was going to have to make the calls and actually talk to the nurses himself. "Okay, you **whiny puke**, just do it and get it over and done with."

He did it.

Then he struggled to reach the calendar hanging on the pantry door. He put large red **X**s on the dates for the appointment, along with the times. Done! He'd committed, whiny puke that he was.

Jake whirled the chair around and headed for the gym, where Calvin was waiting to work his ass to the bone. He drew a deep breath and made a promise to himself that he would give one hundred percent to the workout.

Calvin Winters took one look at Jake, and his first thought was **Oh, shit! Something happened, and I'm going to have to deal with this guy all day long**. He was stunned when Jake yanked his sweatshirt over his head and said, "I hope you had a good night, Cal. I'm ready when you are. Just so you know, I just, five minutes ago, scheduled an appointment to speak with the surgeon, and made an appointment for a workup. I'll need a report from you to take with me."

"Ah...well, good for you, Jake. Sure, no problem. When do you need it?"

"Next week. Friday is my appointment. We good?"

"We're good, Jake. Congratulations!"

"Aren't you going to say it?" Jake needled.

"Say what?"

"The same thing Moose always says, 'Are you going to cancel it?' "

"Why would I say that? I'm taking you at your word. If you say you're going to do it, then I believe you. To think otherwise would mean you're a liar, and I do not think you are a liar. What I think is you're scared, and guess what, man. You have every right to be scared out of your wits. But, even a slim chance you can walk is better than no chance. So, having said that, get your ass in gear and let's make you sweat. You know the drill. Who's the boss here in this room?"

"You are!" Jake said, shooting off a sharp salute.

"And...?"

"I do what you say, when you say it, and how you say it," Jake said smartly.

"Then let's do it!"

At the end of the three-hour session, Jake was ready to cry he hurt so bad. But he'd done everything Calvin had asked plus more. "Whiny puke my ass," he muttered over and over as he made his way to the kitchen for lunch. He was starved, since he hadn't eaten his breakfast. He hoped he didn't fall asleep in the middle of the homemade vegetable soup Moose was making.

## Chapter Six

Gracie Sweet let herself in to Beth's house a little after nine o'clock. She'd lollygagged, an expression her mother used to use all the time when she was too slow doing something or other. She simply was in no hurry to turn on the computer to assess the damage she knew was unfolding. Just thinking about it was scary enough for her, visualizing a nightmare come to life.

Postponing the inevitable moment, Gracie opened one of the garden doors and let Gizmo out. She left the door ajar so he could get back in on his own. Sometimes Giz was quick, and other times he liked to meander in the hopes of treeing a squirrel. She made coffee, then dropped some shrimp flakes into the fish tank. She always spent a few minutes tapping on the tank and talking to the fish. Beth used to do the same thing.

It was just way too quiet in here. But did she really want to turn on the surround sound and drown in countrywestern music? Maybe what she needed to listen to was some crazy rap music to get her dander up. She hated rap music. Golden oldies? Too schmaltzy, reminded her too much of Alex. Maybe a little jazz with some moody Miles Davis. Nah. A stupid game show on TV. No—Beth said all those shows were fixed, so why waste her time. How Beth came by that information she had no clue. It was probably just her own opinion. In the end, she wasn't going to watch or listen to any game show, so the thought was moot.

Gracie heard the garden door click and knew Gizmo was inside. "Did you lock it?" she shouted. A sharp bark was the affirmative response. "Good boy!"

Coffee cup in hand, Gracie walked around to her desk. She hesitated a moment before she sat down. She looked around, knowing she would probably never view this room the same way again once she turned on the computer. She hated change. Of any kind. And yet, that's what life was all about, change.

Gracie pressed the button that took the computer out of sleep mode and waited for it to boot up. She stared across at the colorful fish swimming so lazily in their home. And then it hit her—the phone wasn't ringing. That was part of the silence. The phone should have been ringing off the hook. Mandy and Callie had said they had to take the phone off the hook, or they would lose their minds. And yet the office phones, of which there were four along with two different fax numbers, were silent. None of them were ringing, not the office phones or the 800 number. She reached over and picked up the receivers, one by one, to see if there was a dial tone. There was.

Coffee cup cradled in both her hands, Gracie leaned back in her special ergonomic chair and closed her eyes as she thought about Perfect Match's successes and failures. Who was disgruntled enough to hack into their system? A client? A competitor? Who?

The name Luke Olsen hit her right between the eyes. When Perfect Match was just a dream on paper for her and Beth, they had contacted an architect to redesign the back end of the house to create the spacious office that was now the headquarters of Perfect Match. Beth said they had to do it right, or her brother would have a fit, so that meant hiring an architect and a construction company, because the house, a gift from Beth's brother, would keep him happy. She followed that up with, "If he even cares enough about me to stop by to check on me or his gift of the house." To Gracie's knowledge, the brother had never stopped by.

Luke Olsen was a super good-looking hunk. She remembered how she and Beth both had giggled and primped as they flirted with him. More Beth than her. At the time, Beth had been on the outs with John, and she said it was okay to flirt a little, and besides, it was time John stopped taking her for granted. So it was mainly to make him jealous. It worked, too. For Beth. Luke still flirted with her; then, as time went on and Beth told him to cool it, he got nasty. Maybe **nasty** wasn't the right word. Maybe **sassy, snarly,** something along those lines.

Suddenly, both Beth and she, along with the contractor, had started seeing another side of Luke Olsen. The contractor had threatened to walk off the job unless Olsen started treating him with respect. Beth found herself in a sticky situation where she had to confront Olsen and lay it on the line. Either he toed the mark, her mark, or he was fired.

At that point, the job was almost complete except for painting and a few cosmetic touches. All the inspections had been done, and she'd gotten the COO, so Beth wrote him a check, thinking that was the end of her business with Luke Olsen.

And in a way it was the end; Olsen cashed the check, and she and Beth painted the room themselves. They placed the new furniture where they wanted it, installed the fish tank themselves, then hooked up all the equipment.

How Olsen found out what kind of business they were in was to this day still a mystery. As it turned out, he was one of their very first clients, only he came to them with a different name. The name he filled out on his online profile sheet said he was Phil Parsons, an electrical engineer who owned his own firm. He paid five thousand dollars with a certified bank check in the name of Phil Parsons for his platinum status, which guaranteed him seventeen meet-and-greets.

After five meet-and-greets with no second dates, she and Beth both decided something was off. They discreetly interviewed the five women who had met with him and they all told them the same thing—that all he wanted to talk about was Perfect Match and the woman who ran it. He also broke the first rule of the company, which was on the first meet-and-greet, the couple went dutch. He always insisted, the women said, on paying the entire bill. He also always ordered the most expensive wine or champagne. All of the women thought he was trying to impress them. None of them were impressed, however. They also said he looked good, smelled good, had impeccable manners, but there was no promise of anything. One of the women summed it up by saying that Phil Parsons was the closest thing to a robot that she'd ever come across, and they were all thankful when he never called a second time.

That was when Beth decided to contact two old childhood friends, twin brothers who were lawyers and had investigators at their disposal. She hired one, and when the report came back, needless to say they were both stunned. Phil Parsons was actually Luke Olsen.

Gracie squeezed her eyes shut as she recalled how the two of them panicked when they read the report. In the end, the twin lawyers, Andy and Artie, had sent Luke Olsen a registered letter to his parents' architectural firm telling him that they were refunding his check in the amount of five thousand dollars because he'd misrepresented himself and broken the rules everyone who used the services of Perfect Match had agreed to. All Beth could say over and over was how could someone so good-looking, with a legitimate profile like his, turn out to be such a skunk?

Gracie and Beth over time more or less forgot about Luke Olsen as their business took off like a rocket, and they were both working sixteen to eighteen hours a day. Their clients were ecstatic with the matches Beth and she arranged. The money poured in faster than they could count it. Word of mouth brought them clients in droves, in all age categories.

Two years and three months later, Beth started experiencing panic attacks. She said she thought someone followed her when she went anywhere. She said her cell phone, which she kept on her night table, would ring late at night, but no one spoke when she clicked it on. Twice she said she thought she saw someone in the backyard early in the evening and once a little before dawn. She was adamant that someone was watching her. She begged Gracie to leave Gizmo with her.

Back they went to the twin lawyers and their special investigator. The first person they homed in on was Luke Olsen. It took them all of three weeks to corner him and call the police. Beth was able to take out a restraining order on Olsen, but she continued to have regular panic attacks.

It was with Gracie's encouragement that Beth followed her dream and went to Nashville. She told her she needed to get away from Garden Grove, Luke Olsen, and her brother, Jake being the one at the core of her misery. Beth didn't fight her; she was more than ready to head to a safer climate. Other than telling her brother that she was leaving, and that only at the last minute, her departure was a secret.

And now this. Gracie was convinced that this latest mess had to be Luke Olsen. No one else had a vendetta against either her or Beth. She shivered at the thought and what lay ahead for Perfect Match.

Gracie was off her chair in a second and running around to Beth's desk. She yanked open the bottom drawer and pulled out a file with a big red **X** on the front. She flipped through the pages before going back to the cover profile to refresh her memory.

Luke Olsen, aka Phil Parsons, was definitely a goodlooking guy.

Gracie looked at the four pictures in the file. One was of Luke in a kayak; he was the outdoor sports type. The second was Luke in a designer power suit that looked like it was made for him. The third picture was a younger version of him with his parents, who were just as attractive as Luke was. The last picture was of him in his running gear, spandex shorts, muscle shirt, and a sweatband around his forehead. According to his profile, he was six foot three, 190 pounds. Said he worked out every day and ran twentyfive miles on weekends. He was an architect by training, drove a Porsche, and belonged to two different health clubs. The overall impression was he was a playboy who worked or pretended to work at his own firm. **A stand-up guy,** according to Beth's original note penned in the margin. Later, Beth penned another note in the margin: **not a stand-up guy**.

Beth had penciled on a red flag **No second dates with the same person.**

When Beth had discreetly asked the women how the dates went, they'd merely shrugged and said Phil Parsons, whose real name was Luke Olsen, was like a shiny red apple, but when you bit into it, it wasn't as good as the outside, or words to that effect. "No substance" was another comment. "All eye candy, nothing under the veneer" was another comment. And he refused to follow the rules, insisting on paying for everything. Another red flag penciled in by Beth. Nothing positive, no other notes written by Beth as feedback.

Gracie kept flipping the pages. Luke, aka Phil, had paid for seventeen meet-and-greets, before she and Beth discovered who he really was and cut him off at the knees. Gracie squeezed her eyes shut. That was about the time that they had started to hear ugly rumors about their company, rumors they had to hustle to squelch. They'd burned the candle at both ends as they sought to set up individual as well as group meetings to discuss the ugly rumors that someone was spreading. They organized parties, get-togethers, meet-and-greets till they were like zombies. But, finally, they were able to put a lid on it all. Then came a quiet time for a few months. Yes, they'd lost some clients, but they picked up some new ones, too. And then the dark stuff hit the fan with Beth, who said she was being stalked. It had gotten so bad at one point that she asked to take Gizmo for protection. And now this.

Gracie stared at the screen in front of her. She should have been looking at the company's home page with a couple holding hands. Instead, she saw an animated lightning bolt with the words **Dead in the Water,** which rolled over and over.

Gracie was frantic as she hit key after key only to find all the files and folders empty. She hit the backup key and checked the files—gone. Then she hit the outside stored files at Mozy—gone. How, she thought, swiping at her forehead, was this possible?

Gracie yanked at her bottom drawer and pulled out the shoe box with all the memory sticks that Beth had insisted on. Eight months into their business they'd started backing everything up on the memory sticks at the end of the day. Neither one of them ever walked out of the office at the end of the day until that was done. And of course the handwritten ledgers. Beth called it Rule Number Two. Her sigh of relief was so loud Gizmo reared up to see exactly what the sigh meant. Satisfied that all was well, he dropped his head onto his big paws and watched the fish swim to and fro in the big tank. Eventually, his eyes closed because his world as he knew it these days was right side up.

**Okay, what's my next move here?** Gracie wondered. Do I call Beth and seek her input, or do I go out to Jake Masters's house and apprise him of all of this, or do I just sit here and contemplate my belly button? Who would do this? Surely it wasn't Luke Olsen, regardless of how dissatisfied he was with his treatment by Perfect Match. Then again, he probably wasn't too happy with the restraining order that was in place against him. That alone might be enough to push him into doing something like this.

A competitor was more likely, but which one? A local matchmaking service or one of the biggies? What was the end goal? To put Perfect Match out of business? A client who wanted to get even for some perceived wrongdoing? She quickly negated the latter as she and Beth made it a policy to work overtime with an unhappy client until they found just the right partner for him or her. As Beth was fond of saying, "There is a perfect someone out there for each one of you. We just have to find that person, and that's why we're here." They had only known two failures, and both were men impossible to satisfy. They had cheerfully refunded all fees to both men, wished them well in their pursuit of the perfect female partner, who both women were quick to point out, hadn't been born yet. There had been no blowback from either man, and today they were someone else's problem. In Gracie's mind, it now boiled down to either Luke Olsen, aka Phil

Parsons, or one of their rivals.

Gracie wished, hoped, it was Olsen, because she felt she could deal with him. If it was a rival, the deck was stacked. How to find out? Why wasn't the damn phone ringing? She picked it up and listened for the dial tone again. It droned in her ear. She did the same with the phones on Beth's desk, only to hear the same droning sound.

Gracie swiveled her chair around, and that's when Gizmo growled deep in his throat as he got to his feet. A nanosecond later, every phone in the room started to ring, and the fax machines started whirring as the computer  e-mail pinged an alert that an e-mail was coming through. Giz somehow knew it was going to happen before it did. The dog's hearing was over the moon. She stroked his big head and spoke softly. Battlefield-weary, the big shepherd didn't like excessive noise, and this was definitely excessive noise. In the blink of an eye, she turned all the phones to mute. That just left the soft whirring of the fax machines. She quickly turned off the pinging sound on her computer. The fur on the back of Gizmo's neck went back down, but he didn't lie down. He started to patrol the room. Gracie watched him, all the while talking to him quietly, just the way the military vets had taught her on his return from Afghanistan.

Finally, after fifteen minutes, Gizmo came over and nuzzled Gracie's leg to let her know all was well. She smooched him, tickled his ears, and rubbed the sweet spot between his eyes before she handed over a chew that was as big as her foot. He walked away with it, flopped down, and went to work on it.

Gracie drew a deep sigh as she started pulling papers out of the fax machines. She winced. There had to be four or five hundred from all the different machines, and they were still coming in. At this rate, she'd have to replace the printer cartridge and replace the paper tray.

"I need a Xanax," she muttered under her breath when she clicked on her e-mail and looked at the long list. She knew without picking up the phone that there would be just as many voice mails.

Instead of reading and sifting through what was staring her in the face, Gracie pulled out her cell phone and called Mandy Franklin in New York. She barked a greeting of sorts and said, "Your backup is good, right?"

"It's all old files, Gracie. We're good. Well, not good, but you know what I mean. I put in a call to one of those A-1 Temporary office placement companies, and they're sending me three people to help respond to this disaster. I just got off the phone with Callie in Chicago, and she did the same thing. I haven't been able to touch base with Lily Wexler. Today might be her late day. I'll keep trying. Listen, Gracie. Yeah, this is a big pain in the butt, but thanks to Beth and her iron rules, the bulk of our stuff is safe. A quick look through tells me what the hacker got is all old stuff but still serious. He or she got Social Security numbers, credit card info, home addresses. And, of course, our clients are blaming us for not being more secure. Plain and simple, their identities have been stolen. I see lawsuits all over the place. What's your take on this?"

"Same as yours. I'll call our local temp company and do what you did, so we stay on top of things. I'm going to call the company's legal team and see where we stand. That's why we pay them a retainer. I'll get back to you. If you manage to get hold of Lily, tell her to call me ASAP. Fill her in, but I'm sure she'll have already jumped right on it."

Gracie spent the next thirty minutes talking to the placement services and was promised four temps would be ringing her doorbell within ninety minutes. The placement supervisor was quick to tell her the hourly rate was fortyfive dollars. Gracie didn't bat an eye. "Whatever it takes," was the best she could manage by way of a verbal agreement.

Gracie's second call was to the two-man law firm by the name of Axel and Axel, who were the twin brothers Andy and Artie, and friends of both Beth and Gracie. Perfect Match had quickly become the twins' major client and was on a healthy retainer. Both lawyers agreed to come to the house and bring lunch.

Gracie spent the rest of the morning going through the ugly, threatening e-mails, faxes, and listening to the abusive voice mails. By the time the temporary office workers arrived, Gracie had their work laid out for them, including providing a standard response to any clients who called and, of course, mention of the Axel law firm, which would be handling all communications effective immediately.

Gracie made coffee and set it on the counter next to the bar sink in the office. Everything was operational right up to the moment the doorbell rang.

Gizmo bounded to the door. He loved Andy and Artie and gave them a huge welcome as he herded them toward the kitchen. He eyed and sniffed the take-out food bags, knowing there was something there for him, and, as always, he was right.

The Axel twins were tall and lanky, with dark, curly hair and sharp blue eyes. They looked exactly alike but did not dress alike. Andy favored pressed khakis and a blazer while Artie liked a full suit with pastel shirts and fancy ties. Both had a killer smile and sharp wit. But it was their legal minds that impressed both Beth and Gracie. Neither was married, but as Artie said, both of them were working on it with significant others.

Gracie made a second pot of coffee while Andy set the table once she showed him where everything was. Artie fished around in one of the bags for the food they brought for Gizmo. Six meatballs with no sauce on them and two links of sausage. He cut it up and mixed it with some of the plain pasta. Gizmo watched him like a hawk to make sure nothing fell to the floor. "Here you go, boy," Artie said, setting the dish on the floor. Gizmo looked up at Gracie to see if it was okay to eat, and she nodded.

"God, I wish this dog was mine," the twins said in unison. "Each time we see him, he seems more human than a lot of people I know," Andy added. "Does he still have issues with loud noises?"

"Yes, but it's getting better." She told them about earlier, with all the phones ringing and the pings from the computer.

"I just talk him down, and he's good. He really loves going to the VA hospital on Sundays to help out in rehab. He loves it when the guys salute him. He gives it right back. You're right, though, he is almost human. It's uncanny how he knows or seems to know what each service member needs. He's their cheerleading squad.

"As soon as we get there, the guys all salute him, and he loves it. He wears his dog tags and his battle armor because he knows that means business. They salute him for fun and call him Sergeant Giz. He just drools. The doctors told me Giz does more for morale than anything they can do for the guys. That's how we spend all our Sundays. Believe it or not, Giz knows when Sunday rolls around.

"Okay, 'nuff of that. Let's eat, I'm starved. We can talk business after we eat."

And that's what they did.

It was four o'clock when Andy and Artie packed up their briefcases and prepared to leave, saying they had a handle on it all and they'd take it from here. Gracie was so relieved that she grew light-headed.

"What about New York, Chicago, and California?" she finally managed to gasp.

"We'll work on that tonight from the office. Stop worrying; you're in good hands now. By the way, how is Beth doing?"

"She's planning on taking Nashville by storm." Gracie grinned.

"But she can't sing," the twins said in unison.

"Stop raining on her parade. She's taking lessons."

Hugs were the order of the day, and words that said we're a phone call away rang in Gracie's ears long after the door closed. She checked with the temporaries and was satisfied that all was well, and no one needed anything.

Gracie trotted out to the kitchen, exhaustion finally getting to her. "Let's go for a walk, Giz. I need some fresh air. Twice around the block," she said, buttoning her jacket. Giz liked twice around the block because it gave him more time to check out the kids in the neighborhood, who all wanted to pet him. He allowed it and even barked once or twice to show them who was boss.

**And life goes on**, Gracie thought as she walked along the empty streets. The wind was picking up, and the last of the colorful fall leaves swirled about like someone was blowing a fan on them.

Gracie loved fall. It was her favorite time of year. So many years ago, she'd met Alex at a football rally. He was standing next to the huge bonfire staring at the flames shooting toward the sky. He turned, bumped into her, apologized, and the rest was history. She fell in love that night. Her throat started to close on her, and tears burned behind her eyelids. Gizmo was at her side in a second. "It's okay, Giz. I just had a flashback. I know you have them, too. It's okay."

Twice around the block, Gizmo stayed glued to her side. If he saw a child, he ignored him or her; his job was to give comfort and aid to the woman next to him. A job he took seriously.

## Chapter Seven

Gracie ran her fingers through her mop of hair, trying to smooth out what she called her bed hair, as she looked outside before opening the door for Gizmo, who was acting as frisky as a new pup. It was a bleak-looking day, overcast and gray. The wind was sharp as it whistled through the trees in her small backyard. A typical November day. She half wondered if there would be snowflakes before the end of the day. Possibly. But did she really care? She admitted that right now, right this second, she didn't care about much except the dire predicament Perfect Match was in.

She wondered again, and not for the first time, if she should have played it differently with Beth instead of downplaying the whole mess she was confronted with.

What she needed was some busy-work. She made coffee and scrambled eggs and bacon for Giz, who bolted through the door like a whirlwind the moment he picked up the scent of frying bacon. Gracie turned to look at the big dog and pointed to the door. "You know the drill, Giz. Lock the door." The big shepherd trotted over to the door. His massive paw shot upward. **Snick.** Done. He barked once, sharp and shrill. "Okaaayyy," Gracie said as she scratched at the sweet spot between his eyes. "One delicious breakfast coming right up, big guy."

Gracie nibbled on a slice of bacon that was so crisp it broke apart in her fingers. She scooped it up and dropped it in Gizmo's plate. She had no appetite. She tried to recall when and what she'd eaten last but couldn't remember. She continued to sip at the hot coffee, her thoughts everywhere.

What was she supposed to do today other than go by Beth's house to feed the fish? Go grocery shopping? She had to really be in the mood to go to Whole Foods. Another day, maybe. She'd been meaning to buy a new winter jacket and new boots. Today? She hated clothes shopping almost as much as she hated food shopping. Maybe she'd order something online or through a catalog.

Or...or she could go to Andy and Artie's office and offer her services. Something told her that wasn't a good idea. Andy had called at the stroke of midnight to tell her they were pulling an all-nighter and would have something to report by morning. He also said things were not as grim as they had first thought. Meaning they went through all the computers' hard drives that they had taken with them. Artie had chimed in from the background to say they'd alerted the firm's private investigator, a guy named Jim Mack, and he was already on the job.

She could head out to Jake Masters's house and make a pest of herself. Or she could ignore Beth's brother and visit with Henry, who would make short work of her since she knew diddly-squat about decorating. Henry didn't like people looking over his shoulder or giving him advice. Scratch Jake Masters and Henry.

Gracie was back to contemplating her belly button when the phone rang. The caller

ID showed the name of Beth Masters. She said a breathless hello on the second ring. After listening for a moment, she laughed out loud. "Whoa! Whoa! Slow down and tell me all that again."

The voice on the other end of the line was squealing in pure rapture. Gracie finally figured out what her best friend in the whole world was saying, which was that John got the gig he'd auditioned for and would be working nights with the small band at a place called Rootie Tootie's. And he also got the waiter job at a breakfast-lunch café where the tips were really good. The part that made Beth's voice squeal was the band said she could sing the song she'd written about Jake's lost love. That wouldn't happen for a couple more weeks because she needed more lessons, but the promise was there, and that was all Beth cared about.

When Beth finally calmed down she asked how things were going, but to Gracie's ears she didn't sound like she really cared one way or another how things were going.

Gracie had no desire to rain on Beth's parade. She couldn't remember the last time she'd heard Beth so happy. "I turned everything over to Artie and Andy, and they said things aren't as bad as we originally thought. They have a handle on it."

"That's good. That means it won't be a burden on you. Good, good! Oh, Gracie, I never thought this would happen. I mean I hoped, but you know me. I'm actually going to get to sing with John. John is over the moon. The guys in the band are older and are supernice and they like him. What's not to like when it comes to John Rossmon? You should see this place, Rootie Tootie's. It is **the** place here in Nashville. And John and I just stepped into it. Someone must be watching over us."

Gracie bit down on her lower lip. She almost said, "Just hope it isn't Luke Olsen."

Beth was back to squealing with happiness. Gracie just listened, her mind drifting to what she was going to do with her day. Maybe check her bank and brokerage statements. That was a chore that was long overdue and one she hated almost as much as she hated any kind of shopping, which brought up the question of what **did** she like to do?

Gracie brought herself back to the moment as Beth finally wound down and promised to call her the next day after her and John's first night at Rootie Tootie's.

Gracie poured herself a second cup of coffee as she realized she could stay in her pajamas all day if she wanted to. She could simply dillydally. What a strange term, she thought, as she looked around her kitchen, which she rarely used. Oh, she sat in it in the mornings, had lunch on weekends, but she rarely cooked even though she had a freezer full of food. She looked outside. She couldn't decide if it was a chicken soup or a pork chop kind of day. Why not both? she thought. It wasn't that she didn't like to cook— she did, and she was a good cook. At least according to Beth she was. Not only couldn't Beth sing, but she couldn't cook, either, so her endorsement really didn't mean much. Cooking took up so much time. Prep time. Then you had to watch and stir, or at the very least keep your eye on whatever it was you were cooking but not stirring, so it didn't burn or overcook.

Back in the day, when she'd thought she would marry Alex, she had bought a large eight-quart pressure cooker that was still in the original box in her pantry.

Gracie got up and meandered into the pantry and scanned the shelves for the pressure cooker. She hauled it down off the top shelf, opened it, took out the instructions, then washed the pot. Always read the instructions. Always. She did. Then she shrugged as she went to the freezer, unwrapped a whole chicken, rinsed it off, and dropped it into the pot. She added two containers of chicken broth and a bag of frozen vegetables and several sprigs of fresh parsley that weren't so fresh anymore and looked yellow. Whatever. She dropped them in the pot, added some salt and some cracked pepper, then secured the lid, set the timer, and dinner was under way. She scratched the idea of the pork chops. She'd used up fifteen minutes. Maybe she should make a pie. A frozen one. Everyone needed dessert. She used up another ten minutes turning on the oven and unwrapping a frozen berry pie. She slid it into the oven, set the timer for sixty-five minutes. It wasn't exactly **making** a pie but close enough.

"This is bullshit!" Gracie bellowed at the top of her lungs. Gizmo looked up and waited to see what would follow his mistress's exclamation. When nothing happened, he went back to chewing on his oversized bone.

Gracie Sweet was never one to let things simmer if she could bring matters to a full boil. Nor did she know the meaning of the word **relax.** She was what she called **on,** twenty-four/seven or until she collapsed in bed. It was who she was.

Gracie gave a very unladylike snort as she headed upstairs to take a shower and get dressed. Surely she would find something to keep her busy until she heard from the twins, Henry, Jake Masters, or Beth again. Otherwise, someone would be carrying her out wrapped in a straitjacket.

Thirty minutes later, Gracie was back in the kitchen, dressed in jeans and a stretched-out, worn sweatshirt that said **Fearless** on the back of it. A long-ago gift from Alex that she couldn't bear to part with. Besides, she was a creature of comfort, and designer clothes meant nothing to her. She sniffed the pleasing aromas in the kitchen. Maybe she should cook more often. It was so much easier to buy takeout or call and have someone deliver her food. A homemaker she definitely was not. At this point in time, unfortunately, she wasn't sure what she was. A career woman? A young spinster? Sometimes, it bothered her that she wasn't someone's daughter, sister, niece, granddaughter, or at the very least, someone's godmother. Other times, she thought maybe it was best that she wasn't any of those things. She was Gizmo's owner, and that was enough for her.

Gracie made a fresh pot of coffee, and while it dripped into the pot, she got out an accordion-pleated file folder and pulled out a calculator and almost a year's worth of bank and brokerage statements. She spent a full half hour putting them in monthly order so she could skim through them at the speed of light.

As always, she was amazed and delighted at the bottom lines. She rarely if ever thought about her net worth because it boggled her mind. Years ago, she'd hired a really top-notch broker who said she needed long-term goals and worked toward that end. She'd been devastated in a good kind of way when she'd found out that Alex Samson had named her his beneficiary on a five-hundred-thousand-dollar life insurance policy along with a twelve-store mini strip mall that he'd inherited from his family that was worth seventeen million. While all that was important, it was Gizmo that she valued the most as far as her inheritance went, and she knew that would never, ever change.

It was comforting to know that her old age was taken care of, thanks to Alex. Early on, she'd set up her own 401(k), and it was robust. Should everything fall apart, her own investments along with Social Security would see her through her declining years. Such morbid thoughts. She shoved everything back into the pleated folder and stared at it. Thirty-some million dollars was what she was currently worth. Not too shabby. She carried the file folder to the cabinet under the small built-in desk in the corner and replaced it on the shelf. She wouldn't have to look at it again until March, when her CPA asked for all her files and folders to prepare her personal taxes.

Gracie looked in the oven just as the timer went off. She saw a beautiful, perfectly-browned-on-top berry pie that looked delicious. She set it on the counter to cool, appreciating the heavenly aroma. "Let's go, Giz, we have to feed Beth's fish." With that announcement, Gizmo became a black-and-silver streak as he beelined for the garage door. He loved going in the car.

Fifteen minutes later, Gracie stood in the small foyer in Beth's house, aware of the silence. It was like a tomb. She gave herself a mental shrug to get herself moving. She was starting to dislike coming here to these empty rooms. Her gut told her this was the beginning of the end of Perfect Match. She'd always been one to pay attention to her instincts. She took a moment to wonder if she was overreacting. Something wasn't right, and it had nothing to do with what was going on. **I'm missing something. I can feel it, smell it**, she thought as she made her way to the office so she could feed the fish. She checked the tank, the water temperature, then satisfied the fish were okay, she sprinkled the shrimp flakes across the top of the tank. She watched for a full minute, mesmerized at how the fish knew the flakes were there to gobble down. She sprinkled a few more flakes just in case the fish were extra hungry today. Such a stupid thought. Maybe today was a Gracie Sweet Stupid Day. She'd been having a lot of Gracie Sweet Stupid Days of late.

Gracie turned on the lights, which bathed the office in bright, blinding light. She made coffee at the bar counter, then settled down at her desk, which was bare now that the computers were gone. **What am I missing?** she asked herself again. She looked around, hoping the answer would come to her. When nothing happened, she whistled for Gizmo and opened the

French doors to let him wander the yard. The wind was really kicking up, blowing the leaves in all directions. Gizmo raced after a spiral of them swirling about him. He barked sharply, then did one of his crazy runs around the yard at the speed of light before he skidded to a stop at the door.

Gracie laughed. "Okay, guess that's your exercise for the day." She shivered as she closed and locked the door, then slid a cut-off broom handle into the sliding track. Beth's idea of extra security.

Gracie looked over at the thermostat, wondering if she would be here long enough to warrant turning the heat up. Well, she'd just made coffee, so she had to drink it, ponder her current circumstances, and stare at the fish some more. She walked over and cranked the heat to a reasonable seventyeight degrees. Might as well be comfortable—no sense in shivering.

Gracie settled herself comfortably in her ergonomic chair and sipped her coffee, her eyes on Gizmo, who, for some reason, looked antsy to her. She always got uptight where Giz was concerned when she saw him go into what she called patrol mode, something he had been trained to do by the military. Why would he do that here? He must be picking up on something, and she was almost certain it had nothing to do with her. Something else.

Gracie carefully set her coffee cup down on the desk and leaned forward, never taking her eyes off the big dog. She felt a slice of fear knife down her back as Giz growled. She leaned further forward when the shepherd started to paw at Beth's bottom desk drawer. "Oh, crap!" Gracie muttered as she flew off her chair and around to Beth's desk. She yanked at the drawer and pulled it out as far as it would go. The file with the big red **X** on the cover was gone. "Damn! Damn! Double Damn!" Giz barked loud and shrill as he pawed at the floor. "I know, I know! Someone was here last night! I'm sure I set the alarm. Well, almost sure!"

Gracie whipped around, reaching for her cell phone. She punched in the numbers for the alarm company, who picked up on the first ring. She quickly announced

herself, gave the address, then breathlessly asked, "Was the alarm set last night, and
did anyone activate it at any time during
the evening?"

The woman on the other end of the phone
told her she would check and to hold on.
"The alarm was turned on at quarter to
eight last night by number four twenty-one,
Grace Sweet."

"I'm four twenty-one." **I did set the alarm.**

The voice continued. "The alarm was
turned off at two minutes after three A.M.,
and reset at three forty-five. It was turned
off again but not reset twenty-two minutes
ago."

"That was me, twenty-two minutes ago.
I set it at seven forty-five last night, but I
did not turn it off at two minutes after three;
nor did I reset it at three forty-five."

"Were you burglarized last night, is that
what you're saying?" the voice asked.

"Yes. I have to call the police."

"Yes, you do. You cannot hold us responsible since the alarm was turned off and on
per code. You realize that, right?"

Gracie seethed. "Yes, I do realize that.

Thanks for your help," she said, disgust ringing in her voice. She looked over at Gizmo, who was working himself into a frenzy. She went over to him, dropped to her knees, and spoke softly in his ear. He calmed almost immediately. "You did good, Giz. If I had a medal, I'd pin it on you. Not that you need another one. I had a gut feeling something was awry when I got here this morning. Who knows when I would have gotten around to looking in Beth's desk drawers again. You did my job for me." Then she said the words Giz had lived by for so long from Alex. "Good job, Giz!" The big shepherd nuzzled her neck as he basked in her quiet praise. God, how she loved this big dog with the soulful brown eyes.

"Now we call the police, and after that, I'm going to call Andy and Artie and tell them about this. After that, we'll go for a nice long walk and pick up some lunch. How's that sound, big guy?" The shepherd barked to show his approval.

"I wonder how the intruder got in here. As far as I know, only Beth, John, and I have keys, and we never keep a key outside," Gracie muttered to herself. She'd read enough spy and mystery novels to suspect whoever it was knew how to pick the lock.

While she waited for the police to arrive, Gracie ran through the house, checking to see if anything else had been taken. The hair on her neck and arms moved as she stepped into Beth's bedroom on the second floor. Her gaze raked the room. It still looked lived in. There were still clothes, shoes, coats, and jackets hanging in the walk-in closet. There were still things on the vanity in the bathroom. No wet towels or anything like that, but it still looked like a bathroom that was in use. Her skin crawled as she thought about Luke Olsen knowing that Beth had left. Until now, she'd been so sure that no one knew except Beth's brother and herself plus their help. And they didn't even know Luke Olsen. If it was Luke Olsen who had broken in.

The police arrived in twenty minutes. After that, a forensic crew arrived to dust for fingerprints and examine the lock on the front door. Gracie signed off on the report that said to the best of her knowledge nothing was taken except a file on Luke Olsen that had been in the bottom drawer, a file she'd read the day before. She asked if they were going to talk to Luke Olsen. The officer looked at her, and said, "If you're accusing him, then, yes, we'll talk to him. If you aren't accusing him, then the answer is no. Unless you have proof Olsen is the one who broke in here, there's not much we can do."

And that was the end of that.

Gracie closed and locked the door. Maybe she needed to get a better, more secure lock. How he got the code to the alarm system was the question that really bothered her. She'd seen a movie once where a burglar had a square box of some sort that could spit out an alarm code in twenty seconds. Maybe those boxes were something architects used on a daily basis. Now, that was a crock if she'd ever heard one, yet it came from her own mind. She knew there would be no fingerprints other than her own, Beth's, John's, and the cleaning lady's, who came once a week.

Any burglar worth his salt would wear gloves. "Crap all over again."

Gracie spent the next twenty minutes shutting down the office, checking and rechecking all the locks and windows, turning down the heat, cleaning and unplugging the coffeepot. She felt like she was locking the barn door after the horse was stolen, but she did what she had to do. In the garage, she called a locksmith and made an appointment for ten the next morning to reconfigure all the locks and to install dead bolts. Then she called the alarm company and changed the code, for whatever good that would do.

"Let's walk to the law office, Giz. You need more exercise, and it sure won't hurt me, either. Then we'll go to lunch."

At best, it was a brisk ten-minute walk, which they completed in record time. It was so warm inside Andy and Artie's law offices, Gracie grew light-headed. The receptionist, a pleasant older woman, showed her to the private offices and asked if she could get her anything. Gracie said no, but Gizmo nuzzled the woman's leg as much as to say, "I'll take a cookie if you have one." She did, and Giz barked his thanks.

"Wow! You two look awful. No, no, don't get up. Sorry, I know you said you were pulling an all-nighter. I hadn't intended to come over, but I have news, and that's why I'm here." Gracie quickly related Gizmo's discovery, the police call, and what all they said. "I'm almost positive that it was Luke Olsen. The only thing missing as far as I could tell is his file. I know it was in the bottom drawer because I pulled it out yesterday to read it, then I put it back. So, tell me, what do you think?"

"What we think is this....You were hacked but not really. The person who did it wanted you to think the worst. We spent all night talking with and e-mailing your clients. Yes, they were hacked, but just their e-mails. All of them immediately called their credit-card companies, their banks, etc., and nothing else went awry. It's still early, but we're both thinking it was a scare aimed at you and Beth. If Olsen is your hacker and Beth's stalker, he had to know he could get into some very serious trouble if he misused any information he gathered off your computers. Yes, at first blush we all panicked. Andy thinks, and I agree, that all he wanted to do was get Beth's attention. Even if it was negative attention. I don't remember if you told us this or not, but does Olsen know Beth's gone?"

"I don't know. I checked out her bedroom before coming here because I wondered the same thing. For all intents and purposes, it looks like she still lives at the house. She didn't take all her things. Actually, she left a set of everything behind so if and when she does come back, she won't have to pack a bag and all the junk she carries with her. I think it's safe to say Olsen still thinks she's in residence, but I can't be sure. He's probably waiting with bated breath for her to get in touch with him. Sicko," Gracie said through clenched teeth.

"Well, that's where we are right now, and it's not a really bad place. We're on top of it, but we both need to get some sleep. And then we'll go back at it. Isn't tomorrow the day you set up shop at Beth's brother's house?"

"Yep. I plan on telling him then what's going on. I was going to go there today but thought better of the idea. I also plan on downplaying it all for Beth so she doesn't get her panties in a wad and rush here. Thanks, guys. Keep in touch, okay?"

The twins promised they would and walked Gracie to the front door. She and Giz took the walk back to Beth's at a more leisurely pace than they had the walk to the law office.

"I'm relieved, Giz," Gracie said as she settled herself behind the wheel. "Buckle up, big guy." The shepherd did as he was told. Gracie grinned. He'd fought her when she tried to teach him how to buckle the seat belt, but he quickly got the message when the car didn't move. He also learned that the quicker he did it, the bigger the treat. He barked. Time to get this show on the road, and he was hoping for a juicy cheeseburger.

"Cheeseburgers from McDonald's okay, Giz?"

Gizmo let loose with an earsplitting bark. Translation: more than okay, and don't forget the fries.

# Chapter Eight

D-day!

Gracie took all of five seconds to decide what she was going to wear to her first day at work at Jake Masters's house, the new headquarters, at least temporarily, of Perfect Match. Worn, tattered, lived-in jeans and a fleecelined, equally worn and tattered sweatshirt that said **Sweet** on the back of it was her final decision. Wool socks and ankle boots because her feet were always cold.

Her curly hair was pulled back into a ponytail. She penciled in some eyebrow color, ran the brush over a packet of blush and smeared on some strawberry-flavored lipstick. **Good to go!** Giz barked, his big head tilted to the side. "Right, I forgot!" Gracie spritzed some perfume in the air and danced under it. She laughed the way she always did when Giz held up first one paw, then the other for a spritz. "Now we both smell like a lily field. Okay, pal, let's grab some breakfast. And then we can hit the road."

Midway through a breakfast of blueberry pancakes that Gizmo practically inhaled, Gracie answered the phone. It was Beth calling for an update. Gracie quickly reassured her that all was well, then listened to Beth tell her about her first night at Rootie Tootie's, which was so awesome she didn't have words to describe it. "John was really good, and the audience loved him." She prattled on, then wished Gracie luck with her no-account brother. "Just don't let him get the upper hand, Gracie. If you need to step on him, step on him. He can only intimidate you if you allow him to. To my own dismay, I allowed it. Rein him in. Moose will be on your side even if you think he isn't. Okay, listen, I gotta run. I'll call you tomorrow or maybe later today on your cell, and you can let me know how the first day went."

**Don't let him get the upper hand. Don't let him intimidate you. Step on him. Rein him in.** Gracie looked over at Gizmo, who was watching her. "She must think I'm some kind of CIA operative. Or maybe even a Royal Canadian Mountie. Jake Masters is not going to listen to one thing I have to say. You might have to bite his ass or something, Giz. You know, to get his attention. Yeah, I know he sits all day, so his butt is out of the question. We'll work on that as time goes by." Gizmo barked, an indication he either did or did not understand what she'd just said.

Gracie opened the door for the dog to go out, then tidied up the kitchen. She had things to do—stop by Beth's house, feed the fish, stop by the law office, stop by the post office to mail out some bills, call Henry to make sure he would be done by noon, stop by the dry cleaners to pick up the winter coat that she'd taken in to be cleaned. All busywork. Still, it had to be done.

"Okay, Giz, let's get this show on the road."

Gracie sat quietly in the car outside the open gates of Jake Masters's estate. She hated the way her heart was pounding, hated that she was so nervous, her hands were actually sweating. She hated that Giz was picking up on her nervousness. "God, how did I ever let Beth talk me into this? How?" Giz whined and tried to nuzzle her neck. "It's okay," she said soothingly. "I'm just being a wuss today. I just need a few more minutes before...before I...whatever it is I'm going to do when I get in there."

Gracie stared out the windshield. Were those snow flurries she was seeing? Yep. Amazing, but then again, maybe not so amazing; it was, after all, coming up on the end of November. She shivered, but she wasn't cold. Try and figure that one out. Fear. Yeah, yeah, it was fear. Fear of a man in a wheelchair. Fear of letting Beth down.

Gracie took a deep breath as she struggled to get her cell phone out of her jacket pocket. She hit the speed dial and, within seconds, was speaking to Henry and asking if it was okay to come in.

"We're just wrapping up here. The guy, the one in the chair, hasn't seen our work yet. We've been more or less waiting for you and dragging our feet till you got here. Then there's the lunch thing. That guy

Moose gets in a snit if we aren't ready to eat when he's ready to serve us his food, which I have to say is pretty good. You can have lunch with us. Today is Mexican something or other. Where are you, Gracie?"

"Outside the gates in the driveway trying to screw up my courage to drive through and enter the house. I'm also trying to calm Gizmo down. He doesn't know what's going on, and you know how he hates change of any kind. Okay, okay, don't say another word. I'm coming in. I know the layout, so I'll just go straight to the office door."

Gracie ended the call and stuck the phone back in her pocket. She took a massive breath and let it out in a loud **swoosh** of sound. She barreled through the open gates and parked at the foot of the steps that led to the big veranda. Her eyebrows shot upward in surprise as she noticed that each step sported a pumpkin. Did the cranky guy named Moose put them there or did Henry? Not that it mattered one way or another.

Henry opened the door the minute Gracie

stepped onto the veranda. He made a big production of tickling Gizmo and pulling a treat out of his pocket. "I hope you're ready, Gracie. I have to say, it all came out better than expected. Even if you hate it, tell me you love it because you know I can't take rejection. You can actually walk in, connect all the stuff you ordered, and sit down to work. But not till after we partake of Mr. Moose's Mexican lunch. Let's go," Henry said, leading the way to the newly renovated office.

Gracie's hands flew to her mouth in shock and surprise. The first thing she noticed was the dotted Swiss curtains. She swooned. "Beautiful! It almost looks like our office in Beth's house, except for the curtains. Oh, Henry, you did a super job. I can see my reflection in the floor. How many coats of varnish or whatever you used are on here?"

"None. The wood comes like that. Steve and Wayne laid it all down last night. We just cleaned it up this morning. We had a little trouble with the pump on the fish tank, but I got it to work. Keep your eye on it, and if it stops working, call me. Everything is under warranty. The phone company was here at seven this morning and hooked everything up. Everything is operational.

"Terry hung all the pictures late last night. Your rogue's gallery, as she called it. I have to say, it makes the room. Your first successes. Good memories. We were able to recess the big-screen TV by taking out the top half of the closet. The built-ins are great, so the room looks a lot bigger than it actually is. Wayne brought the last of the greenery in about an hour ago. Make sure you water it. He left instructions on the desk. The only thing you might have a problem with is the area for the guy in the chair. As you can see, I carved out a nook for him next to the fireplace. His chair will fit there nicely and give him swing-around room. You didn't say, but I figured you did not want the same desk arrangement you have at Beth's house, where you and Beth sat facing each other. I did take that liberty."

Gracie sighed with relief. "Thank God you did!"

"Like I said, all you have to do is hook up your equipment and hit the gas starter on the fireplace, and you are all set. So, you like it, Gracie?"

"Oh, Henry, I love it. I can't tell you how I love those curtains. I just love dotted Swiss, and I know they don't use curtains anymore, but these windows just begged for them. Did you take pictures? If you didn't, you need to do that now and send them all on to Beth. She can't wait to see what you did."

While Henry walked around taking pictures, with Gizmo on his trail, Gracie walked around touching this and that, poking at one thing or another, and nodding her approval. She bent down, pressed the gas starter, and blinked when flames shot upward. Ambience. It was all about the ambience. She was confident she could make it all work. As long as the guy in the chair didn't throw stumbling blocks in her way.

A knock sounded at the door. Henry stopped what he was doing and waved a hand at Gracie, which meant "do not open the door." She didn't. When he was satisfied with the pictures he'd taken and sent them off to Beth, he gave Wayne the signal to open the door and wheel in the food cart, piled high with food.

"We're kind of informal," Henry said, filling his plate and sitting down on the hearth. Gracie joined him. Gizmo walked from one person to the next for samples.

"This is good," Gracie said, smacking her lips. She decided she shouldn't eat too much when she remembered the chicken soup she'd cooked the previous day, which was tonight's dinner.

"What do you think the guy is going to say?" Henry asked anxiously.

"Who knows? Not anything very flattering, that's for sure. He'll probably say it's a girly-girl thing, with the curtains. Since I'm the one who will be locked up here working eight to ten hours a day, it's me that counts. I don't think he's much into light and airy—more dark and dismal and dungeonlike. According to Beth, the guy is in a dark place in his head. When all is said and done at the end of the day, it is what it is. If this doesn't work, I just go back to the house and pick up where I left off. I'm simply following Beth's plan. He'll be the loser in the end, and Beth will have to learn to live with it all."

Henry got up and carried his plate over to the serving cart. He dusted his hands dramatically and said, "Our work here is done. So, Gracie, if you're satisfied, we'll be on our way as soon as I notify the master of the house that it's time to pay up and sign off on the work. Actually, what that means is I call Mr. Moose and tell him he can come for the cart and have him bring his boss in for the final inspection."

Gracie eyed Henry, and the way he was tapping his foot. **He's nervous,** she thought. The truth was, she was just as nervous but didn't want to admit it.

"Okay, guys, you all got your gear packed up?" Everyone nodded. "I'll meet you outside in a few minutes. Warm up the van. I heard it's only thirty-six degrees out there today." Henry placed his call to Moose, then wheeled the serving cart out to the hallway. He looked at Gracie and took a deep breath.

Gracie, Henry, and Gizmo stood to the side of the closed doorway. They heard the sound of the motorized wheelchair before they saw it. The hair on the back of Gizmo's neck went straight up, and his ears went flat against his head. "Damn, I forgot. Oh, crap," Gracie cried, as the shepherd started to growl and whine at the same time.

"What? What's wrong with him?" Henry asked anxiously, sweat beading on his forehead. He swiped at it with his arm.

"Gizmo knows what a wheelchair is. He's a therapy dog. I take him every Sunday to the VA hospital—you know that, Henry. The guys love him, and he loves them. The problem is he isn't wearing his dog tags and body armor. This is outside his routine, and he's confused. He's not sure what's going on. It's the chair that is confusing him."

Gracie tried to put herself between Gizmo and Jake Masters, who was staring, mesmerized, at the huge shepherd. "Listen to me carefully, Mr. Masters. Please. Gizmo is a therapy dog. He thinks you're a wounded vet. He's confused because he isn't wearing his body armor and his dog tags. So, please, just salute him and call him Sergeant Gizmo. He'll do the same, and everything should be okay. Please, Mr. Masters, just do that."

Jake looked confused, his eyes blinking rapidly. He'd never seen such a damn big dog up close. He did as he was told and snapped off a smart salute. Gizmo sat up on his haunches, brought his paw up to his eye, and snapped off a salute that was just as crisp and smart as Jake's. Gracie let loose with a long sigh.

"Gizmo is a soldier, Mr. Masters. He has medals and commendations out the yin yang. He's the only dog in the whole world to receive the Congressional Medal of Honor. The whole world! His handler was killed in Afghanistan. He was a friend of mine; his name was Alex Samson. The military gave the dog to me when he returned Stateside. He has some issues, like loud noises, but otherwise, he's fine. He is an asset to the VA program where he does his therapy work every Sunday. Right now, he's not sure what's going on here. It's up to you how you make friends with him. Like I said, it's the chair."

"Could you guys...um...do all this later? My people are waiting for me outside. I'd like you to inspect the room, Mr. Masters, so I can be paid." Henry swung the door open wide enough to accommodate the wheelchair Jake Masters was sitting in.

Gracie kept one eye on Masters and the other on Gizmo, who was trotting alongside the wheelchair. He knew the drill.

If she hadn't been looking so closely, Gracie would have missed the tears she saw building up in Jake's eyes. He turned to Gracie, and said, "My sister's bedroom, when we were growing up, had windows and curtains like this." He let his gaze rake the room and nodded. "Definitely a big difference. The floor is nice. The chair will move more easily. You did a good job." He turned to Moose, and said, "Pay Mr. Neunsinger."

Jake's attention immediately returned to the dog standing next to him. They eyeballed each other, then Jake laughed.

Gizmo barked.

"Sergeant Gizmo, huh?" Giz barked again. "I'm Jake. He held out his hand, and Giz lifted one big paw and slapped it down dead center and barked again.

Gracie didn't realize how tense she was until she saw the handshake. Everyone was happy. She started to mutter to herself as she set about hooking up the computers and fax machines. She stopped once to give Henry a big hug. He said he'd call her for dinner one day next week. She watched Jake and Gizmo out of the corner of her eye as the shepherd tried to push the chair closer to the windows. Jake got the drift of what he was trying to do. Giz wanted him to see the world outside the confines of a room. She grinned to herself. Maybe in the end, Gizmo would be the one that would save Gracie's brother. It looked to her like they were bonding. She took that moment to stare up at Moose, who looked happier than a pig in a mudslide. **Well, well, what have we here?** Whatever it was she was sure she'd figure it out before long.

The moment everything was hooked

up and the computers booted up, Gracie whistled sharply, and Giz flew across the room. Jake looked at her questioningly. "Was that whistle for the dog or me? All you have to do is call me by name."

"Very well, Mr. Masters, it's time for us to sit down and for you to tell me how much you know about your sister's business so we can divide the work evenly. You really need to understand how this business operates—and make no mistake, this is a thriving business. Once I have a grasp of your understanding, we can progress from there. Your workstation is by the fireplace. As you must have noticed, I hooked up your computer, your fax, and your phone. Click on the home page, and you're all set. So, fill me in here, Mr. Masters."

Jake bit down and started to chew on his lower lip. "Well, um, I really...the thing is...I haven't had...think about it, my sister just..."

"I think what you're trying to say is you don't know any more than you knew five weeks ago when your sister turned this business over to you," Gracie said, ice dripping from her words. Gizmo reared up.

He'd never heard that tone of voice from Gracie before.

"Listen...I..."

"No!" The one word exploded from Gracie's mouth like a gunshot. "**You** listen to me. Your sister hired me to oversee this business. She assured me that you would be cooperative. I told you on day one that I have no intention of losing this job because you are a lazy laggard, a king-sized pain in the ass, full of daily pity parties and full of yourself because you are a whiny puke, and because jobs that pay like this one do not come by very often. I work hard, but I'm not going to do your job, too. I have a life. It's obvious to me you do not have one with the exception of what your sister calls your pity parties. If you screw me over on this, I will drag your sorry ass through every court in the land. What part of **I need this job** don't you get?" Gracie snarled as she slammed a folder down on the desk.

Gizmo was on his feet in a nanosecond. He didn't like any of this. He growled deep in his throat as his big head turned first to Gracie, then to Jake.

"Think quick, Mr. Masters, before Sergeant Gizmo takes matters into his own hands. I'd be real quick if I were you."

"Look, I didn't sign up for this. I thought my sister was...I don't know...trying to get me to do something I didn't want to do. And another thing, I do not believe my sister said all those...those things about me."

"Oh, she said them all right. She also said I shouldn't trust you because you say one thing and do another. That's where she got the 'lazy laggard' from. I think. Let's be clear right now. As of this minute, you know absolutely nothing about Perfect Match, is that right? Oh, one last thing. Your sister also told me not to believe anything you tell me because you lie."

Jake started to sputter. Who the hell was this woman standing in **his** house talking trash to him? He was careful to keep one eye on the dog and the other one on the angry, snarling woman giving him what for. "So I didn't read anything, okay? I'm not in the matchmaking business. I told my sister that, but she refused to listen to me. I do not lie. I do-not-want-to-be-in-the-matchmaking-business. I told my sister that over and over, but she refused to listen to me. I don't have time for this. I went out on a limb and allowed you in here. I allowed you to tear up this room, which was perfectly good to start with, but I still okayed it. It was my understanding you were running my sister's company and doing it out of my house. This," he said, waving his arms over his head, "does not work for me."

"Well, it's a little late for that, Mr. Masters. I'm here, ready to go to work, and I am going to need your help. I don't have time to play games with you. I work. I work because I want to fund my 401(k), so I can have a secure old age and not have to depend on someone like you to take care of me. I have a work ethic. Obviously, you do not. So this is what I'm going to do because it's obvious I am in charge. You are going to sit there at your workstation and read everything your sister dropped off for you. It tells about all the inner workings of the company. You will sit there until I say otherwise."

"What? Lady, where do you get off telling me what to do in my own house? Screw you and the horse you rode in on," Jake shouted.

Gracie laughed. An ugly sound to Jake's ears.

"Giz, **hold and stay.**"

Gizmo sailed across the room and pushed the wheelchair to the workstation. Two mighty shoves, and Jake Masters was facing the computer on the built-in desk. Gracie walked over and plopped down three file folders, duplicates of what Beth had dropped off on her last visit to her brother. "When you finish these, just raise your hand, and I'll quiz you."

"Now just a damn minute. You can't tell me what to do in my own house. "Moose!" he bellowed at the top of his lungs. When nothing happened, Jake shouted again. He stopped in midbellow when Gizmo smacked him on the arm with his paw.

"There's something you need to know, so there is no mistake on your part, Mr. Masters. If I say the word e-n-e-m-y," Gracie said, spelling the word, "Giz will topple you out of that chair and put his paw on your throat. He can hold that position for **hours.** Then if I add a second word and say e-n-e-m-y c-o-m-b-a-t-a-n-t, he **will kill** you. You make the decision if you want it the easy way or the hard way. It goes without saying that there is a release word that I will not share with you for obvious reasons. Just to keep the record straight, Giz has had seventeen release incidents. You might want to keep that in mind." Good God, did she just say and do all of this? **Oh, Beth, the things I do for you.**

Jake thought about it. He'd never seen a more determined, angrier woman in his life. As for the dog...well, that was a no-brainer. "Ha! There's a phone here, right on this desk. I'll just hit nine-one-one."

"Go for it!" Gracie snarled. "Giz, no movements, no phone calls." She almost laughed when Giz's big paw shot out and knocked the phone onto the floor. He replaced the receiver in the cradle and made sure it was out of reach of the man in the chair.

Jake cursed loud and long. Who the hell did this crazy woman think she was? He shouted for Moose again.

Gracie's eyes narrowed when she heard a soft knock on the office door. "Come in," she said sweetly. Moose poked his head in the doorway but didn't say anything.

"About time. Will you please call the police and get this wild woman and her dog the hell out of here," Jake bellowed.

"Why would I do a stupid thing like that, Jake?" Moose asked.

"Why? Why? Because I told you to, that's why. I am your boss, in case you forgot that little fact," Jake continued loudly. "Are you blind? This woman and that damn dog are holding me prisoner. That's considered kidnapping here in South Carolina. Home invasion or something like that. Get me out of here! That's an order, Moose!"

"Oh well, if that's the case, then I quit. If the police come, it will hit the news. You keep saying you don't want anyone to know where you are, and on top of that, they'll find out you're involved in a match-making service. Get it through your head, Jake, you can't have it both ways. In the end, who cares? I quit! What do you want me to tell Calvin?"

Gracie jumped into the fray before Jake could say anything. "Tell Calvin, whoever Calvin is, that Mr. Masters is unavailable until I say otherwise. That might be tomorrow, it might be next week. It all depends on how cooperative Mr. Masters is and how much of a quick study he is."

"Okay, no problem," Moose said happily. "Before I pack my bags, would you like me to make you some coffee?"

"That would be so lovely, Mr. Moose. Hazelnut, if you have it."

"I do. What can I get Sergeant Gizmo?"

"Well, right now, Sergeant Gizmo is on duty. But a couple of carrot sticks would be lovely for when he takes a break."

"What the hell..." Jake exploded.

"Giz, I'd appreciate some silence here. Your charge is throwing me off."

Giz looked from Gracie to Jake. His ears went flat, and he tucked his tail between his legs as he moved closer to the chair. With all the power in his body, Giz spun the chair around and around, and Gracie got dizzy watching the spinning motion until Jake and the chair were flush with the desk. Giz barked three times.

"Three barks means Sergeant Gizmo is tired of your shenanigans. Open your mouth again, and his foot will be in it. Now **READ**! Make sure you absorb what you're reading because I will quiz you, and if you fail, we're back to square one. Consider yourself lucky, Mr. Masters, that you had the brakes on the chair. If the brakes had been off, I'd be peeling you off the ceiling about now. The next time, you might not be so lucky."

"Goddamn Nazi. That's exactly what you are! This is my house, my room, my office, and you are a paid employee."

"How's that working for you right now, Mr. Whiny Puke?" Gracie cooed. **Oh, God, she didn't just say that, did she?**

Moose thought he was going to choke to death on his own laughter. This was the most fun he'd had since they'd moved here after Jake's accident. He could hardly wait to get out to the kitchen so he could call Beth on the sneak.

# Chapter Nine

Moose Dennison punched in Beth Masters's cell phone number and waited for it to be answered as he ground the hazelnut beans that Gracie Sweet had requested. The machine turned off just as Beth announced herself on the other end of the line. For no reason other than that he loved talking to Little Beezer, as he thought of Jake's sister, Moose started to laugh on the open line and couldn't stop as he spooned coffee into the wire basket in his hands.

"Stop cackling, Moose, and tell me what's going on," Beth said in a nervous voice that carried clearly over the line.

"Your girl has your brother on the run. Beezer, I wish you were here to have seen and heard it. That dog...God Almighty, he is one fierce animal. Right now, he's got Jake pinned to his desk, and let me be the first to say I have never seen fear in your brother, but he is scared out of his wits at that dog. No, let me take that back. I think he's more afraid of Gracie Sweet. She might look like an angel, but she was nothing but a devil in that room not ten minutes ago. She let him have it with both barrels."

"Good! Good! Moose, you do realize that's not who Gracie is, right? She is the sweetest woman alive and does not have a mean bone in her body. She's just following the plan I laid out for her. Sounds like it might be working. What did Jake do?"

"Well, he tried to fire her. She set him straight about that. Then I quit."

"You quit every day, so that's nothing new," Beth said.

"This time I'm going to the Holiday Inn for a few days. To teach him a lesson once and for all."

"What about Calvin?"

"Here's the thing with Calvin. Gracie said to tell him she'll let him know when she's going to release Jake. Said it might not be till next week, so I sent Calvin home but paid him for the time off. The dog is guarding the phone, so Jake can't make any calls. Jake actually wanted me to call the police, do you believe that?" Moose said, indignation ringing in his voice.

"I believe anything where my brother is concerned. You told me yesterday that he made an appointment with the surgeon and the shrink for next week. What are the odds he will keep either one, Moose?"

"Your guess is as good as mine, Beezer. I've lost count over the past three years how many times he scheduled appointments, then canceled them. He sounded like he meant it this time, but I just don't know."

"Yeah, I know. Do you think Gracie can hold up to him?"

"Well, she sure got his attention first crack out of the gate. We both know Jake doesn't curse, but man oh man, he let loose with some cusswords I ain't never heard before."

"Locker room vernacular," Beth said, laughing. "I'm going to take that as a good sign. Don't laugh, Moose, but maybe, just maybe, Jake will actually go through with the surgery just to get away from Gracie. Whadda ya think?"

Moose went off into another cackle of laughter. "Anything is possible. Beezer, is that dog all she says he is?"

Beth laughed again. "All of that plus a bag of chips. I really love that dog. I used to dog sit him when Gracie had somewhere to go where she couldn't take him. He's more human than some humans I know. But you always have to remember. Giz is a trained soldier and used to obeying commands. You'd cry your eyes out if you knew half of what that magnificent dog went through in Afghanistan. Did Gracie tell you he and two other military service K-nines got special medals from the president? Giz was the only one who got the Medal of Honor, though. He did, and the ceremony was held in the Rose Garden at the White House. I saw the video. I actually cried when I saw those three dogs salute the commander in chief. Alex would have been so proud of him. It was awesome. Really awesome."

"No, she didn't tell me about it, but I agree that dog is awesome. We haven't talked much. Mostly it's eye contact. I didn't want Jake to get suspicious."

"So, you're really leaving? How will Jake manage tonight without you?"

"I guess we won't know till tomorrow morning when Gracie reports in to you. I don't have her cell phone number to call her, so if you want to give it to me, now is a good time." Moose punched the numbers into his phone right after Beezer's number, which was on his speed dial.

"Hold on, Beth. How's Gracie going to get on the property tomorrow and into the house? She doesn't have the code to the gate or a key to the house. That's my bad. I should have thought of that."

"Not to worry, I'll call her tonight. Do you still keep a key under the light fixture by the back door?" Moose said he did. "Then no problem. What's the code?" Moose rattled it off.

"So, how is Nashville treating you, kid?" Moose said, changing the subject.

"I love it! Just love it. I'm meant to be here, Moose. John loves it, too. He already has a gig and a job part-time as a waiter. Did you ever hear of a place called Rootie Tootie's here in Nashville? It is the place to be seen, the hottest spot in all of Nashville. He plays there every night. It's the place to be and be heard here in Nashville. Moose, I don't think I've ever been this happy in my whole entire life. I'd be over the moon if Jake...never mind, no sense going there. It is what it is."

"Nope, never heard of the place, but if you say it's the place to be, then that's good enough for me. Nice talking to you, Beezer. Don't worry about anything here. Your gal has it going on, and that dog... well, like I said, don't worry."

"Okay, I won't—worry that is. Oh, Moose, one more thing. Does Gracie know you're on our side?"

Moose cackled again. "I think she does now."

"I'll call her later tonight and clue her in just to be on the safe side," Beth said happily. "I can feel it, sense it, almost taste it, Moose. It's all coming together just the way I planned. Listen, enjoy your stay at the Holiday Inn. And stop worrying about Jake. He's a big boy, and big boys have to take responsibility for their actions. You know what you always say, Moose. Either you're part of the problem or you're part of the solution. And on that thought, I'm hanging up. Love you," Beth said.

Moose watched the last of the water dripping into the carafe. His thoughts were far away as he fixed a tray for Gracie. He deliberately set one cup and one saucer on the tray with a pretty paper doily. He set a small plate with some of his home-made sugar cookies next to the cup. He cleaned and added two big carrot sticks and wrapped them in a wet paper towel for the dog. He looked at the tray and knew it was missing something. Something girly. With no flowers to be had at this time of year, Moose meandered out to the backyard and cut a few sprigs of holly and a small bouquet of evergreens that he tied with red butcher's string and laid them across the tray. Now, that was more like it.

Moose eyed the tray and wondered if he could safely carry it down the long hall to the office without spilling or dropping it because of his arthritic hands. He shrugged and pulled out the serving cart and set the tray on top. Simple as one, two, three. He trundled down the hall, rapped softly on the door, then opened it and wheeled in the cart.

"Is this break time?" Jake asked nastily.

"For me, yes, for you, **NO!**" Gracie all but roared without taking her eyes off the computer screen.

"Where would you like me to set this up for you, Miz Sweet?"

"Anywhere is just fine. Oh, that coffee smells heavenly. This is just so sweet of you to make this coffee for me. Giz will appreciate the carrots later when he takes a break. And, please call me Gracie. Is it okay to call you Moose?"

"Absolutely, it's okay to call me by my nickname; everyone else does. Sometimes I forget my name is Orville. I'm sorry we're not going to get to know each other better. It's like hello and good-bye all in one. Enjoy," Moose said.

Moose looked over at Jake, his face sad. "I'm going to miss you, Jake. Good luck."

"Knock it off, Moose. We go through this

every other day. Where are you going to go? You don't even have a home to go to. You need me, so cut the crap and bring me some coffee."

"Good-bye, Jake," Moose said, closing the door softly behind him.

"Aside from all your other bad faults, you really are an ugly person, you know that? No one should be spoken to like that. That man has taken care of you forever is what your sister told me. What will you do without him? Don't expect any help from me. I bet you can't even cook. How do you get in and out of the shower? I rest my case," Gracie said as she sipped the delicious hazelnut coffee.

The silence in the room was total, so it was hard not to miss the sound of the coughing, sputtering pickup truck as it tore down the driveway.

"He's just going to the market or the drugstore; he'll be back in an hour or so after he calms down," Jake said, ignoring Gracie's other comments.

Gracie couldn't resist a smart retort. "You wanna bet, Mr. Masters? A hundred bucks says he's not coming back. Can't say as I blame him. Personally, I find it depressing working with you. I can't even begin to imagine what that poor man goes through coddling you like a baby. Have you looked at the man lately, really looked at him? He's old. Old people deserve respect. And kindness. You should be taking care of him, not the other way around. Whiny puke," she muttered under her breath just loud enough for Jake Masters to hear.

Jake ignored her and kept on reading whatever he was reading. Gracie only hoped he was retaining whatever it was.

The afternoon wore on. It seemed to Gracie that Jake and Gizmo both had their ears tuned to the outdoors and any sounds that might filter through. There was nothing to be heard but the wind slapping tree branches against the windows.

Gracie looked at her watch. It was 5:50. Ten minutes to quitting time. The afternoon had gotten away from her. Since she'd been so adamant about closing up shop at six o'clock, there was no time for a quiz, which meant she wasn't going to be able to tell Jake about the hacking job or give him the details on Beth's stalker. Tomorrow would be soon enough, she decided. Gracie whistled for Giz, who was at her side immediately. "Time to go home."

Giz looked first at her, then at the man in the chair. "He's on his own," she said to Giz.

"I'm leaving now, Mr. Masters. I'll go over the material with you in the morning."

"Aren't you afraid I'll call the police when you leave?"

**Tit for tat.** "It's your word against mine. Aren't you afraid I'll go to the **Post and Courier** and volunteer to do an interview with their star reporter? They might even pay me. Then again maybe not; you're a has-been football player these days, so I doubt you'd generate all that much interest. I'd probably have to do the interview for free. I hate doing free things, but in your case, I'll make an exception," Gracie snapped coldly.

"I bet you take ugly pills every day to be this nasty, don't you?" Jake barked, his eyes spewing sparks.

"Yep. The minute I got the skinny on what a whiny puke you are, I started taking them. I'll see you in the morning. I hope you can ace the quiz. If not, we're going to have a real serious problem. I want you to think about that all night long. From where I'm standing, your future looks pretty darn miserable but, then again, I think you actually thrive on misery. Good night, Mr. Masters."

Jake Masters sat bug-eyed as he listened to the big dog's paws on the new floor. He strained to hear the front door close and the **snick** of the lock sliding into place. He snorted as he realized one Miz Gracie Sweet would be unable to return in the morning without a key or the code to the gate. He didn't know if he was elated or depressed at the thought. Whatever, Moose would let her in. Damn the man; it was six o'clock and he wasn't back yet.

Worms of fear settled in Jake's stomach. Moose never stayed away this long. He wondered if he'd had an accident in that crappy old truck he refused to give up. No, he decided, he would have heard by now.

Jake was antsy now as he wheeled his chair out of the office and down the hall to the back end of the house, where Moose had his apartment off the kitchen. He blinked when he saw the door to the apartment standing open. He wheeled himself to the doorway and stared inside at the immaculate room. He scooted through to the bedroom. It, too, was as tidy as the living room. The bed was made, and there was not a wrinkle in the spread to be seen. The closet door was wide open. It was empty. There wasn't so much as a scrap of paper or a thread to be seen. He looked over at the dresser, where Moose kept a gallery of pictures of him and Beezer. They were gone.

Jake felt a frenzy of fear overtake him as he yanked at the dresser drawers, all empty. Maybe he missed something. He squeezed his eyes shut, then opened them. The little apartment looked the same, like no one had ever lived there. He couldn't even smell Moose's Old Spice shaving cream.

Moose was gone.

Jake's eyes burned as he wheeled himself out to the tidy kitchen. He looked around. By now there should have been something bubbling on the stove or baking in the oven. The table should have been set. He swung back around and looked in the refrigerator. There was food. Food that needed to be prepared and cooked. Well, that wasn't going to happen since he didn't know how to cook. He corrected the thought; he could boil eggs, but there weren't any eggs in the fridge. He poked around, hoping to find something in a container that he would have to just heat up. **Nada.**

Everything in the freezer was frozen solid, and there were no leftovers, like spaghetti or soup, in containers. Jake banged his fist on the refrigerator door and wasn't surprised to see that he'd made a dent. His next stop was the pantry, which was virtually empty. Moose believed in shopping daily and eating only fresh food. It took Jake just seconds to realize there was nothing in the pantry that he could sink his teeth into.

Takeout! Aha! He wouldn't starve after all. He just needed to call someplace and ask them to deliver.... Then he remembered Moose telling him once they were two miles past the delivery routes. Scratch takeout.

Jake was seething now. How could Moose do this to him? He slumped in his chair. Being honest with himself, he knew how. Moose was fed up with him. Who could blame him, being tied to a cripple in a wheelchair. Sometimes, and this was one of those times, life just out and out sucked.

Jake pulled his cell phone out of one of the pockets on the chair. All he had to do was call Moose and apologize. Like he'd done so many times before. His finger hovered over the keys. This, he knew now, wasn't like before. This was where the rubber met the road. Moose was done with him. The ache he felt made him almost physically sick. What the hell was he going to do without Moose? Especially now with that Nazi storm trooper calling the shots, not to mention that killer dog, who was just dying to sink his teeth into him.

Something perverse in him made him tap in his sister's phone number. For some reason he felt the need to talk to her, to hear her sweet voice encouraging him. The call went to voice mail. He hung up. He was so desperate to talk to someone, to rant and rave and whine and piss and moan that he was tempted to call Gracie Sweet. That thought flew in and out of his mind neutron swift. The Nazi, no matter how good-looking she was, was the last person he wanted to talk to. When, he wondered, did he decide she was pretty? Since he couldn't remember making that decision, he decided Moose must have mentioned that he thought the young woman was pretty. Yeah, yeah, that would explain it, because most of the time she looked like an unholy devil, in his opinion.

Jake swore then, making up new curses as he went along, and made his way to the elevator that would take him to the second floor where his bedroom was located, along with his at-home theater.

Now that he was here, what was he going to do? Watch his old games on the big screen? He'd seen them all a kazillion times and knew each play by heart. Jake looked down at his legs and winced. Every sportscaster in the world had proclaimed him the best running back in the history of football. And look at him now. "Yeah," he muttered to himself, "look at me now."

Before he knew what he was doing, he yanked his laptop from one of the bags on the side of his chair and powered it up. He hit the Google button and typed in **K-9 war heroes in South Carolina**. Almost immediately, a full picture of Gracie Sweet's dog filled the screen. Then he hit the arrow that would allow him to see the video in the Rose Garden at the White House. He sat staring, mesmerized at what he was seeing. He could feel his throat closing up as he watched the three magnificent animals parade in front of their commander in chief. He almost lost it when he saw all three animals offer up a salute, and the commander in chief snap one off that was just as impressive.

Jake watched the medal ceremony, then Giz and the president alone as the man presented the Medal of Honor to the dog. He watched each dog shake the president's hand. The dogs fell back into line while the president took to the microphone to read aloud to the world what these three fine warriors had done for their country. He watched, tears rolling down his cheeks, when the first two dogs were joined by their handlers, followed by Gizmo, who walked alone because his handler hadn't returned with him. He did lose it, then, when the marine band took over. He swiped at his eyes as, out of sight of the camera, a young woman dressed in a bright-flowered sundress stepped next to Gizmo and walked with him out of the garden where reporters gathered to interview the handlers. Gracie Sweet **was** standing in for Sergeant Alex Samson, Gizmo's handler. A beautiful woman and a one-of-a-kind magnificent dog.

The dog had been to war and back. He'd survived. His skills on the battlefield, which the president had extolled, rang in Jake's ears. They were so impressive, Jake could feel his eyes fill up again when he compared his own life to the shepherd's. Man, he was so far down on the rungs of the ladder, he didn't even count. No way could he even come close to comparing himself to Sergeant Gizmo Samson Sweet.

Jake tried to remember the last time he'd actually cried, shedding real tears. Maybe when he was ten years old. Not that he hadn't wanted to cry many, many times, but his father's words always echoed in his brain. "Big boys don't cry."

"Bullshit!" Jake bellowed to the silence that surrounded him. He repeated it again, "Bullshit!"

The only thing as far as he could tell that he had in common with Gizmo was they were both famous. He through football and the shepherd through war. The shepherd had earned it. All he'd done was run around a football field. No comparison at all. None. The thought rocked him.

And at that moment in time, Jake Masters took control of his life. He straightened up in the chair and headed for the bathroom, where he struggled to get out of his clothes and into the shower. On his own, with no help. Thank God for his upper-body strength. No one was more surprised than Jake himself when he managed it all on his own, even dressing with no help. He was exhausted, but at the same time, he was exhilarated. He rested for a few minutes before he headed back to the chair and out to the elevator.

**Sustenance.**

Jake poked around the refrigerator and found some cheese, a tomato, a cu-cumber, something that looked like sprouts of some sort, lettuce, and some sliced pumpernickel bread in a baggie. He spotted a sweet potato at the back of the vege-table bin and popped it into the microwave oven. He knew, because Moose told him, that sweet potatoes were good for something. Cholesterol, he thought, but wasn't sure. It looked like he wasn't going to starve after all.

Early in the morning if Moose wasn't back, and Jake knew he wouldn't be, he'd call the market and order some groceries. He remembered Moose telling him that the market had a whole section of cooked food, rotisserie chickens, meat loaf, fried chicken, stir-fry, and just about any other food you could mention. He could always go online to one of the food networks and look up recipes if he didn't like the cooked food, although Moose said it was almost as good as his own. How hard could it be to cook something? This was all assuming Miz Nazi herself and her killer dog didn't work him to the bone or to the point he was too tired to cook.

Jake Masters stared off into space.

He needed a plan.

A plan that would work.

For him.

And put Miss Nazi Storm Trooper in her place.

Jake chomped down on his sandwich, and while it wasn't as good as one made by Moose, it was still good. He ate the sweet potato, skin and all, and felt like he'd done something good for his health. Health. He needed to take his pills and his vitamins. The only problem was the pill bottles were lined up on the windowsill over the sink and he couldn't reach them.

Jake wheeled himself into the laundry room and returned with a broom. He used the long handle to swipe all the pill bottles into the sink. He reached down and lined them up on the counter. He looked at them, wondering why he was taking so many pills, because he could no longer remember what they were for. Moose had always just handed them to him with a glass of water, said, "Take these," and he took them.

Well, Moose wasn't here now, was he? With one swipe of his arm, Jake sent the pills, bottles and all, into the sink. Screw it!

Things were different now. Now he was in charge. As much as he hated to admit it, it was a great feeling. He left the mess and headed for his family room, where he turned on the gas-driven fireplace, hit the remote for the eightyfour-inch TV on the wall, tuned it to ESPN, then put it on mute. He scored a long-neck Budweiser from the bar fridge and settled down to read, again, everything Gracie Sweet had given him to read. He would ace her damn quiz if it was the last thing he ever did.

# Chapter Ten

Gracie felt all woolly headed as she sat in Jake's driveway. She wished she was anywhere but here. Gizmo, in the seat next to her, was whining, so it was a good bet he wasn't any happier than she was at the moment. She thought about Beth's late-night phone call, and everything she'd told her about Moose. She had felt depressed after the phone call and tossed and turned all night. She had dark circles under her eyes and felt jittery. She was out of her element, and she knew it. She turned to the dog, and said, "I wish I had never let Beth talk me into any of this. I wish, I wish, I wish. And now I'm stuck. Just the thought of spending all day in that room with Jake is making me crazy." Gizmo continued to whine.

"Look outside, Giz. Is this a perfect day or what? Any other time, we could have gone out to one of those farms and picked pumpkins and the fall apples for

Thanksgiving dinner. Blue skies, just the right temperature, the sun is out. And here we are. Tell you what, we'll go out for lunch. Actually, we don't have a choice, with Moose gone now. It's either bag it, which we didn't do, or go out. We'll need a break by lunchtime, I'm thinking."

Giz barked. Time to move. Gracie punched in the code that would open the massive iron gates. Was Jake Masters keeping people out or keeping himself in? Like it mattered at this point in time.

Gracie drove around to the back of the house and parked. She found the key to the kitchen door with no problem. She let herself in and looked around at the messy kitchen. It had been neat and tidy when she'd left yesterday. She eyed the coffeepot and started poking around for the coffee container. That's when she noticed all the prescription bottles in the sink. Her eyebrows shot upward. Jake Masters was a tall guy, six-three or -four. Sitting in the wheelchair, he should have been able to reach into the sink if the bottles toppled over by accident. Why hadn't he done that? Or had he tossed them in the sink deliberately? Well, that wasn't her problem.

The hair on the back of Gizmo's neck moved. She heard the whirring of the wheelchair; then, out of the corner of her eye, she spotted her nemesis.

"How'd you get in here?" Jake barked.

"With a key." Gracie held up the key to make her point. "I didn't break in, if that's your next question. Moose gave me the code to the gate, and here I am." She eyed the dripping coffee and had her cup ready the moment she heard the last plop of sound. She'd only made two cups, just enough to fill the oversized coffee mug she'd brought from home, a gift from Alex. The script on the side of the cup had at one time read **You are the love of my life**. The letters were faded and worn off now, but she couldn't bear to part with the mug. She added the last of the cream, then tossed the bottle into the trash container under the sink.

"Let's go, Giz, we have a long day ahead of us."

From his position in the doorway, Jake couldn't see the counter past the center island and had no way of knowing the coffeepot was empty. "I take mine light with two sugars."

Gracie made a production of looking around to see who Jake was talking to. "I don't see anyone else here in the kitchen, so I assume you were speaking to me, right? Well, I'm not your maid. Let's get that straight right now. You want coffee, make it yourself. Make it quick because we have a lot of ground to cover. By the way, did you sleep in your clothes? You look awful. You also need to shave. Just because we're working from home doesn't mean you should look the way you do. Now, if you'll excuse me, I need to get ready for this workday."

Jake had no other recourse except to move his chair in reverse so Gracie and Gizmo could get through the door.

Jake looked around at the mess he'd left the night before. He winced. If Moose saw the mess he'd created, he'd pitch an unholy fit. Well, Moose wasn't here.

**Coffee.** He couldn't remember the last time he'd made coffee. Come to think of it, maybe he'd never made coffee. How hard could it be? He looked around, wondering where the container was. He finally found it. He was hopping mad now. Why couldn't she have made enough for him, too? This was his house and his coffee. "I'm not your maid," he said, mimicking Gracie's words. He tried to spoon the coffee grounds into the wire basket but missed by half an inch. Coffee grounds flew everywhere. A string of obscenities filled the air.

He was back to mimicking Gracie Sweet again. "Did you sleep in your clothes?" Well, yeah, he had, but so what? "You also need to shave." Like I don't know that. Damn Nazi.

Jake eyed the coffeemaker again. He really wanted a cup of coffee. He didn't come alive until his second cup. He sucked in his breath as he wheeled himself over to the sink to fill the pot with water up to the two-cup line. That's when he saw all the pill bottles in the sink. "Shit!" He decided his best bet was to ignore the pill bottles just the way he was ignoring the mess he'd made. This time he made sure the coffee grounds made their way into the wire basket. One scoop for each cup, plus one for the pot. He wondered how he knew that. Probably Moose had said it at some point, and for whatever reason, he now remembered. He heaved a huge sigh of relief when he turned the on button into position and watched it turn bright red.

Two things hit him at once. He needed to clean up his language. He'd never been one to curse and swear, but lately that seemed to be all he did. He decided a few **hells** and **damns** along the way didn't count. The second thing he needed to do was to find a housekeeper. Stat. Somewhere in one of the drawers, Moose kept a list of the tradespeople he dealt with. From time to time, he'd used a domestic service to help with the heavy cleaning. It took Jake close to ten minutes, but he finally found the book. He rifled through the pages until he found the page he wanted. In the blink of an eye, he

punched in the number, announced himself, and stated his needs. He listened,
and said okay from time to time. Finally, he
said, "And have her stop at the Emporium
for food. There is nothing here. I have an
account there. No, she will not be living
in, but I want her here at six every
morning. She can leave at five as long
as she prepares dinner before she goes.
I understand the salary scale. Fax me
whatever it is you need me to sign." Jake
rattled off his fax number, then gave the
lady he was talking to the code to the gate.
"I'll leave the kitchen door open. The door
chimes, so I'll know when she gets here.
One last thing. I'm handicapped and am
in a wheelchair. If that makes a difference,
tell me now." The voice on the other end of
the phone said that was no problem.

Jake leaned back in his chair, feeling
like he'd just scaled a mountain. Not only
had he made coffee, but he'd hired a housekeeper. Yahhh, Jake Masters.

Jake had just settled his special coffee
cup into the special holder on his chair
when he looked up to see Gizmo in the

doorway staring at him. He forgot how ticked off he was that Gracie used the last of the cream for her coffee and left none for him. To his credit, he didn't cuss, but his stomach muscles tied themselves in a knot.

Eyeing the dog, Jake spoke softly to the big animal. "I'm not having a very good morning, Sergeant. As you can see," he said, waving his arms about. "You look really smart, so I'm assuming you know I'm not in top form here. The truth is, I don't know if I'll ever be in top form again. Something tells me you've seen it all, and I'm a pretty poor example of mankind. It's getting away from me, as much as I hate to admit it. The thing is, Sergeant, I have no one to blame but myself. I've been blaming everyone else to make myself feel better. It doesn't work. Okay, enough, right? Lead on, Sergeant, and I will follow you."

Gizmo tilted his head to the side and stared at Jake and the chair. He advanced into the room and stopped directly in front of the chair and looked up at Jake. He let out a soft **woof,** then a second **woof.**

Then he held out his paw for Jake to shake. Jake grinned. "You get it, don't you? Well, damn. Okay, let's go show that Na—your boss I'm not the lazy laggard and whiny puke she thinks I am."

Giz backed up and walked alongside the wheelchair. He stepped aside to let Jake power through, then took up his position again. Gracie looked up and immediately knew something was different, but she couldn't figure out what it was. She hated it when she couldn't figure something out. Time.

Gracie wasted no time. She swiveled her chair around and maneuvered it to the center of the room so she could see and hear Jake better. "You ready?"

"As I'll ever be, but first let me suggest something to you. How about if I just tell you my thoughts after reading through everything you gave me? That might save us some time. Then, if I missed something, you can call me on it. Does that work for you, Miz Sweet?"

"Actually, it does, Mr. Masters. Go for it!"

Jake took a deep breath and exhaled

slowly. He tried to center himself the way his therapist had taught him. "I went into this knowing absolutely nothing, and I do mean nothing, about the dating game or the matchmaking business. To be honest, I'm not even sure I knew there was such a thing. I am referring to back in the day when my sister started up this operation. In today's world, I see commercials all the time on TV for matchmaking. I have to say when I do see a commercial for a dating service, I switch the channel because, for some reason, it offends me.

"When Beth, my sister, started up her business it was at the beginning, and to me it was like the Wild West, a new frontier. There were no rules, no regulations. Dog eat dog, you kill what you eat, and all for the dollar. The fly-bynight companies sprang up everywhere, most overnight. People flocked to them, thinking the grass was greener on the other side of the fence. People, especially the younger ones, dumped their current partners hoping to find the perfect mate, who just might be rich and love them into eternity. How'm I doing so far?" Gracie nodded for him to continue.

"And then the crazies started coming out of the woodwork, and things weren't kind of so wonderful anymore. Applicants were lying right and left, sending pictures of other people who looked better than they did. The meetand-greets turned into horror shows, and the clients started demanding their money back. They do not do background checks on the Internet, so anyone could and did sign up.

"The services started to scuttle and scurry, not wanting to lose the gold mine that allowed them to make money hand over fist while sitting at home in their ratty bathrobes. The million-dollar matchmaking service eventually turned into a billion-dollar-a-year business. The owners of the companies started to tighten up on the Web sites, and started charging a fifty-dollar monthly fee. Then they initiated tiers, silver, gold, platinum, with the platinum costing five thousand dollars. These were called VIPs, and they had access to the Web site and local in-person functions.

That costs extra, usually seventy-five a month for the silver tier for a once-a-month event, usually something at a restaurant, or maybe an art gallery. Something different every month. It's a hundred-dollar-a-month fee for the gold tier. Gold entitles the applicant access to the Web site and special video matchup. The set-up cost here is five hundred and costs a hundred dollars a month.

"I found that the silver and gold tiers are not as stringent as the platinum. Platinum tries to weed out the losers; they do in-depth interviews, and each applicant is guaranteed five dates. All for five thousand dollars. If you don't meet your match after five dates, you have to start all over again and plunk down another five grand." Jake stopped and looked straight at Gracie. "It's a hell of a way to make money. Should I continue?" Gracie nodded.

"I can give you some statistics. There are 54,250,000 single people in the United States.

"The total number of people in the United States who have tried online dating is 41,259,000.

"Annual revenue from the online-dating industry is $1,249,000,000.

"Average amount of money spent by dating-site customers per year is $239.

"Only 10 percent of the customers leave after the first three months.

"Percent of male online users is 52.4.

"Percent of female online users is 47.6.

"Should I continue?"

Gracie realized Jake had indeed read the material she'd given him and also committed it to memory. "Let me ask you a few questions. I'm sure you read the write-ups on the other online services that I included. Tell me what, at this point in time, sets your sister's service apart from the others."

Jake didn't miss a beat. "She had the good sense to scale back after the wild-frontier days. She went smaller and more secure. She made her bag of money first crack out of the gate. Then she made that money work for her. I have to say I admire what she's done. In a million years, I wouldn't have thought she was capable of running a company, much less something like this, and sustaining it. I see hands-on all the way. I'm impressed, for whatever that's worth.

"I'm also impressed that Perfect Match has three satellite offices, in New York, Chicago, and Los Angeles. The managers appear to be top notch. I just don't know where I'm supposed to fit in to all of this.

"In case you haven't figured it out, I made the decision to have the surgery I have put off for too long. I go in for my first workup Friday, the day after Thanksgiving. I expect the surgery will take place the following day but no later than Tuesday. Just so you know, I won't be coming back here for a while because I'll be going straight to rehab. I'm not trying to shirk my duty here or weasel out on my sister. It is what it is. Anything I can do on my laptop at the center, I'll be happy to do. Probably not until week two, just so you know."

Gracie gave Jake a steely eyed stare. "Are you just mouthing words here, or is this for real? Your sister told me you planned to do this seven or eight times and chickened out each time. If you're serious this time, then I can work around you and shoulder your share of the work. If you weasel out—"

"If I weasel out, what?" Jake snapped.

"You don't want to know, Mr. Masters. Suffice it to say it won't be pretty. Now, I want you to listen to me very carefully because what I'm about to tell you is very important. It concerns your sister and her safety. Beth was stalked in the past. She had to get a restraining order against the stalker. That was months ago. The other night, her house was broken into, and a file was stolen. The file on the stalker. Nothing else was taken. We—the police and I—think the stalker made a key when he did some work for Beth last year when she converted the long back porch of her house into her new office. It's the only thing that makes sense. I turned it all over to a law firm. Andy and Artie Axel are twin lawyers and friends of Beth. There's more, so listen carefully.

"We, Perfect Match, got hacked several days ago. We think it was Beth's stalker.

At first we all panicked, but came to realize that it wasn't nearly as serious as we first thought. We've been working around the clock to make it all right. The good thing is that the hacker just got all the old clients, who are no longer with us, but we still have to deal with it all. The firewalls of the new system Beth switched over to are impossible to break through. Plus, she insisted on paper copies, just the opposite of what everyone else does. Computerize, computerize. Not Beth. She's in love with pen and paper and made a convert out of me. Plus, we have all the good files on memory sticks."

Jake slapped at his forehead. "You're just telling me this now! You said it happened a couple of days ago. Why did you wait till now?" Jake snarled. "That's my sister you're talking about! What are the police saying?"

"I can't believe you just asked me that, Mr. Masters. First things first. If your sister wanted you to know, she would have called you. I had to ask her permission to even tell you now. You have not exactly been forthcoming about anything, and you've made no bones about not wanting to be involved in any of this, so why would I involve you even more? The police are not saying much of anything. We cannot prove the stalker is the one who broke into Beth's house. We can't accuse without proof. The lawyers hired a private investigator to tail the stalker, who, by the way, is named Luke Olsen. He also goes by the name Phil Parsons when he does online dating. He's an architect by profession. As I said earlier, he did some work on Beth's house."

"I know who he is. He did work here when I first bought this place. Beth must have remembered the name and hired him because he worked here and knew I would approve the work he was doing for her. his is insane. I have to do something. Get her security or something. My God, why didn't she tell me! I have to protect her!"

"Aren't you a little late in the worry department, Mr. Masters? What's going to be insane is if the private detective can't locate Mr. Olsen because he is trailing

Beth in Nashville."

"Can you forget you took your ugly pill this morning and cut me some slack here? Beth is my sister. It goes without saying I'm concerned for her well-being. I might not know much about the matchmaking business, but I know a lot about stalkers. I was stalked myself by some groupie fans during my career. It's not pretty, and it sure as hell isn't nice looking over your shoulder all the time. You should have told me the minute you found out, so I could help."

"Like I said, if Beth wanted you to know, she would have asked for your help. John Rossmon is with her. They've made friends in Nashville. Beth is no fool; she knows how all this works. She never goes anywhere alone. Please give her some credit.

"We filed a police report for all that's going to do any of us. Beth said she was going to take her paperwork on the restraining order to the police there in Nashville, a paper trail, so to speak. If she wanted security guards surrounding her, she certainly has enough money to hire them. She was quite clear that she doesn't want or need your help. You need to accept that.

"One more thing. It is certainly not my place to say this, but I'm going to say it anyway because I actually feel bad for the two of you since you're all each other has. I don't know if Beth will ever forgive you. You need to give that a lot of thought and see what you can do."

"Do? Do? Is that what you said? I did everything but turn myself inside out. She won't take my phone calls, she ignores my text messages. I sent dozens of e-mails. Believe it or not, I do get it. She's done with me. But I'm not done with her. She's my baby sister. I went off the rails, but I'm getting back on. You don't like me. I get that, too. But do you think you could put aside all your ill feeling and help me out here? Not me personally, but help me to help Beth."

Gracie didn't think she'd ever seen such torment on a human's face. She almost felt sorry for Jake, but then she remembered Beth's meltdowns where her brother was concerned and how she had cried hysterically over her brother's rejection of her. If it wasn't for John and her, Beth would have had a complete nervous breakdown. How do you forgive something like that?

"I don't know what to tell you, Mr. Masters. This is a family situation, and I have no place advising you. Beth is my boss." It was a little white lie—so what. Then she couldn't resist having the last word. "Beth is counting on you to help run this business, so why don't you do just that and let the authorities handle the rest."

"You really are a coldhearted woman, aren't you? Do you even have a heart?"

Jake's words stung Gracie to the quick. She could feel her eyes start to burn. **I will not cry. I will not. I do have a heart, and it's been broken. I'm trying, but sometimes a broken heart is impossible to mend.** She needed to come up with a snappy comeback, and she needed it now. "I think that's a question you should direct to yourself, not me," she responded in a voice that could have chilled milk. "Can we please get back to work here? We have hundreds of e-mails and phone calls to make, and I wanted to schedule a conference call with New York, Chicago, and Los Angeles to introduce you to Mandy, Callie, and Lily."

Jake threw his hands in the air. "Business as usual. The dollar comes first is, I guess, what you're saying. Never mind that my sister is in harm's way. The business of making money comes first. That's bullshit, Miz Sweet," Jake snarled.

"Well, that's the way it is per the boss's orders, and by boss I mean Beth Masters. I just do what I'm told. That's why they pay me the big bucks. So, what's it going to be?"

"What it's going to be is I'm going to call Luke's firm, talk to his parents, see what I can find out. Then I'm going to call my old coach, whose father works for the CIA, and ask for his advice. Then I'm going to call my surgeon and postpone my surgery until I know my sister is out of harm's way. If you don't like it, then get the hell out of my house and don't come back. Wait, wait! I didn't mean that last part. I'm upset, okay?"

"Like hell you're upset. Beth sure was right about you. You're using your very own sister, whom you pushed under the bus, so you can get out of the surgery just like you've done in the past. How low can one person stoop?"

Jake looked flabbergasted at Gracie's words. He struggled to find the right words and knew it wasn't working by the look of disgust on Gracie's face. "I can see how you'd think that right off the bat, but it's not true. Once I go into the hospital, I won't be good for anything. Hell, I'll be lucky if I can tell you my name. The painkillers turn you into a blithering idiot. The therapy about kills you. I won't be able to help. This way I can do whatever I can even if it seems minuscule to you. I have to do it this way. Why can't you understand it?"

"Maybe because of your track record. Maybe because Beth doesn't want you to do anything. Maybe because it sounds like a cop-out. Do you want me to continue?"

"God no," Jake said wearily. His voice was resigned when he said, "You must have taken two of those ugly pills this morning. Excuse me, I think I hear the arrival of my new housekeeper. After I talk to her, I'm going to shower and shave; and then we can get down to work. You do what you have to do, and I'll do what I have to do. And I don't want to hear another word from you, or this time I will bounce you and your dog right out of here. On second thought, the dog can stay, and you go."

"Oooh, you're scaring me, Mr. Masters," Gracie needled. Gizmo barked long and loud to show he was on someone's side, it just wasn't clear who that someone was. Gracie watched as the dog followed Jake out of the room. It was all she could do not to laugh out loud. She quickly punched in Beth's number and waited for her to pick up. Unfortunately, that didn't happen, and the call went to voice mail. She left a quick, concise message, knowing Beth would smile when she heard it.

In the kitchen, Jake looked at the woman who was standing in the middle of the room staring at the mess he'd made. "I'm Jake Masters. And you are?"

"Ilsa Gloom. I brought the food from the Emporium. The receipt is in one of the bags. Tell me what my duties are so I can get started." She waved her big arms and hands around, and said, "No more of this!"

Jake nodded. "It was an accident." He waved his arms about to indicate the mess.

"What do you want for dinner?"

"Pork chops," Jake said smartly.

The woman nodded and pulled an apron out of a black bag she'd set on the table. "You can go now. I'm allergic to dogs."

"Oh, well now. You see, that's going to be a problem. The dog stays." Gizmo barked shrilly.

"It won't be a problem if you keep him out of the kitchen."

Jake weighed his options and realized suddenly he had no options to weigh. He nodded. **Damn it to hell, Moose, where are you when I really need you?**

"C'mon, Sergeant. How would you like to take a ride in the elevator?" Giz didn't bother to bark, he just raced ahead and pressed the round button to open the elevator door. He waited until Jake was safely inside before he entered. Jake grinned when the big dog pressed the button that would stop the elevator at the second floor. "I wish I was half as smart as you are, Sergeant. Your owner has me down as some lowlife, no-account, good-for-nothing, whiny puke. She's right—that's the sad part. Well now, wait a minute. She's only half right. I'm working on...on my issues. You got any input, I'd like to hear it. Like now would be good."

Jake laughed when the big shepherd sat down on his haunches and stared at him. "I'm on my own is what you're indicating. I guess. Okay, I get it. Does that work for you, big guy?"

Gizmo lowered himself to the floor and dropped his head onto his paws, his signal that he was okay with it all.

Jake felt proud of himself that it only took him the better part of an hour to shower, dress, and shave. He refused to admit he felt drained when he heaved himself back into the chair. Giz was at his side, immediately nudging his leg and offering up his paw. Jake knew in his gut the dog did this same thing with the vets at the rehab center. His way of offering encouragement. "Good boy," he said softly and gently as he cupped the dog's big head in his hands. "Good boy."

## Chapter Eleven

"Jake Masters reporting for duty!" Jake said as he wheeled himself into the office. He eyeballed Gracie as he rolled the chair closer to her desk. "I think we got off on the wrong foot, Miz Sweet, and I'm willing to take the blame for it. So, my suggestion is, let's start over. I'm Jake Masters. Call me Jake," he said, extending his hand. A smile as wide as the Grand Canyon spread across his face. "Your dog likes me, so that has to give me a little bit of an edge, doncha think?"

The playful tone of his voice did not go unnoticed by Gracie. She reacted in kind.

Gracie automatically reached for his hand. She couldn't help but feel the calluses on the palms. **It must be some kind of trick,** was her first thought. Giz did seem to be enamored of him. Dogs, especially trained dogs like Giz, were astute judges of character. "Gracie Sweet. Nice to meet you...um...Jake."

Gizmo barked his approval, not once, not twice, but three times. The shepherd definitely approved. Gracie grinned in spite of herself. "Ah, Gracie here," Gracie said, withdrawing her hand, which suddenly felt like it was on fire.

"I apologize for everything and anything. I want us to work together. I want to do whatever you think will work for my sister. I admit I panicked a little while ago when I said I wasn't going to go for the surgery. I am. The thought of spending the rest of my life in this chair is just not an option any longer. I'll do whatever I can do up until next Friday. I won't argue with you, I won't fight with you. I've always been pretty good about following orders even when I don't like the orders.

"I think I understand this business, but I'm sure I'm going to screw up along the way, so just set me straight. And about those...ugly pills...I didn't mean that."

"Yes, you did mean it," Gracie said coolly. "Otherwise, you wouldn't have said it."

Chagrined, Jake did agree. "Okay, at the moment I said it, I sort of, kind of, meant it.

But I don't...I was just angry. I apologize."

"Apology accepted. I need to say something, too. Your sister, Beth, my boss, told me all her life all she wanted was your approval. Before she left for Nashville, I guess that would have been after she came here, she said she had to accept the fact that no matter what she did, she would never get that approval. She said she finally accepted that fact, and that's what made her more certain than ever that going to Nashville was the right thing for her to do. Perhaps I shouldn't have told you this, but unless you say the words out loud, you can never be certain the other person understands. Do you understand, Jake?"

"Nothing like hitting me smack between the eyes! No, I did not know Beezer felt like that, but it certainly explains a lot of things. Unfortunately, we both know you can't unring the bell. I never felt that way. I never judged my sister. I knew she was trying to find her way, trying to figure out what she wanted to do with her life. I never, ever, begrudged anything I did for her. I just wanted her to be happy. I can't deny that I went off the rails after the accident. I regret that now. More than you will ever know."

Gizmo did his three-bark song, his "yes" signal that enough was enough. It was also clear to Gracie that the big dog was on Jake's side. She had to respect that, but she still felt a little jealous. "Anything else you want to unload to clear your conscience?" she said coolly. Nice eyes. Repentant eyes. A person could drown in their dark depths. Now, where did that thought come from? Gracie hated the ring of heat that was creeping up from her neck to her cheeks.

Jake laughed. It was an alien sound to his own ears, a clear indication that he rarely if ever laughed these days. She was smiling at him. At him. He wondered what it meant. A really lovely smile. Maybe the ugly pill was wearing off, or she had some devious trick up her sleeve. Gracie smiled at the sound because it sounded genuine to her. "Nope! My conscience is clear now, so I'm good. So what do you want me to do?"

"Start calling our clients. Just identify yourself as Beth's and my assistant. The reason for that is the guys might get caught up in your football history if they match the name to the sport. If you have to leave a message, do so, but ask them to return your call. We need to make this personal and show we're on top of things. I'm going to be doing the same thing. We'll break for lunch, then we have the conference call with Mandy, Callie, and Lily, and later this afternoon, the lawyers are stopping by to update us. At the moment, I think we're in pretty good shape, but that can change on a dime. I'm going to make some coffee. Would you like some?" **Good Lord, did I just ask him if he wanted coffee? It must be the repentant brown eyes.**

"I would. Thanks for asking." **Uh-oh, she is being way too nice all of a sudden. She really must be up to something because she's still smiling. At me.**

Gracie grinned all the way to the kitchen. Well, she'd whipped him into shape in short order. Then she laughed out loud because she knew Jake was thinking he had whipped **her** into shape. She could hardly wait to send a text to Beth.

Gracie took one look at the sour, dour housekeeper, and reared back. "I was just going to make some coffee."

"Not in my kitchen, you aren't. I will make it for you. I told Mr. Masters the dog can't be in the kitchen," said the woman.

"But you don't know how I like my coffee. The dog is not in the kitchen—he's standing by the door."

"You'll like the way I make it," the sourpuss said coldly.

Gracie whirled around, Giz on her heels. She raced down the hall and into the office. "Hey, Jake, do I have your permission to fire that...that...woman?" The brown eyes sparked with something Gracie couldn't define.

"Oh, God, please do it. I didn't have the guts. Wait a minute, though. I have to pay her. I'll call the agency to send someone else." The wheelchair moved faster than Gracie thought possible. Jake was back within minutes, with a check in hand. "Lock the door after she leaves and make sure Giz pushes her out the door. She's not allergic to dogs. I called the agency, and they said she just doesn't like cleaning up dog hair. Do you need me for backup?" he asked anxiously.

"I think Giz is all the backup I need." God, he was acting so nice, so normal, and he was trusting her to fire his housekeeper. Hmmmmm.

Gracie trotted back to the kitchen. She handed over the check, and said, "Mr. Masters regrets that you and he are not a good fit. He'd like you to leave now, and he also said to thank you for your efforts."

"Well I never..." Ilsa Gloom sputtered.

Gizmo barked shrilly as he nudged the woman toward the door. She grabbed her coat and handbag off the hook by the back door but didn't bother putting her coat on. Gizmo barked again, and the minute the door closed, he slammed his paw on the lock.

"Good job, Giz!" Gracie reached into the pocket of her jeans and pulled out a

Greenie and handed it over.

Ten minutes later, Gracie had two cups of coffee poured and on the tray that she carried back to the office.

"How'd it go?" Jake asked fretfully. "She didn't bite you or anything, did she?" Well damn, he actually sounded like he cared. Hmmmmm all over again.

"Giz ran her off. Now what are you going to do for a cook?"

"The agency is sending someone else. I was very explicit this time around. When I hired Ilsa Gloom, I was desperate, and she was the only person available. The woman at the agency said the person she was sending would be a good fit and that she had a sunny personality and loves animals. Thanks for the coffee. My turn next time. I know how to make coffee. I did it yesterday. Of course, it wasn't nearly as good as yours is today."

**A compliment. Would wonders never cease? He sounds sincere, but then, I do make good coffee.** "What next time? You're getting a housekeeper to take your turn." Gracie laughed at her own joke.

Jake grinned. Her laugh sounded a little rusty but infectious at the same time. He didn't know how he knew, but he felt like Gracie Sweet didn't laugh much. "You have a point. Well, she's going to want a day off here and there, or she might be too busy to stop and make coffee. Then I'll take my turn."

**He's being waaayyy too pleasant,** Gracie thought. She wondered if Jake had a trick or two up his sleeve or if he actually was turning himself around. She hoped for the latter because she hated being so mean spirited. It was just not who she was. "Okay, that works for me."

"Hey, Gracie," Jake said like they were bosom buddies. "Are you sure you don't want me to call Luke Olsen and fish around? Or I could phone the firm, talk to the parents, and see what I can glean from them. I know you're calling the shots here, but what could it hurt? Think about it."

"It isn't such a bad idea overall, but let's wait to see what the lawyers say this afternoon when they get here. They should have a report from the private investigator they hired. We don't want to rock the boat. If they don't come up with anything, then I'd agree to call. Will that work for you?" That all sounded good to her ears, like she was including him in the decisions and at the same time giving value to his opinions. Maybe he was all tricked out and was actually being nice because underneath that facade he really was a nice guy. **Hmmmmm.**

**She's being too nice. Too cooperative.** Maybe they had just been rubbing each other the wrong way, or the ugly pill was wearing off. Jake winced. He needed to get off that ugly-pill business. Nothing could make Gracie Sweet ugly, and he knew it in his gut. As much as he hated to admit it, he knew he was the one who was being ugly. Well, he was dedicated now, and nothing was going to throw him off his game.

With Gizmo sitting next to his chair, chewing away on his oversized Greenie, Jake made call after call, following all of Gracie's instructions. Lunch came and went, and the afternoon took off at a good pace. Before he knew it, it was three o'clock, and Gracie was holding up her hand to signal she wanted to talk after he completed his call. He had a nice phone voice, professional and yet soothing. For some reason, that surprised her after all the snide comments and barking he'd done where she was concerned.

Jake turned the chair around and wheeled himself over to Gracie's section of the office. "I'm all yours!"

**And what would I do with you if that were true,** Gracie wondered. She knew she was supposed to comment but she felt tongue-tied. This was not good. "Our conference call is in fifteen minutes." Now that was absolutely brilliant. Obviously, Gizmo thought so, too, because he barked loud and long. Gracie felt confused.

"If you can spare a few minutes, I'd like to ask your...your advice on something."

Gracie blinked. **He wants my advice. Another trick of some kind.** "Ask away." **Another brilliant comment.** She really needed to update her repartee. She waited, wondering what kind of advice she could possibly give this man in the wheelchair. It looked like Gizmo was wondering the same thing, because he kept nudging Jake's hand so he would continue to tickle his sweet spot.

"It's Moose. I screwed up. The second biggest mistake of my life. The first, of course, was Beth. I don't know how to make it right with either one of them, but right now I'm concentrating on Moose. If Beth were talking to me, I'd ask her, but I have to wing it. I sent Moose dozens of texts and lost count of the phone calls that went to voice mail. I don't know what else to do. I don't even know where he is. If I did, I'd find a way to go there and ask him to come back. This is his home. It will always be his home till the day he dies. I even put his name on the deed to this house."

"Did you tell him that?"

"What? That I put his name on the deed? No. Should I have?"

"Well, yeah," Gracie drawled. "But, somehow, I don't think that would have mattered one way or the other to Mr. Moose.

I really don't know him, so maybe you are asking the wrong person for advice. I more or less thought he was a father image to you or something along those lines."

"Oh, he is...was. Sometimes over the years, we had this love-hate relationship. He turned himself inside out to get me to where I am today. He made me do the therapy, took me to the doctors, and all that. He cooked for me, did my laundry, helped me shower. I would have died without him. He was my rock."

"Did you ever tell him that?"

Jake squirmed in his chair. "I thought I did. I don't know if I said those exact words. I assumed it was understood."

"Wrong. One should never assume; nor should one ever presume. That's Beth's Rule Number Three. Works every time. Beth's Rule Number Four is that you cannot put a price tag on love or loyalty. And she's on the money on that one, too."

"Really! Those are my sister's rules?"

"To live by. Yessiree, they are her rules. I agree with both of them."

"Obviously, I not only didn't know my

sister as well as I thought I did, but I also didn't know Moose, either."

"You see, that's where you're wrong. You did know. In your heart. But when you went off the rails, as you put it, all you thought about was yourself. I can even understand that. To a point. But there comes a time when you have to man up and take responsibility for your actions. You drove your sister out of your life. Then you drove Mr. Moose away. Now you're sorry and want to make it right. How am I doing so far?"

"Spot-on," Jake said grudgingly. "What do you think I should do? A female point of view, so to speak."

Gracie smiled. "They say confession is good for the soul. Bare it all and mean it. Sincerity carries on one's voice. I don't see any other recourse for you. Everyone is entitled to a mistake or two along life's highway. I've found that people are very forgiving when they're given the opportunity to forgive as long as nothing else is expected except for the forgive-ness part. By any chance are you asking me to intercede with your sister? Is that what this is all about?"

"I thought about that at first, but the answer is no. This is something I have to do myself. Even I know that. Actually, I thought about writing letters to both Beth and Moose, but I have no clue where to send them. The written word is more powerful than a voice mail. I figured I could pour my heart out to both of them, and they could either toss the letter or read it again and again until they decided I meant everything in the letter."

Gracie thought about all the letters and e-mails she'd saved from Alex and how she read them over and over until she knew them by heart. It was all she had left of the man she'd loved with all her heart. They were locked away in a metal box on a top shelf, way back in the corner of her closet. A closet that was to have been shared by the two of them someday. She no longer needed to read the letters since she knew them by heart. It was how she fell asleep at night, whispering the words to herself until her eyes closed.

"Perhaps you should write the letters and hold them until you locate Beth and Mr. Moose. I guess you will have to keep calling and leaving messages. It's not enough to walk the walk; you have to talk the talk, too. Anything else?"

Jake shook his head. "How'd you like lunch?"

"I thought you said she was a good cook."

"That's what the agency said. Too much salt, right? Too bland. I can't teach her how to cook because I don't know how. You have any pointers to give her?"

"Are you asking me to train your cook?"

"No! No! Pointers! Clues. Hints! I just thought that most women know how to cook, and you're most definitely a member of the female persuasion. Most of those of the male persuasion, and I admit to being one of them, have no clue how to put something together that won't taste like glue and cardboard. Moose is an exception to the rule. He cooks like a five-star chef. It's about spices and herbs. At least that's what Moose said. My new lady didn't read the same book Moose read, I guess. Never mind, forget I asked. I said too much already."

Jake looked pointedly at his watch. "I think it's time for the conference call."

**He looks nervous,** Gracie thought as she pressed in the digits, mumbled a few words, pressed in more digits until she heard Callie's, Lily's, and Mandy's voices. She introduced Jake as Beth's brother. Everyone said hello, then they got down to business.

Mandy went first. "Gracie, I called in a techie, and he assured me that no real damage has been done. He thinks the hacker just wanted recognition. We've been on the phones for over twenty-four hours, and so far no one's bank accounts or credit cards have been hacked. We urged every member to cancel out their cards, notify their banks, and change all their passwords. Everything has been reported to the various agencies, and I'm confident enough right now to say we're ninety-five percent contained. There are always those stragglers that put off responding for whatever reason. We'll follow up, of course. But that's where we are right now here in New York."

Callie's and Lily's reports were virtually the same.

Gracie offered up a three-minute pep talk, complimented the three women on all their hard work, and told them to stay alert. "The lawyers are coming by later this afternoon, and I'll send you an update before I close for the day. I think it's safe to say our hacker is Beth's stalker, but until we can prove it, there isn't much we can do. I am hoping for a good report from the private investigator. I'll also send that along. Now, does anyone have anything they want to add or say?"

No one did. The three women welcomed Jake to Perfect Match before saying good-bye to him. He thanked them in a husky, sexy voice, then winked at Gracie, whose jaw dropped. Gizmo threw his head back and let loose with a howl of sound. Jake laughed out loud.

This guy had a sense of humor, Gracie thought to herself. Who knew?

Jake pointed to the pictures of the three

women next to their regions on the wall map next to Gracie's chair. "Lily is one smoking-hot babe. Callie could probably snag some big, rich, power broker, and Mandy is the best eye candy I've ever seen. It's a shame that not one of the three is my type." Gizmo snorted his acceptance of the comment and went back to sleep.

"Well, Mr. Masters, that smoking-hot babe is married to a guy who looks like George Clooney and has four kids. Callie is married to a Lutheran minister, and eye candy Mandy is gay." Her voice was so tart, her mouth started to water. What was his type? She didn't mean to give voice to her thought, but the words somehow just tumbled out of her mouth. "What is your type, Jake?"

Jake pretended to think. "Oh, I don't know, maybe someone along your lines, with your intelligence, but maybe with a little more meat on her bones."

Gracie didn't know if she should be flattered or insulted. Probably a little bit of both. She supposed she was to give some kind of snappy response, but words simply failed her. She turned away, her cheeks burning. "Finish up. The lawyers will be here within the hour. I could use some coffee. Your turn to go to the kitchen."

"Okay," Jake said agreeably. "Do you want some cookies, or maybe some brownies? Like I said, you could stand to gain a few pounds."

"Don't concern yourself with my weight. I'm right where I'm supposed to be weight-wise. Actually, Jake, I am in perfect health. Oh, and my teeth are good, too. On second thought, I'll take two brownies, and bring some sugar cookies for Giz. I brought them with me this morning. I left them on the counter by the stove."

Gizmo was up like a shot the minute he heard the words **brownies** and **sugar cookies**. He also knew he only got the white brownies, never the chocolate ones.

Gracie leaned back in her ergonomic chair and closed her eyes the minute the door closed behind Jake. She needed to process everything and do it quickly, but right this moment she felt like Alice about to drop through the rabbit hole.

But before she toppled over, she had to try to make sense of one thing. Was Jake Masters flirting with her? She cracked one eyelid and stared at Gizmo. "Tell me the truth, was he flirting with me, Giz?"

Three sharp barks. Affirmative. "You sure?" Three more sharp barks. "Well, I'll be damned." Gracie backed away from the rabbit hole and laughed out loud.

# Chapter Twelve

The doorbell rang promptly at four o'clock. Gizmo was on his feet in a nanosecond as he waited for a command. Gracie shook her head to indicate the big dog was to stay in place. "It's Andy and Artie," she called out to Jake, who was finishing up the call he was on and, like Gizmo, waited for instructions. "I assume your new housekeeper will go to the door and bring them back here, right?"

Jake shrugged. "We really didn't get into a list of her duties. I planned on sitting down with her at some point today to tell her what I expected. I'll do that this evening."

A moment later, there was a soft knock on the door. "Come in!" Gracie called, and the two lawyers entered the room and stood, if not dumbfounded, then spellbound. Both lawyers were loaded down with what looked like stuffed-to-overflowing briefcases. "This looks just like Beth's old office," Andy said in awe.

"Except for the curtains," Artie agreed.

Gracie got up, hugged the two lawyers, and introduced the twins to Jake, who said he was happy to meet them. Giz barked for attention, knowing somewhere in one of their pockets a treat awaited. The minute it was forthcoming, Giz carried his prize over to the door and lay down in the middle—his signal that no one was to leave the room until he moved. He was also smart enough to know that in order to get him to move, he got a second treat.

"Time is money, people," Andy said. "So let's get to it."

"You guys look tired," Gracie said, concern ringing in her voice.

"We've been working around the clock. Beth pays us to be thorough, and there is no way we would ever let her down. Here goes...Artie and I did a video conference with Lily, Mandy, and Callie. We're satisfied with the results there. We conferenced some of the clients, and while some of them were annoyed, they understand the socialmedia scene and the hacking that goes on. No one is threatening a lawsuit—

that's the good news. We sent out legal letters on everyone's behalf to the credit card companies and the banks. Also legal releases from all the clients. It was a major effort, but it had to be done. For now, at least, you are in the clear. Our techies, who, by the way, are the best of the best, are ninety-nine percent certain that the hack job was to get Beth's attention, nothing more. It's like you see on television; the guy or gal who is doing it wants to be noticed. It's like they're shouting, 'See, I can get to you anywhere, anytime, so pay attention to me.' The trick is to find the person, but whoever did it used a server in Budapest and bounced his signals all over hell and back, so it's someone who knows his way around cyberspace. That's just another way of saying it's impossible to track. The guy counted on that, I'm sure. Right now, he's feeling pretty smug, thinking all he did was leave an untraceable footprint, which puts him in control."

Artie swiped at his curly hair and gave up a weak, tired grin. "We didn't do so well with our private detective, Jim Mack. Since we think, and I say **think,** because we can't prove that the hacker is Luke Olsen, there wasn't much to find. Jim went to the office, posing as a possible client, and was told by the mother, who is a full partner in the firm, that Luke was out of town on business. She didn't give up anything else. Either she doesn't know when he'll be back or simply wasn't going to tell me.

"She did offer up her services, but Jim said he wanted Luke. She didn't seem suspicious and was very open and chatty. She did give him Luke's cell phone number, but when you call the number, it goes to voice mail. The mother said if Luke called in, she'd give him Jim's name and number. When Jim asked her when he left town, she said she thought it was four or five days ago. A rush job of some sort. Other than that, it was a dry hole."

Andy picked up where Artie left off and opened his bulging briefcase. "With no one to follow, all Jim could do was make the rounds and interview people who know Luke. And surprise, surprise, Luke Olsen really doesn't have any friends. He said, and it is all in his report, that he has acquaintances and customers but that seems to be it. He doesn't golf or play tennis. He has a gym membership that he uses maybe once a month. He couldn't find a single person he ever confided in. The consensus was the guy is a good architect and knows his business. Olsen goes to Starbucks twice a day and sits there and drinks his coffee and flirts with the baristas. All three women said he was a hunk but a creepy hunk. Which brings Jim to his next question. Do you want him to go to Nashville to see if he can pick up the trail there? He's convinced Olsen is in Nashville."

"Hell, yes," Jake said, the words exploding from his mouth like gunshots.

The twins looked at Gracie for confirmation. She nodded.

"One other thing," Artie said. "Jim lifted some fingerprints from Beth's house. Now I know what you're going to say—he worked there overseeing the renovations, so there is bound to be a stray print or two even from years ago—and you would be right. But the prints Jim found— again, this is all in his report—were found in Beth's bathroom and bedroom as well as in the office. Fresh prints."

Gracie took that minute to look at Jake, who looked like a deer caught in the headlights. She felt the fine hairs on the back of her neck move. This was not good. Definitely not good.

Jake's gaze sharpened. In a cold, controlled voice, he said, "I guess this is where you have to give up my sister's location or get in touch with her yourself, so she can take appropriate measures for her safety. I'll leave the room so you can keep your promise to Beth to not tell me where she is." He wheeled his chair so fast, the tires actually screeched on the new flooring. Giz was up like a shot and following him out of the room.

Gracie bit down on her lip. She didn't like this turn of events. She stared at the twin lawyers and shrugged as she scribbled off Beth's address. "This isn't feeling right to me."

"It is his sister. It doesn't matter what

went on before, what matters is the here and now. I understand you have to honor Beth's wishes, but maybe it's time to call her and alert her to the seriousness of this situation," Andy said.

"Stalkers are not predictable people. At some point, this guy is going to get frustrated just looking from afar. I talked to a cop friend of mine, and he clued me in on how those guys work. And by the way, there are women stalkers out there, too. Being as high-profile as Jake was when he was playing football, I'm sure he heard or saw some of what goes on firsthand. Sooner or later, our guy is going to want a face-to-face with Beth. Stalkers are also known for following their victim, not hiding out in the shadows, so to speak, and appearing out of the blue, so the victim gets just a glimpse of them and goes into panic mode. Which is exactly what the stalker wants to happen," Artie said.

"This is really creeping me out. You guys know how independent and fearless Beth is. She's not going to want guards or someone watching over her. She'll say she can take care of herself and that she has John at her side. The thing is, John now has a part-time job, so he isn't with her all the time. Yes, at night, I assume Beth goes with him to the club where he works. She'll come up with every excuse in the book," Gracie said.

The twins threw their hands in the air simultaneously. "Then how do you think we should proceed from here on in? Beth has to be made aware of how dangerous this can get. She has to take this seriously. Do you want us to call her?" Andy asked.

"I have a better idea. Let's all call her. I can put us on speaker so we can all hear. That way, the three of us can say what we want to say. Assuming she picks up the phone. Sometimes, she just lets it go to voice mail. Then there's Jake. I don't feel right or good about this, and no, I am not switching up sides here."

"Do it!" Artie said.

Gracie hit the number one on her speed dial and waited. She sucked in a deep breath and exhaled only when she heard Beth's cheerful voice.

"I was just going to call you, Gracie. Guess what? John said he's off over Thanksgiving, so we're going to come home for the day. If you buy all the food, I'll cook. We'll just blow in, visit, eat, and blow right back out because John has to work Friday night. You okay with that, Gracie?

"Oh, I'm going to invite Moose for dinner. Have you talked to him? How's it all going?" Beth asked breathlessly.

"Well, now that you asked, I want you to listen to me very carefully. Artie and Andy are here. We're all here in the office at Jake's house. He's out in the kitchen at the moment. That's the reason for this call."

Gracie signaled to Andy to start the ball rolling. He did, but three minutes into the conversation, they all realized that Gracie was absolutely correct. Talking to Beth was like talking to a brick wall. Artie chimed in, reading stats on stalkers from a form in his hand. As with Gracie, Beth pooh-poohed it all away. To her credit, she did listen. But she was having no part of it.

"Listen, Beth, you know I'm not one to sound the alarm bell, but I'm sounding it now. Everyone is worried sick about you. Stalkers start out like Peeping Toms and graduate to different stages. I want you to think about something. What if, for instance, this guy comes up behind you and puts you in a choke hold and damages your throat. What if you can never sing again? Don't you dare say something stupid like you'll start wearing scarves. Do you hear me, Beth?"

"I think the whole town of Nashville can hear you. Okay, okay, I will not go anywhere alone from this moment on. Maybe when I come home for Thanksgiving, you'll let me bring Gizmo back with me."

"Oh, no. No, no, no! Giz stays with me. I'm not giving him up even for you because you're being bullheaded. Don't ever bring that up again. Jim Mack, the detective, will be leaving for Nashville today, so be nice to him when he gets there. Help him out. I don't know why, Beth, but I feel you need him. Humor me, okay?"

"Sure, whatever you say. Such a waste of time, manpower, and money. How sure are you about this?"

"I am one hundred percent sure, and Andy and Artie agree. So does your brother. And if you tell Moose, he will agree also," Gracie said.

"Anything else?"

"Isn't that enough?" Gracie shot back. "Listen, Beth, be careful, okay? Just keep remembering that Luke Olsen's fingerprints were all over your bedroom and bathroom. He broke into your house. That means he's moved up several levels since you took out that restraining order against him. He's wanting more now."

"I get it, Gracie. I really do, but I'm not going to live my life in fear. I will stay extra alert, and I promise not to go anywhere alone. I'll talk to John about it all, too. We've made some really nice new friends here, and we can put them on alert also. Stop worrying about me, okay? Is Jake working out?"

"I was born to worry, you know that, and yes, Jake is working out. He's got a good grasp on the business now. He's very cooperative, and Giz loves and adores him."

Beth mumbled something into the phone that didn't sound complimentary. Gracie didn't bother to ask her to repeat what she'd said, and ended the call. She looked up at the twins and threw her hands in the air. "You heard what I heard. The only thing I think that got to her was the possibility of this guy's coming up behind her and injuring her throat, so she can't sing. I think that really got to her. My advice—send Mr. Mack to Nashville ten minutes ago and tell him not to take his eyes off her. I think it will be good if he reports in every six hours. That's not too much to expect, is it?"

"Is it safe to come in? Did you all get Beth to agree?"

Artie looked over at Jake, and said, "Your sister is as stubborn as a mule, but you already know that, I assume. We're sending the detective to Nashville today. He's a good man and has a friend on the police force there. He'll know what to do if things get sticky or out of hand."

Jake glanced over at Gracie and hated the look of worry he saw on her face. He wished there was something he could do but had no idea what, if anything, that something was. He turned and steered his chair out the door and down the hall and out of sight. He pressed in the digits to Moose's cell phone and talked from his heart. For a full ten minutes. He ended with, "I really need you, Moose. Beezer needs you, too. Please, come back so we can all work together to keep Beezer safe. Please, Moose."

Forty minutes later, long after the twin lawyers departed, Gracie jerked upright, as did Giz, when they both heard the chugging, wheezing sound of Moose's truck.

Jake laughed out loud, then blessed himself. Moose to the rescue. God, how he loved that man. Giz, sensing the exuberant mood in the room, ran out the door and raced down the hall to be a welcoming committee of one.

Gracie stayed in the office, nibbling on her thumbnail as she waited for Moose to come by and say something, anything, an indication that he was just visiting, staying, or picking up the rest of his belongings. She also wondered how, if he planned on staying, it would work out with the new housekeeper. Gracie hated waiting. She bit down on her lower lip and decided she could sneak down the hall and listen outside the kitchen. Of course, she knew that eavesdroppers never heard anything good about themselves, but then again, this wasn't about her—it was about Beth.

Gracie didn't stop to think. She acted, running out of the room and tiptoeing down the hall. She could hear voices, then she heard the sound of a car engine. The new housekeeper leaving? She childishly crossed her fingers that Giz wouldn't pick up her scent and come barreling through the door. She flattened herself against the wall and unashamedly listened.

"God, Moose, I gotta tell you, I didn't think I could miss anyone as much as I missed you. Tell me that you're here to stay. I'm sorry. I had no right to take you for granted, and that's exactly what

I did. It was all about me, me, me. If it takes me the rest of my life, I promise to spend it making this all right. Right now, though, this isn't about me, it's about Beth. I'm hoping you can talk some sense into her."

Moose played it to the hilt. Gracie grinned, her fist shooting in the air.

"I don't know if I'm staying or not. That's going to be up to you, Jake. I've heard all those promises so many times I've lost count. Right now, though, I don't care about you. I'm here to offer whatever help I can to Beezer.

"I have to say, Jake, I did admire how deftly you discharged that little lady you had messing up my kitchen. I didn't know you had it in you to be so kind."

"That was a low blow, Moose." Jake held up his hands, palms outward. "But I deserve it, so let's move on. And before you can ask, yes, I am going ahead with the scheduled surgery. Everything is in the works. Did I miss anything?"

"A few things," Moose snapped. "How is it working out with the little lady in the office, and what about this monster dog?" Giz let loose with a loud bark, then growled to show he wasn't fond of Moose's words. Moose reached for a dog treat in a clear plastic canister sitting on the counter. "I meant that as a compliment, Sergeant."

"I think it's safe to say Gracie and I have a truce of sorts. She does have a sharp tongue at times. If you take a real good look at her, Moose, she's pretty. She has expressive eyes and, once, I actually saw her smile. I actually like her, but I'll never tell her that. She looked like the Mona Lisa when she smiled. I kid you not. I've done everything she asked me to do. In other words, Moose, I've been a perfect gentleman. You can be proud of me. I mean that.

Beth's business is safe, and that's because a lot of people who care about her pitched in and worked around the clock. I learned more about my sister in these past few days than I knew about her all our lives. Did I say that right, does it make sense?

"I should have spent more time with

her. I don't know if I can ever make that right, but as long as I'm breathing, I'll keep trying. As for the dog, he really is one of a kind. I think he likes me. When I get back here after surgery and rehab, I'm going to look into getting a dog like Giz. He's a therapy dog, did you know that? Gracie takes him to the VA on Sundays to give moral support to the veterans there for therapy. You gotta admire that, and the dog. Like I said, he likes me."

Outside in the hallway, Gracie's hands flew to her mouth in shock. She turned around and ran down to the office, where she collapsed into her ergonomic chair. He thought she was pretty. He wasn't crazy about her sharp tongue, however. And he thought she looked like the Mona Lisa. Gracie didn't know if she should be flattered or insulted, because she thought that in the Mona Lisa paintings she'd seen, Mona looked homely.

Gracie squeezed her eyes shut and wondered what it would be like to glide across a dance floor with Jake Masters. Like that was ever going to happen. He thought she was pretty. Hmmmmm.

Back in the kitchen, the conversation continued. "What's our next move here?" Moose asked.

Jake shared everything he knew right up to the part where the private detective, Jim Mack, was heading for Nashville today. "Your turn, Moose. Don't tell me you haven't been in touch with Beezer, because I know you have. You love her as much as I do. Help me out here, okay?"

"I have spoken to her, but the conversations are mainly about her career and what she hopes will happen down the road. She's really excited about her singing lessons and John's gig, as she calls it. She said she and John have made a lot of new friends. She doesn't ask about you, if that's your next question. She called me just as I pulled into the driveway to invite me for Thanksgiving dinner. She said she and John are coming back just for the day. She's cooking at her house. No, you are not invited."

"I didn't think I would be, Moose. It's okay. I already planned on ordering a complete dinner from Zabar's in New York. I plan on psyching myself up for Friday, and I need to be alone to do that. Not to worry—I called a medical transportation service to take me to the hospital Friday morning, so don't worry about that. Spend as much time as you can with Beezer and John.

"Look, I've goofed up here long enough. I have some stuff I still need to go over with Gracie before we call it a day. If I could stand up, I'd hug you, Moose."

Moose almost lost it then at the sincerity in Jake's voice. "What do you want for dinner, Jake?" he asked gruffly.

Jake looked stunned. "You're cooking?"

"Well, yeah. I like to eat at least once a day. How does three big juicy rib eyes sound, with twice-baked potatoes, salad, and some of my mango relish?"

"It sounds like I died and went to heaven. Three steaks?"

"For the big guy here," Moose said, pointing to Gizmo. "You want to stay for dinner? Rib eye steak that will make you drool for me. My specialty. Whadda ya say, Sergeant?"

Gizmo barked three times.

"That means yes. Gracie said when he barks three times, it means yes. Two barks is no. Oooh, I don't know if she'll let him stay for the night. You better check with her before you cook his steak."

"Why don't you do that, Jake? Check with her, I mean."

Jake squirmed in his chair. "What if she says no?"

Moose snorted. "Use your powers of persuasion. And doesn't the dog have something to say about it?"

"The dog can't ask permission. This might be overstepping my bounds here.... Okay, okay, I'll ask her," Jake said, turning his chair around. He looked back over his shoulder, and said, "I love you, old man, you know that, right?"

Moose made another snorting sound as he bent down to pick up his suitcase to take into his room. The moment he closed the door, he did a little jig and shot both fists high in the air.

The minute Jake entered the office, he got right to the point. "Moose is going to grill some rib eyes tonight and he invited Gizmo for dinner. The dog barked three times meaning, according to you, yes. I realize he is your dog and what you say goes, so if you don't want him to stay, it's okay."

This was the last thing she expected to hear from Jake. Should she say yes or should she say no? If she said no, what would he think of her? She looked over at Gizmo, and asked, "You wanna stay for dinner and spend the night?" Giz let loose with three sharp barks as he danced around in a circle. "Okay then. Go tell Mr. Moose you're staying." The dog was off like a shot.

Gracie homed in on Jake. "Don't think you're going to steal my dog's affections."

"Gracie! How could I possibly do that?" He grinned.

"Yeah, well, you wouldn't be the first person to try. Look, I'm tired, so let's call it a day and get an early start in the morning."

"That works for me. I'm kind of tired myself."

Gracie packed her stuff, gathered up her

coat and backpack as she wondered why she hadn't been invited to dinner. Maybe they thought she wasn't worthy of one of Mr. Moose's rib eyes. Something hot pricked at her eyelids.

Jake heard Gizmo bounding down the hall, so he could walk Gracie to the door. He wondered now why he hadn't invited Gracie to dinner. Or why Moose hadn't suggested it. Come to think of it, she'd looked stunned that the dog was invited but not her. Not cool, Jake. Not cool at all.

# Chapter Thirteen

Beth Masters plopped a heavy, accordion-pleated file folder on the table of her cozy breakfast nook and proceeded to lay out stacks of forms and papers in orderly rows. She looked at the clock on the kitchen wall, then down at her cell phone, and finally at the piles of papers. She sighed deeply. She felt out of sorts, discombobulated, as John liked to say. She knew he was standing in the doorway watching her, waiting for her to say something. She hated it when he looked at her like he was looking at her now. She bit down on her lower lip.

"Wanna talk about it, Beth? I have time before I have to head on out. Good dinner, by the way. Sometimes, talking about it helps." He grinned, then said what he always said in situations like this, "Wanna get married?" At which point Beth always giggled and waved her hands in the air. Translation: I'm not quite ready yet.

Beth stared across the room at the love of her life. Her anchor. Her port in a storm. They'd been together almost all their lives, except for John's stint in the Marine Corps. She'd written him every single day for four solid years. John wrote once a week if he was lucky, short letters that she devoured and memorized. She loved him heart and soul and knew no one could or would ever be able to take his place in her heart. There was nothing she wouldn't do for this man. Nothing. The mess on the table was proof of her love and devotion.

John Rossmon was six-two and tipped the scales at 180. Paul Newman blue eyes, adorable dimples that he hated, a sizzling, sexy smile that drove women crazy, and her name was at the top of that particular list. He wore his hair high and tight, the same way he'd worn it in the marines. A hunk. And he was all hers. He'd been all hers since they were ten years old. He had mowed their lawn, and she'd taken him glasses of lemonade that he would share with her. He walked her to school, sometimes carrying her book bag.

He'd taken her to all her proms and kissed her for the first time under the old oak tree where he had carved their initials when he was thirteen. He had magic fingers with his guitar and could sing like a bird. If she had a wish, it would be that he found his place here in Nashville and got to head up the charts. Every night, right before she fell asleep, she prayed that it would happen for John. If there was anything she could do to help things along, she'd do it in a New York minute.

"Yeah, I guess. I'm not trying to keep anything from you, John. It's just that I needed a little time to think about Gracie's phone call. And Moose's call. I planned on telling you later tonight." Beth threw her hands up as she started to talk, bullet fast. She finally wound down. "So, yes, that's the reason I'm not going to the club with you tonight. I want to stay here and plan out a course of action. I'm not afraid, but I am concerned. Neither Gracie nor Moose are alarmists, and right now they're both ringing alarm bells loud and long. I have to pay attention to that."

John digested all he heard, then slid into the leather booth behind the table. "What about Jake?" he asked, reaching for her hand and squeezing it.

"Jake, according to Gracie, and Moose, too, wanted to postpone his surgery and come up here and beat some sense into my head. He saw the error of his ways and backed off. The detective Andy and Artie hired is on his way here as we speak. He should get here around nine, just when you hit the club. That's another reason I'm staying home tonight. Gracie and Moose both badgered me to agree to letting him stay here with us. We have a spare bedroom, so I said yes. I knew you wouldn't mind and that you'd be relieved. It is what it is, John. I have to deal with it, and I'm not going to run and hide and live my life like that. I absolutely refuse to let some screwball drive me to the ground. Don't suggest going to the police. We have no proof of anything, and you know as well as I do that you cannot accuse someone of something this serious without proof."

"Marry me, Beth."

"You were supposed to say something good about the detective moving in here and watching over me. Besides, you know the rule—you only get to ask me to marry you once a day. Two times does not count. And...you know I can't marry you until Jake can walk me down the aisle. Having Moose do it isn't the same. I was thinking, though, they could both walk me down the aisle when it's time." Her voice was so angry, so defensive, and yet sad, that John burst out laughing.

"Go ahead and laugh, John Rossmon, but I know that Jake is going to walk again. This is his last chance. I had to push his face into the reality of it all, or he'd never get out of that chair. No way am I going to back down now after all this. He's going for the surgery, and that was the biggest hurdle. He knows this is it."

"Well, I'm not leaving here until the detective arrives. I want your promise, Beth, that you won't go anywhere alone from here on in. I know it will cramp your style, free spirit that you are, but still, I want your promise."

Beth smiled as she promised. "I asked Gracie to let me have Gizmo, but she refused. Do you believe that? She refused! She also told me Giz adores Jake, and Jake loves the dog. She sees this as a big plus where Jake is concerned. I think that's why she won't let me have him. Oh, and get this. Jake and Moose invited Giz to dinner and to spend the night. Gracie sounded to me like she was a little put out about that. I'm kind of thinking she got her nose out of joint when she wasn't invited. For dinner, not the sleepover."

John laughed out loud. "Beth, you are as transparent as window glass. Your goal has always been to fix up Gracie and Jake. You said it yourself more times than I can remember that they are the perfect match, they just don't know it. Yet."

Beth sniffed, then grinned. "Admit it, John, they are a perfect match, and you know it. I wanted them to be my first clients, but it didn't work out that way. In the end, as we both know, this will all work out just the way it is supposed to."

John pointed to the mess of papers on the table. "You made up your mind?"

"Actually, Mr. Hudson, my voice teacher, who by the way said I should call him Alfie, said I should start making arrangements to book everything for February. He said by then I should be ready to cut the CD. I'm doing our song, the one you and I wrote. You said you were okay with it, right? When I finally book the dates, you'll have to block out the time with the band and the café. Did you change your mind about singing the song at the club?"

"Well, yeah, Beth. I don't want to tip our hand. The minute we record it, I got the guys to agree to let us do it at the club. I'm not going solo on that. That's your baby. Did you ever tell Jake you got the inspiration from his first love?"

"No, and we are never going to tell him, either. If he puts it together, that's fine, but we are not volunteering anything where Allison is concerned. She didn't care about Jake. All she wanted was to be seen with a big football star. She cheated on him left and right, and he was so sappy he couldn't see it until one of his teammates showed him pictures. It took him forever to get over her. All he could say over and over was 'What was I thinking?' Hence the title for the song."

"Jake's pretty astute when he wants to be. I'm okay with whatever you want. Oooh, there goes the buzzer. Must be your private eye. I'll let him in, then head for the club. I'll call you, okay? Promise you are in for the night."

"John, I am in for the night. I promise," Beth said, crossing her heart. "Go!"

Jim Mack was a fiftysomething man who looked to be in tip-top shape. Introductions were made, hands shaken, and they all sat down with coffee. "Appreciate you all letting me camp out here. It will make my life a lot easier. I promise not to get in the way."

Beth eyed the man carefully. Square jaw. She liked that. Shrewd, clear gray eyes that looked right through you. She liked that, too. In size and weight, he was head to toe with John. He wore a regulation haircut that looked like he'd just come from the barber. He even smelled good, all woodsy and citrusy. She liked that, too. But what she liked most about him was how he was dressed—pressed khakis, blazer, T-shirt underneath, and Docksiders. He'd blend in perfectly here in Nashville, where his clothing was pretty much the standard uniform of the day.

His credentials were impressive. Twenty-five years at the FBI for starters. That alone told Beth she was in good hands if this guy was watching over her. Luke Olsen would be hard-pressed to get past someone like Jim Mack. Her gut told her this guy had seen and done it all, and nothing would go unnoticed. Plus, if Andy and Artie said he was good, then he was golden in her opinion. Also the double plus was Mack's last five years at the Bureau as their top profiler, which would definitely give him an added edge. The bottom line was that just sitting here next to him made her feel safe. She knew she was in good hands as long as she did her part. That was going to be the hard thing.

John looked at his watch. "Gotta go, guys. My public awaits. Don't want to disappoint them." He eyed Beth before he kissed her good-bye. He whispered in her ear, "Do what this guy says, okay? I like him."

"Hmmmmm. Don't fall for any groupies tonight." Beth giggled.

"I'll do my best. Lock the door behind me. I want to hear you do it, Beth."

"That's okay, John. I'll follow you out. I have to get my bag out of the car, and I'll lock up. Call me if you see or hear anything out of the ordinary tonight or from here on in."

"Will do. Take good care of my girl for me. I have to admit, I'm a little scared about that nut job out there." The two men shook hands and parted ways, John to his Ford Ranger, and Jim Mack to his Beemer.

If John hadn't been so preoccupied with thoughts of Beth and the new detective, plus shivering in the cold, he might have spotted the tall, solid-looking man at the entrance to the parking area. As it was, the man observing John stepped back into the shadows, allowing him to confirm that it was John Rossmon in the Ford and a stranger heading back into the building.

The observer hopped into his black SUV and followed John. The man gave himself a mental pat on the back for being astute enough to check the utility records to find out where John and Beth lived.

As he drove along, three cars behind Rossmon, Luke Olsen again congratulated himself. It had only taken him four days to come up with Beth's address and now, tonight, he was going to find out where Rossmon worked.

Olsen liked Nashville. The city was alive. Walking the streets, getting the lay of the land these past few days, allowed him to get the rhythm of the city, the people, the traffic, the day-to-day life, then the night life. He liked the way the city breathed. He knew he could be happy here with Beth Masters, but first he had to get rid of that pesky John Rossmon. With his newfound euphoria in check, he let his mind wander to who the man was that Rossmon had been talking to in the parking lot. Tenant? Friend? Stranger? Not that it mattered right now.

Luke did wonder where Beth was. Was she at home? Did she go wherever it was Rossmon was going? Some club, obviously. He'd made that astute deduction when he saw him carrying his carry bag and guitar. Where else would he be going but to work at nine-thirty at night? Nashville just started to liven up at that hour. He likened Nashville to New Orleans even though he'd only been to the Big Easy once, years ago. The beat. It was all about the beat of the city. And damn if he didn't love the beat. Yessiree, he and Beth could be really happy here.

While Luke Olsen was congratulating himself, Beth Masters was having an intense conversation with Jim Mack. "I get it, Jim. I really do." She was getting really weary of repeating over and over that she would do as she was told.

"So what is," Mack said, waving his hand over the clutter and piles of paper on the breakfast nook table, "that mess?"

"The reason I came here. I came here to

find my fame and fortune. I plan on taking Nashville by storm at some point. I'm knee deep in singing lessons, and this mess that you are referring to is all the paperwork for me to cut a CD sometime in February. Along with John. I need to get all this paperwork in on time."

Mack eyed Beth, and said, "Really?"

Beth looked away. She was right about this guy; he had eyes that could look into a person's soul. At least that's the way it seemed to her at the moment. "Why do you say **really** like that? It sounds like you don't believe me."

"You forget what I used to do for a living, before I retired. You do know what profilers do, don't you?"

Beth nodded. "I noticed you've been studying me since you got here. You didn't fool me, Mr. Mack. I already knew everything you said. I promised to cooperate the moment you got here. So the rest of the time you've been studying me and coming to some kind of conclusions. How am I doing so far?"

Mack laughed. "Spot-on. Is it okay to call

you Beth? And, of course, you can call me either Jim or Mack. No one calls me Mr. Mack, and I've retired the title of Special Agent Mack."

Beth didn't like the way the conversation was going. She faked a yawn and said it was time to turn in. She didn't mean to ask what Mack's conclusions were, but the words tumbled off her tongue almost at the speed of light.

Mack grinned. "You sure you want to know?"

Beth wasn't sure at all. Her head bobbed up and down. She knew she was going to regret this. She stiffened her shoulders.

"You're a phony," Jim Mack said gently.

"And you know this...how? An hour of studying me, and you can tell I'm a phony?" There was outrage in her tone. And fear.

"Yes. Am I wrong?" Mack's voice was still gentle, but softer somehow, as though he was apologizing for his opinion.

Beth's mind raced. She was right about her original assessment of the private detective. He could see right through her. She hedged. "I suppose you could make that statement about most people. Everyone has something they don't bring out into the open. That doesn't necessarily mean they're phony. It just means they don't want to share certain aspects of their life."

"A phony is a phony no matter how you look at it."

Beth sucked in a deep breath. "What makes me a phony, Mr. Mack?"

"See, you're calling me Mr. Mack. We agreed a little earlier to go with first names. That alone tells me I struck a nerve. But since you asked the question, here goes. You came here saying you wanted to be a famous countrywestern singer and to take Nashville by storm. Everyone I've talked to has told me you can't sing worth a darn. And yet here you are, and you're taking vocal lessons. You're planning on cutting a CD sometime in February. Even though a few months of lessons won't guarantee to put you on the charts. You came here for John Rossmon. You want him to make the big time because **he is good enough**.

Pretending to want to do this was the only way you could get him to agree to come along for the ride. John is the one with the talent, not you. I'm just surprised that you would be okay with all the negative things your friends and vocal teacher said about you. How am I doing so far?"

Beth shrugged. "I love John. I believe in him, and I know he can make it. I have no talent whatsoever. I'm not so stupid that I don't know that. I'm just going through the motions for John. Please don't blow my cover. It was the only thing I could think of to do to get him here, so he could follow his dream. He loves playing at Rootie Tootie's. He actually has fans. People show up just to hear him. I've never seen him happier. I don't know where all this will go from here. Maybe nowhere, and he'll be stuck playing in a small band at a full-every-night club. That just wasn't happening back in Garden Grove. I'm hoping someone will discover him. He's that good." This was all said defiantly, with sparks shooting from her eyes.

"Little lady, I admire the hell out of

you. I don't know anyone, and that's the God's honest truth, who would do that for their partner. I also admire what you've done, or perhaps the correct term is **not done**, for your brother, Jake. You have my vote, and do not worry, your secret is safe with me."

Beth's shoulders sagged with relief that now someone else knew her secret. She now had an ally. It really was time to go to bed. She said so.

"We good here, Beth?" Mack asked quietly.

"We're good, Jim."

"Then I guess we can say good night. What time do you leave for your singing lesson?"

"Nine-thirty. John leaves the house at six because he works at a café as a waiter for the breakfast and lunch trade. Then he comes home and sleeps till dinnertime. It's a long day for him, as he doesn't get home till around two."

"Good night, Beth," Mack called over his shoulder as he made his way to the guest room.

"Night, Jim."

Inside her room, with the door closed, Beth fell back on the bed and started to cry. Outed by a profiler. The one thing that had never entered her head in all the plans she'd made. Damn.

# Chapter Fourteen

Rootie Tootie's wasn't exactly an institution in Nashville, but it came close. There were so many wild stories about the origin of the hundred-year-old establishment that no one was sure what was truth and what wasn't. People just called it an old club where musicians and singers got their start on the road to fame.

The building was gray clapboard set back deep in an alley. To the naked eye, it looked like an eyesore, a dump as some called it. But every night it was filled to overflowing with people lined up at the rope line, all the way to the end of the alley, waiting for someone to leave just so they could spend a few minutes inside and brag that they had at least spent some time at the famous establishment when they returned to wherever home was.

Rootie Tootie's was owned by a little man. No one ever, as in ever, used the word **dwarf** when describing Arnold

Stonebridge. By day, Rootie Tootie's was a soup kitchen, where Arnold fed down-and-out musicians and performers. He served a robust breakfast to start the day and a fine, nutrition-packed dinner. Speculation as to where the money came from was rife, but no one could pin it down. Arnold always paid his bills on time, paid the band, his waitresses and waiters primo wages. The inside of the building was up to code and kept in immaculate condition. If closely examined, the outside was just as sturdy and well maintained, but with a different aim in sight. Arnold wanted the building to look shabby. No one knew why, so in the end, it was what it was.

All manner of rumors floated around Nashville, but only one person was truly in the know, and that was Arnold Stonebridge himself. Because he was a little man, he had insecurities that he tried not to show; but they were there. In his secret dark-time life, he was a frustrated singer. Only he knew what an outstanding voice he had, was born with, but his stature and his insecurity only allowed him to sing for his own pleasure. He had been born to wealth and privilege. Because his socialite mother and political father hadn't wanted a blight on their lives, he was given away, with a multimillion-dollar trust fund that had tripled and quadrupled with expert management. A couple raised him far away in the Ozarks, where no one could or would ever put two and two together about who his parents were. There was even a death certificate saying the baby born to his mother had died an hour after birth. He was educated, cared for, but never loved. He learned early to stay to himself to avoid ridicule and to keep his secret passions secret. Of course, he whimpered at night when he laid his head on the pillow, but by morning he was always resolved to do good somehow, some way.

When he turned eighteen, the family attorney, an uptight son of a bitch, turned his massive trust fund over to him and wished him luck, along with a warning to stay out of his parents' life. The consequences, if he didn't do as he was told, would bring the trust to an end. That was fine with Arnold because he knew that the family, which consisted of two brothers and two sisters, had washed their hands of him. That morning meeting with the attorney, thirty-five years ago, was when he knew the rubber met the road. He told himself he couldn't possibly miss something he never had, nor did he even want to meet the people who had thrown him away like so much trash. Arnold decided right then and there that his mission in life was to help people, and that's what he started to do. He bought the building in the alley, not knowing exactly what he was going to do with it. He cleaned it up, made all the necessary repairs, and sat back to wait.

While he waited, he spent his days singing inside the empty building. He recorded all his songs, which no one would ever hear but himself, and through the years played them over and over. Some of the recordings he redid because, as he believed, everything in life was a learning experience, and he was learning every day how to make things better, even his old recordings.

As time went on, and nothing happened to improve his life, Arnold realized he had to take the bull by the horns and wrestle it to the ground. He went looking for people to help. Many, because of who he was and what he looked like, turned him down, but he didn't allow himself to get discouraged. Gradually over time, people did find him, kind people who thanked him for helping them and getting them back on their feet. Before he knew it, word had spread, and he had more on his plate than he could handle. That's when the idea to open Rootie Tootie's as a club came to him. Musicians always needed a helping hand because Nashville was cold and cruel to newcomers. He joyously became the helping hand. The only thing he ever asked of anyone that he helped was if they made it in the music world, to come back and give back. To pay it forward, as they say nowadays. They all did. Every single one. And every year at Christmastime, more checks arrived. That's when Arnold Stonebridge knew he had been blessed beyond anything he could have ever imagined. Some nights, with no fanfare, a big-time celebrity would take the stage and blow everyone's socks off. They never failed to thank the little man who gave them their start just the way they never left without leaving a check for those who were still struggling. Arnold called these people his true treasures, and the reason he was put on earth was to take care of them.

Arnold Stonebridge hopped out of his specially equipped car and walked around to the back of the building. It was still early, six o'clock, to be precise. He hadn't been able to sleep, so he'd gotten up early, a little after four, and decided to go for an early-morning drive. He liked driving through the city before it came alive. For some strange reason, it always seemed to fortify him to get on with the day. The sun wasn't quite over the horizon yet. As always, he was the first one in to get ready for the breakfast rush. He looked up at the bulletin board to see what was on the menu. Blueberry pancakes, sausage, and bacon, along with scrambled eggs. All the orange juice and coffee a person could drink, and one to go if the person wanted it. Especially in this cold weather.

Everything in the kitchen was made to order for him, including the special pad that looked like a mat with an attached automobile jack, which would, with a few quick pumps, elevate him to worktable height. As long as he was standing on the pad, he could wheel it about to open the giant refrigerator, reach the monster coffee urns and the machine that crushed oranges for the pitchers of juice that appeared on every table, and the huge deep freeze. Over the years, he had discovered that it paid to buy in bulk.

One by one, his help trickled in, always with smiles on their faces. What was better than getting fed prime food and being paid to prepare it? It was win-win for everyone.

Arnold's only rule was everyone had to smile. He absolutely would not tolerate frowns, moaning, and groaning. No one ever disappointed Arnold. And yet Arnold had no idea how much he was loved and adored. No idea at all.

While they all worked in harmony, laughing and talking, the food was always ready sharply at eight o'clock, when the first guest arrived. Today, the talk was about the newest member of the band. Arnold's ears perked up. He'd listened to the young man for the past few days and decided that with the proper guidance, the boy would make it.

"Word got out about the new guy and how good he is. You all must have noticed we were packed to the walls these past few nights. They're coming to see and hear him," a chubby redhead giggled. "The guy is a real hunk, and he can sing. What do you think, Arnold?"

Everyone stopped what they were doing for a moment to hear the wise one's opinion. The whole world knew Arnold was stingy with his praise. If he said you were good, then you were damned good. If he said something vague, like "I think he or she has a little way to go," or "in time he or she might get up there," then that meant the person had a lot of work to do.

"Two nights, and he had the whole room on their feet. That young man has a humbleness to him. I like that. I heard he's an ex-marine, did two tours of duty in Iraq. I take that to mean he's seen more in his young life than most people, and most of what he's seen hasn't been good. He's got charisma. He's also got a set of lungs on him, and a smile that makes you want to hug him. And, he has a pretty little gal who appears to be crazy about him. She sits ringside and has the nicest smile. It's easy to tell they're in love." Among other things, Arnold Stonebridge was a romantic.

And with those kind words, John Rossmon's career was on its way. He just didn't know it.

The club doors opened for the evening the moment the dinner hour was over and everything put back to where it belonged. Now the interior looked like what it was, a nightclub and not a soup kitchen. The lights came on— subdued, of course. The little vases of fresh flowers along with small candles were distributed to each of the tables by one of the waitresses. Snacks were served, free, of course— pretzels, chips, nuts, candies. Drinks were a dollar each. The limit was three to a customer. Arnold's other rule was no one left his establishment inebriated. No one. His patrons knew a good thing when they saw it and monitored each other. It all worked. That's why the line all the way out to the alley was the same every night, even in the rain and the snow.

Arnold was always on hand when the doors opened after the dinner hour. He shook hands, smiled, asked after families, congratulated and commiserated with his guests for a solid hour; and then he disappeared to his quarters on the second floor. The only access to his private quarters was an elevator that stayed in the locked position once he was in residence.

Here, in his private sanctuary, everything was built to accommodate him and his height. It wasn't lavish, but it was on the high side of comfortable. He'd told the architects, a firm from out of state because he didn't want the locals knowing his business, that he wanted warm and cozy, a nest. The project had taken a little over two months, with the architects and their young son staying in a rental apartment a mile away. A strange young boy he had never warmed up to, as Arnold recalled. His only special request aside from warm and cozy was that he have floor-to-ceiling bookshelves to hold all his treasured books, which numbered in the thousands. The contractors had to reinforce all the walls as well as the floors to hold the weight of the books. His true treasures, and he'd read each and every book on the shelves. Some of them, like the classics, more than once.

It was the architects' suggestion to put in a one-way mirrored window similar to the ones used in Las Vegas casinos, so Arnold could observe what was going on down below. He'd demurred at first, then finally agreed. In the end, it turned out to be just perfect. Some nights, when the band was in superior form, he would sit in his chair and watch and listen and dream that he was on the small stage with them, singing his heart out.

Something was off tonight. He could feel a different kind of energy. He likened it to one other time in his life, when he was sitting right where he was sitting and watching the happy customers until an entourage walked in and headed for a reserved table. Governor and Mrs. Able Stonebrook—his parents—and his siblings. He remembered how his little heart had started to pound in his chest. What were they doing here? Had they called for a reservation? If so, no one had told him. But, then, why would they? His parents had changed his name, not their own. Still, having the governor and his family show up was something that would make the morning papers. Stonebridge, Stonebrook. No reason for anyone to link the two together.

Arnold watched as the mood in the room, which was always electric, fizzled. It took only an hour before people started to leave, and the band took a half-hour break. He watched as his mother looked around with disdain, while his father tried to question one waitress after another. Finally, one of his tall, handsome brothers got up and stomped his way to the door. The others followed him, all regal in stature, all of them looking embarrassed that no one cared about their appearance. A note was left behind, which was given to him the next day. He still had the tattered piece of paper locked away. Just a little scrap of paper that read:

**Dear Arnold,**
**I brought the family here tonight to see you. I'm sorry you were indisposed. Please, call me at this number.**
**Love,**
**Dad**

Well, Dad, aren't you like sixty-five years too late?

Arnold remembered how he'd cried so hard he made himself sick. He never called the number and left strict orders with all his employees never to allow the governor or any member of his family to get to the entrance of the alley, much less into the building. Because if they did, they would be on the unemployment line the very next day. As far as he knew, none of his family had ever returned to Rootie Tootie's.

Arnold shook his head to clear away his ugly thoughts and concentrated on what was going on down below. It took him only a second to realize it wasn't the guests, it was the band. No, not the band, it was John Rossmon. His beat was off. Only someone like himself or the other members of the band would pick up on it. No one else seemed to notice. Arnold slid off his chair and went to find his glasses. Ah, now he could see all the way to China. He homed in on Rossmon. He looked normal. Clean-cut, freshly shaved, recent haircut. Pressed khakis, white shirt, sleeves rolled up. No tie. No wrinkles on the shirt, which had been ironed; he could see the creases on the sleeves. He was smiling but it wasn't the same smile he'd seen the past few days. The man was worried. Arnold could tell. Maybe he was behind in his rent. Maybe he couldn't make his car payment. He hadn't showed up for breakfast or dinner, so that told him he had enough money to eat.

Arnold did notice that Rossmon's gaze kept going to ringside, to the table where his blond friend had sat earlier in the week. She wasn't here tonight. A spat of some kind? Maybe she was sick. The flu had been going around early this year. He shook his head. Whatever it was, he wasn't going to find out sitting here watching. When you wanted to know something, the best way to find out was to ask. He hated doing that. He'd always tried not to get involved in his guests' lives. If they approached him and asked for help, that was okay. He never turned anyone away. He also hated gossip of any kind. Consequently, his employees shared very little of what was actually going on, and that was fine with him. He had eyes and ears.

Arnold frowned when he saw Dick Breme, the leader of the band, give Rossmon a sour look. He himself had winced at a sour, off-key note. Even from up here, Arnold could see that Rossmon was aware of his shortcomings tonight. He could see the apology in his eyes when he nodded at Breme.

At eleven o'clock, Arnold couldn't stand it a second longer. He'd go sit ringside in the hopes that Rossmon would shake whatever it was that was bothering him. He couldn't explain why, even to himself, he'd taken such an instant liking to the ex-marine. Maybe it was because when they had met, Rossmon hadn't given any kind of sign that Arnold was other than just a man he was shaking hands with. This was a man who was not judgmental. He had kind, gentle eyes and a smile that lit up the room. Just a regular all-around good guy had been his final decision. Someone he might want to get to know better.

When he hit the main floor, Arnold signaled to one of the waiters and told him he wanted the ringside table. With five minutes to go till the band broke for a fifteenminute intermission, Arnold felt confident Rossmon would join him.

When the stage lights dimmed, and the band laid aside their instruments, Arnold raised an arm at Rossmon and pointed to the chair next to him. John hopped off the stage, walked over to the table, and held out his hand to shake Arnold's. "I'm sorry, sir. I'm having an off night. It's personal, and I won't let it happen again. It's just... it's not me...well, it is me, but it's...Oh, hell, I shouldn't be unloading on you like this. Sorry, Mr. Stonebridge."

Arnold did something then that he'd never done before, and he wasn't even sure why he did it at that moment. "Call me Arnold. Can I call you John?"

"Um...sure. I mean great. I've only been here a few days, but everyone calls you Mr. Stonebridge. I thought...I guess I don't know what I thought. But okay, I'm a pretty informal person myself."

"Can I buy you a beer, John?"

John almost fell off his chair. Out of the corner of his eye he could see people watching him and the little man, especially Dick Breme. He wondered if he was going to get fired. The first thing Breme had told him was that Stonebridge did not socialize with the help and that he never, as in never, drank with them. For sure, he was going to get fired. God, with all that was going on with Beth, how could he tell her he got fired after only a few days? "I'd like that, Mr....Arnold."

Arnold held up his hand. He called over his shoulder, "Two Bud Lights. Make sure they're ice cold."

When the beer arrived, Arnold held his out and clinked it against John's. "Let's drink to your future success."

John thought he was going to faint. Maybe he wasn't going to get fired after all.

"Let's talk about it. That means you talk, and I listen," Arnold said. "Even upstairs, I could hear that you were off. You also look off. Talk to me, son."

Son. John started to feel warm all over. And to his own surprise and chagrin, he began to talk. He spoke bullet fast as he related his life with Beth, the marines, Jake Masters, coming here, and Beth's immediate problem. He wound down with, "And the private detective arrived this evening and will be staying with us. He'll be with Beth when I can't be."

Arnold listened attentively as he tried to

make sense out of what he'd just heard. No wonder the young man was off. Before Arnold could even think about what he was going to say, the words tumbled out of his mouth. "I have all kinds of top-notch security here even though you can't see it. I also have a spare bedroom if you think your young lady would consider using it. If that's not something that works for you, then how about this? I have extra security that I can loan out to your private detective. All you have to do is ask. Tomorrow, have your detective stop by here so we can have a chat. He doesn't know this town like I do. I'll be glad to do whatever I can do to help."

John was flabbergasted. "Why, sir? You just met me. Why would you do this—go out of your way for someone you barely know?"

Arnold chuckled. A pleasant sound to John's ears. A welcome, pleasant sound.

"As strange and as hokey as it may sound to you, I believe I was put on this earth to help people. The truth is, it's all I know how to do. So you see, you aren't putting me out, and I'm not going out of my way. I'm simply doing what I always do. Think about it. Now, I want you back up on that stage, and I want you to perform like you did the first night you were here. Pretend I'm Beth cheering you on. Can you do that, John?"

"You bet, Arnold. Listen, about what I just—"

"Your business will never leave my lips. Go on, get up there; your fans are waiting." John laughed out loud before he extended his hand again. Arnold placed his own tiny hand in John's, then felt John's other hand clamp down. In that moment in time, Arnold Stonebridge knew he'd made a friend for life. A true friend.

Dick Breme looked at John and grinned. "You back on track, kid?"

Kid. Well, he supposed he was a kid compared to Dick and his guys, who were in their late forties. "Yeah. Let's have some fun. This crowd looks like it's about to go to sleep. Can I use that sax over there?" Dick nodded. "Let's wake them up with 'When the Saints Go Marching In'! I know it's not your thing, but I think the little man will get a kick out of it!"

"Well, in that case, hit it, boys!"

Arnold laughed so hard he cried as he clapped his tiny hands in a show of appreciation. He knew he was right about the kid. Knew it in his gut, his heart, and in his mind.

When the band called it a night a little after 1:00 A.M., John packed up, his spirits so high nothing could have dampened them. He struggled to find the right word to describe how he felt, and the only thing that came to mind was **euphoric**.

"See ya tomorrow, kid," Dick called out as he led the parade into the hall and the service entrance all the help used.

"Yeah, see you tomorrow. And, Dick, sorry about the poor start tonight. It won't happen again."

"Don't sweat it, kid. We all have an off night from time to time."

John reached for his down jacket, slipped into it, then zipped it up. He reached into the pocket and pulled out a bright red watch cap that Beth had knitted for him a few years ago. He settled it on his head and looked around to make sure he had all his gear. He did. Still, he lingered. He walked back into the main room, just off the edge of the stage, and looked upward. He had no idea if his new best friend could see him or not, but he offered up a salute and a big smile.

Arnold Stonebridge stood behind the two-way mirror and clapped his tiny hands and smiled. This was what he called the perfect ending to a long night. He continued to watch as the cleanup crew went about its business of righting the room so it would be ready for breakfast. He was still smiling when he made his way to his bedroom. He knew he was going to sleep like a baby tonight, and he wouldn't be doing any four A.M. drives through the city.

Downstairs, John Rossmon opened the door to a blast of arctic air and a swirl of snowflakes. Snow. He loved snow. He laughed out loud as he made his way to his SUV. If he hadn't been so in tune with the events of the past hour and the swirling snowflakes, he might have noticed the parked car, the exhaust pluming backward. But his eyes were on his own Ford Ranger, and the falling snow.

If John had looked in his rearview mirror, he might have picked up on his tail, but he was too busy playing over and over in his mind his brief encounter with Arnold Stonebridge.

When he reached the mini parking area at the apartment complex, he was in too much of a hurry to see or pay attention to the car that followed him. He hopped out, grabbed his gear, and sprinted toward the staircase that would take him to his and Beth's second-floor apartment. He hoped she was still up, so he could share the evening's events with her.

# Chapter Fifteen

It was almost dawn when John steered his SUV around the corner and into Beth's driveway. He was tired, and he had eye strain from driving through the night. He'd hoped that Beth would stay awake and talk to him for the long drive, but she'd curled up in the backseat and slept the whole trip. Because...as she put it, she had to cook, whereas he could sleep until dinner. It did make sense, so he didn't argue with her. Right now, all he wanted was a hot shower and a warm bed. Beth, he knew, would head straight for the kitchen to start the turkey.

"Hey, sleepyhead, wake up! We're home!"

Beth stirred. She was groggy as she tried to focus. "Already? Oh, my gosh, it is really snowing out. We hardly ever get snow here."

"Duh. The good news is it is not sticking to the ground, and it is letting up." John laughed. He slid out of the car in time to see Jim Mack swerve into the driveway and park right behind him. A wave of relief washed over him. For some reason, just looking at Jim Mack made him feel safe. Beth had said the same thing.

"We're crazy, you know that, right?" John teased. "Who in their right mind drives seven hours, spends all day cooking a huge dinner that is consumed in twenty minutes, cleans up, and then gets in the car and drives seven hours again and goes to work. What were you thinking, Beth?"

"I was thinking I wanted to be in my own house for Thanksgiving dinner, a dinner that I cooked myself. I miss my fish. I miss Gracie, Moose, and Giz. I feel closer to Jake here even though I'm not going to see him. Any other questions?" Beth snapped irritably.

"Nope. I see smoke coming out of the chimney, so I guess Gracie was here to turn up the heat, and I bet you a dollar there is a fire going in the fireplace. What time is Moose due?"

Beth threw her hands in the air. "I thought he'd be here by now. He could be. Maybe someone dropped him off or he put his truck in the garage. Ooops, I spoke too soon. I hear his truck."

John peered through the swirling snow and, sure enough, there was Moose turning into the driveway, followed by Gracie. "Looks like the gang's all here! And I'm off to bed. What about you, Jim? Giz is here, so I think you can safely hit the sack."

The detective nodded in agreement as they all trooped into the warm house.

Gracie frowned when she heard Beth let loose with a mighty sigh, a dreamy look on her face. Something just wasn't adding up where her friend was concerned. Even though she and Beth had been friends as well as business partners for what seemed like forever, Gracie realized there was still a lot about her friend that she didn't know. Like this return trip home for Thanksgiving in the midst of all that was going on. And a dinner she was going to cook herself. Beth's cooking abilities were on a par with her singing abilities, about as nonexistent. She wished it was Moose who was doing the dinner. Thanksgiving dinners were supposed to be special. She seriously doubted this dinner would be special. Something just wasn't adding up. Maybe, by the end of the day, she'd figure it out. If not, oh, well. In the meantime, she'd keep a sharp eye on Beth and try to figure out what she was missing.

By ten o'clock, the twenty-pound bird was prepped, dressed, tented, and in the oven, with Moose doing most of the work. He'd taken one look at Beth and her rubber gloves and made her sit down to watch.

Both Beth and Gracie watched as Moose moved about the kitchen like a seasoned, five-star chef. Moose announced that the vegetables were their job. They started hacking away the moment he turned to continue with a bourbon pecan pie his bingo partner had shared with him and which he served with a special maple whipped cream. After his pumpkin chiffon pie, which was his own concoction, he considered this pie his specialty even though it wasn't his recipe.

By noon, everything was as ready as it could be, even Gizmo's chicken breasts, which were being cooked separately as he couldn't eat turkey. The table was set with Beth's good china, compliments of her grandmother. The crystal and silverware were compliments of her mother. The linen tablecloth and matching napkins were her own, purchased the first year she'd moved into this little house.

Beth studied the table and pronounced it festive. Only Moose saw the sadness in her eyes. He pretended otherwise.

Gracie noticed, too, when the conversation petered out.

"How about some cheese, crackers, and coffee in front of the fire?" Moose suggested. "We can play catch-up, and you, Beth, can tell us what's going on in Nashville." The women agreed and retired, along with Giz, to the living room, where they dropped down and sat by the fire on plush cushions.

Beth knew she was on what Moose called the hot spot. For a moment, she resented both of them, but for only a moment. They cared about her, worried about her. She hoped she didn't look as shaky as she felt on the inside. She knew she was going to have to fess up about Luke Olsen's being in Nashville. Why in the world she ever thought she could handle that on her own was mind boggling.

No sooner were they settled than the doorbell rang. Gizmo was on his feet, the hair on the nape of his neck straight up. He started to quiver and waited for a command from Gracie. "Go!" She ran after him, and both skidded to a stop at the door. Through one of the windowpanes on opposite sides of the door, Gracie could see a delivery truck with a sign on its side that said EDIBLE TREASURES. She motioned for Gizmo to sit and opened the door. A young ish girl in a bright orange outfit held out a huge, cellophanewrapped cornucopia filled to the brim with fruit, nuts, and berries. Gracie blinked as the girl handed it over.

Moose, right behind her, reached into his pocket and withdrew some crumpled bills that he held out. The girl smiled, thanked him, and turned to walk away. Gizmo growled. Gracie hushed him as she set the arrangement on the floor. "Check it out, Giz!" she said as she ripped away the shiny, crackling paper. Giz whined, growled, then upended the basket, the contents rolling all over the floor. He sniffed each and every item, pawed the horn, then stepped back and barked twice. "We're good here," Gracie said, gathering up the contents and stuffing them back into the horn.

"Who is it from? Jake?" Moose asked.

"Don't know. The card is addressed to Beth, so I guess she should open it."

Beth stood in the doorway, watching her friends walking toward her. Giz got there first and licked at her hand. "Throw it in the trash," Beth said coldly.

"Aren't you going to look at the card to see who sent it?" Moose asked.

Beth fixed her steely gaze on Moose, and said, "It's not from Jake. It's from Luke Olsen. He wants me to know he knows I'm home. If you don't believe me, look at the card. Yesterday, he sent me some flowers, a fall arrangement, the kind you put on your Thanksgiving table. I threw them away before John could see them. He wants me to know he's wherever I am but out of sight. Throw that away, Gracie!" Beth shrieked.

"Okay, okay! You never told me he sent you anything in Nashville." She eyed the colorful little card that was stapled to the cellophane. She swallowed hard at the wording.

**I will be thinking of you as you sit down to Thanksgiving dinner. I plan to give thanks for having you in my life. I'll see you soon.**

There was no signature, just two entwined, hand-drawn hearts. Gracie read the words, then held the card up. She ripped it into small pieces she carried over to the fireplace. The trio watched the flames eat up the offensive, ugly little bits of paper.

Gracie whirled around and eyeballed Beth. "You knew he was already in Nashville when I called to warn you, didn't you, and you didn't say a word? What were you thinking, Beth?"

"I thought...I thought he'd go away as long as I ignored him. I didn't want to upset you. You have enough going on here as it is. I'm sorry, Gracie. I never should have involved you in any of this. Jake...the business...and now this."

"And **now this** is right. Beth, he was here in your house, he went through your things. He was in your bedroom, your bathroom. He stole the file you had on him. Then he followed you to Nashville. And you kept it all a secret from John! I don't believe this," Gracie all but snarled. "This...this...arrangement he sent has to mean he's back here in town, and he followed you back from Nashville. He's goading you. What did the message on the flowers he sent to you in Nashville say?"

"He...he made it sound like we were a couple already. I told you, I threw them away. I was going to go to the police the day you called me. I know there is nothing they could do, but I just wanted to have something on file in Nashville. It's not against the law to send someone flowers or gifts, so other than ask them to call the police here for a report, there isn't anything they can do. I never saw Luke in Nashville. You know as well as I do that you cannot accuse someone of something as serious as stalking without ramifications. I might act like a fool once in a while, but I am not a fool. I know he's deranged, but there's nothing we can do about it until he does something that is against the law. I had every intention of telling John, too. But you beat me to it all. And now, here we are."

Gracie turned around and looked at the door. "He's out there!"

"And there is not a thing we can do about it unless he comes on my property. It's not against the law to park on the street. It's a public thoroughfare. He knows all that. He isn't going to make the same mistakes he made the last time."

Moose decided it was time to voice his opinion. "Are we saying that crazy loony tune is out there in the snow, parked in his car and watching this house hoping you're going to go out there and talk to him or invite him in for dinner? Maybe we should wake up that dee-tek-tive, who is sound asleep upstairs, and have him and this here dog go out there and scare the bejesus out of that man."

"No! That's what he wants. He wants a face-to-face with Beth. If she acknowledges him, then he wins. Going out there and confronting him, if he's even out there, will just escalate the situation. I'm going to dump this outside in the trash can and hope he sees me doing it," Gracie said.

Gracie walked through the kitchen to the garage and raised the heavy door where two large blue trash cans sat at the side of the house. She made a production out of lifting the lid and dumping the contents in the can even though she seriously doubted Luke Olsen could see her through the snow flurries. On the other hand, if he had binoculars, he would have a crystal-clear view of her and what she was doing. In a fit of anger, she offered up a single-digit salute and marched back into the house.

"Did you see any cars out there?" Beth asked.

"No. He could be parked around the corner or down at the end of the block with binoculars, but I couldn't see that far with the swirling snow. It's not sticking, though, so don't plan on riding on your sled any time soon." At best, it was a feeble, lame joke, and no one laughed.

For the next two hours, while their Thanksgiving dinner was cooking, the three of them talked ad nauseam about Luke Olsen until Beth threw her hands in the air, and said, "Enough already. We're just making ourselves crazy over this. Today is Thanksgiving. We need to talk about how good our lives are. This business with Luke Olsen is just a rock in the road. We'll deal with it. I've missed you, Gracie, and you, too, Giz. I even missed you, you old curmudgeon," she said to Moose. "Now, tell me what I need to know about Jake. What are the doctors saying? Are they hopeful he will be able to walk again? I'm not saying running or playing football, simply walking and not having to live in that damn chair."

Moose sighed as he got up to toss another log on the fire. "Jake is keeping it all pretty close to the vest this time. As you know, we had that little spat. Well," he drawled, "it was more than a little spat. He had to do some heavy-duty thinking, and everything he's doing seems to be working so far. In my opinion, he's done a one-eighty, and this here dog helped him a lot. He likes the animal. I heard him say to the dog that when he's walking again he's going to go out to the yard and throw a ball for him to fetch. Is that wishful thinking? I don't think so. He's not afraid these days. It was fear and the drugs that kept him glued to that chair. You shook him up, Beth. The minute he started worrying about you, he stopped worrying about himself.

"If he makes it through the operation, and he said the doctors are confident he will, the only thing he has to contend with is the killer therapy. For whatever it's worth, he's up to it. He really is. He's had enough of the chair."

"What is he doing today? Please don't tell me peanut butter and jelly sandwiches," Beth said.

"He told me the other day he ordered

a complete Thanksgiving dinner from Zabar's in New York. It was delivered last night. All he has to do is warm it up today. Don't look like that, Beth. Even if you had invited him today, he would have said no. He is doing what you expect of him. You drew the line in the sand, and he isn't going to wheel across it. In time, he'll be able to step over it, but not yet.

"He has not asked for my help, and as far as I know, he hasn't asked anyone else either. He's taking full responsibility for himself. A medical van is picking him up tomorrow even though I offered to drive him to the hospital for the workup. I'll be there when they operate on him even though he said he didn't want me there. No one should go under the knife without someone on the outside worrying about him."

Beth nodded. "I should be there." No one disputed her words, and she started to cry. "I should have let well enough alone and not badgered him. I was a bully. I forced myself on him, just dumped everything on him, and walked away," she said, sobbing.

Gizmo knew what tears and sobs were because he had comforted Gracie when her memories took her to dark places. He bellied over to Beth and forced her to take his head in her hands and smile. He licked at her and whimpered until she hugged him so hard he yelped, but he didn't move until Beth stopped crying.

"Don't be so hard on yourself, Beezer. If you hadn't done what you did, none of us would be sitting here, and Jake wouldn't be eating Zabar's and dreaming about walking again. He's doing it, thanks to you. You need to move on from that guilt and let the chips fall where they may. The rest is up to Jake," Moose said. "Be back in a minute. Gotta check on my pies. Don't say anything bad about me while I'm gone."

Gizmo barked as much as to say, "Not on my watch."

"Moose is right, Beth. Jake is doing what he needs to do, thanks to you. If you hadn't laid down the law, he might never have gotten up the courage to go back for the operation."

"I was being selfish, Gracie," Beth hiccuped. "Not totally, but I was thinking about myself. I can't marry John unless Jake walks me down the aisle. I made that promise to myself years ago. It has to be Jake. John gets upset with me, but it is what it is. Now that we're where we are, I keep asking myself if Jake will even want to walk me down the aisle. Until recently, I never even gave that a thought. See how selfish I am? I just assumed he would; now I'm not so sure." She started to wail again.

"Beth, your brother loves you, and I know you love him. You're all each other have in the way of a blood family. Jake knows that. I can tell. I know you know it, too. In the end, as we are both fond of saying, it will end just the way it is meant to end, no matter what you or Jake do. So, tell me about Nashville," Gracie said, hoping to divert Beth's line of thought to something that made her happy.

Beth's face lit up like a beacon. "Well, for starters, I love Nashville. I love the people. So does John. Oh, Gracie, the move was so worth it. I've never seen John so happy. He's got a great job with the band. His day job isn't too taxing, and he's making enough money to pay his share of everything. You know how proud he is. My singing lessons are going…okay. I'm really working it. Will I ever be famous? I seriously doubt it, but it won't be for lack of trying. I have all the paperwork and forms and deposit requirements ready to be filled out so I can cut the CD in February. You have to reserve the recording studio like three months in advance. I was just starting on all of that when Jim Mack showed up. It's all still sitting on the kitchen table back in Nashville. I'll get to work on it when we go back. We made some new friends, really great people. It's so interesting how everyone seems to look out for each other.

"And then there is the club, Rootie Tootie's. It's magic, Gracie. Wait till I tell you what happened to John the other night at the club. The owner…"

# Chapter Sixteen

Beth Masters's kitchen took on a life of its own the moment the clock struck three. As Moose put it, "We're coming into the home stretch now, time to make the gravy, let the bird rest, and get all the side dishes going so everything gets to the table hot."

"That's impossible," Gracie muttered under her breath. A lively discussion followed when Moose guaranteed everything would be hot. "It's all in the timing."

Jim Mack and John appeared in the kitchen doorway, looking freshly scrubbed, rested, and hungry. Together, they asked if they could help.

"Only way to help is to stay out of the kitchen, because it isn't big enough for all of us," Moose growled.

Beth, her person half in the refrigerator and half out, started to babble about the cornucopia and Luke Olsen, to both men's dismay. "He's out there watching the house," she said, whirling around, a bowl of cranberry sauce in her hands.

Gracie chirped up. "I think you two should get dressed and take Giz for a walk around the neighborhood to see what you can see. I doubt Olsen is on this block, and I think he's probably got a pair of binoculars. Giz will know. Just keep him on the leash and let him go where he wants to go."

"And you didn't wake us!" Jim Mack exploded.

John Rossmon threw his hands in the air, an expression of disbelief on his face.

"Listen, you two," Beth said, her voice fierce. "Think about it. A delivery van brought the fruit basket. A young girl rang the bell. It wasn't Luke Olsen. What would you have done, sweated the poor thing, grilled her, scared her out of her wits and ruined her whole day? All she did was deliver a basket of fruit that Gracie immediately threw in the trash. You were both tired, you drove all night and needed the sleep. Listen to me.   There-was-nothing-youcould-have-done-even-if-you-were-standing-right-in-thedoorway."

Jim and John both sheepishly conceded

Beth's point.

"I have an idea. I still have the blueprints Luke drew up when he did the work on this house. I have no idea if his scent would still be on them, or even if Giz can still pick up on it if it is. I think it's worth a try. Let me fetch them. They're out in the garage, and it was Luke's idea to wrap them in a plastic sleeve to preserve them, as he put it. I've never looked at them from the day I put them out there on the shelf." She was gone in an instant and returned minutes later, with a dusty, plastic cylinder in her hands. She ran into the laundry room and cleaned and dried it off.

"Come here, Giz!" Beth called. "Gracie, tell him what he has to do."

Gracie laughed. "You don't tell Giz, he tells you. He already knows what's going on. If Luke Olsen is out there, he'll find him."

They all watched as Beth unrolled the blueprints and spread them out on the kitchen floor. They continued to watch as Giz pawed the yellowing paper with all its blue lines and shadings. He sniffed every corner, then pawed the paper a second time. When he looked up at Gracie, he let loose with three sharp barks.

"He's got it, guys. He's the alpha, so let him do his thing." Gracie bent over to hug the big dog and praise him. He barked again. Giz loved hugs and praise.

"Second fiddle to a dog," Jim Mack groused.

"This isn't just any dog, Jim. Giz is a special dog. I'll tell you all about him on our walk," John said as he tickled Giz between his ears. The big dog literally purred his pleasure.

Beth rolled up the blueprints and inserted them back into the plastic sleeve, which she returned to the garage. Then she went into the laundry room and scrubbed her hands until they turned beet red.

"Enough already, Beth! You scrubbed him away. Giz and the guys are on it. We sit back and wait now."

"Gracie, tell me the truth. Do you really think Luke Olsen would...would hurt me?"

Gracie drew in a sharp breath. "I wish I had the answer, Beth. I don't. I have personal ideas and opinions, but how much weight they hold, I have no clue. What I do know is what I read—that stalkers start out one way, then, when rebuffed, switch gears. They want what they want. They're delusional. Like those two hearts on the card in the fruit basket. And like the card you said was on the flowers he sent. He thinks you want him as much as he wants you. He has convinced himself of that. It's not you I am worried about at this moment, it's John. And I admit, I could be wrong. Luke hasn't taken that next step, at least I don't think he has, where he has to get rid of the person he sees standing between you and him, but I think he's thinking about it now. I could be really off base here, but I don't think so. Mr. Mack pretty much verified what I've just said. Any good profiler will agree. I think."

All the color left Beth's face. "I'd just up and die if anything happened to John. Just plain old up and die," Beth cried.

"Nothing is going to happen to John. He's a big guy, he's a marine. That alone should comfort you. I changed my mind about Giz. I'm going to let you take him back with you. That dog is a one-man army. The thing is, you're all going to have to stay together until we get a handle on el jerko and formulate a plan of some kind. That means no more putzing around on your part, Beth. Everything out in the open. No more secrets, and you can forget that part about actually believing you are Superwoman. Either you give me your word right now, this very minute, or I'm outta here. I mean it, Beth." Gracie was relieved to see the color returning to Beth's cheeks.

"Okay, Gracie. After dinner, when the guys clean up, you and I will go upstairs and talk. Are you serious about my taking Giz back with me?"

"As a heart attack," Gracie shot back.

Beth threw her arms around Gracie and hugged her tight. "You're the best friend in the whole world. Even better than Arabella."

Gracie snorted. "Arabella was a figment of your imagination, a pretend friend when you were five years old."

"Yeah, well, she was my only playmate back then. I loved her. You're flesh and blood, and I love you more. Jake had a make-believe friend, too. He'll never admit it, but I remember. His name was Skid, and Jake blamed him for everything when he got himself into trouble, which was about every other day. And he'd say Arabella was a witness. It all made our parents crazy. Enough of this nonsense. We need to get back to the kitchen to help Moose."

"Gravy's made," Moose announced proudly. "How do the pies look?" he asked, hoping for wild compliments. Beth and Gracie both said they looked heavenly. Satisfied, Moose beamed. "The boys are not back yet." It wasn't so much a question as it was a statement. The girls shook their heads. "Well, somebody better call them because dinner will be ready in exactly twelve minutes."

Gracie dropped the spoon she was holding and ran to the door, where she whistled sharply. Giz would hear the whistle and return. Hopefully, the guys would have enough sense to follow him.

It was cold out. Gracie stood in the open doorway, her arms wrapped across her chest. It was a typical Thanksgiving day, all gray and overcast, with gusty winds blowing the last of the autumn leaves every which way. It was still flurrying, but there was no accumulation, so that was a plus in her opinion.

Gracie heard a shrill bark, and even in the distance could see the black streak that was Gizmo headed down the road at ninety miles an hour. She couldn't see Jim or John but knew they were out there. She also knew there was no way they could either keep up or outrun Gizmo. The big dog skidded to a stop, panting and pawing the ground. "You're the bomb, Giz! Good work. Bet you worked up an appetite. Damn, I wish you could talk. Did you spot the jerk out there?"

Giz let loose with three sharp barks, then sat back on his haunches as he waited for the two slugs who had walked him to appear. In spite of herself, Gracie laughed. "Giz, they're just human. Give them a break; you have four legs, and they only have two." Giz looked at her as much as to say, "Can't you count?" "Yeah, right, okay, four legs between them. Your point, pal."

Jim and John, to make it look good, jogged the last few yards to the front door, sheepish looks on their faces, which were red with the cold.

"The dog spotted the car, and he took off. He was parked around the block on the corner and had a clear view of the front of Beth's house," Jim said. "Now he knows we're onto him. He's going to have to change his game plan now."

"We can talk about this over dinner. It's ready. Moose does not like to be kept waiting, and he wants to prove that every dish on the table is hot. So make sure you comment on how hot the food is. Wash your hands and get ready for Thanksgiving dinner."

Giz headed straight for the kitchen and the heavenly aromas wafting his way. The guys headed for the lavatory and laundry room to wash up.

"Dinner is served!" Moose announced as he carried the golden bronze turkey to the table. "I'm carving!" No one argued. "I'm also saying grace." Again, no one argued. "You can start passing the bowls around while I carve. Miz Gracie, do you want to fix the dog's bowl or should I?"

"I'll do it," Gracie said. Giz's plate wasn't a bowl but a platter, which she fixed with loving care. A whole chicken breast, boned and cut into pieces. Mashed potatoes and giblet gravy, a side of sweet potatoes with marshmallows and honey, honey-glazed carrots, string beans, cranberry sauce, and two biscuits. For dessert, he would get the pumpkin chiffon pie because pumpkin was good for a dog's digestive track. She looked at the plate, knowing it was a feast and more than what Giz normally ate. She'd have to run him later. She thought about Alex then, and how he said when they got home Giz was going to eat only what he ate. She remembered talking to the military vet that she took Giz to for check-ups and what he said. "I've never seen a dog in better condition. Keep doing whatever it is you're doing because it works."

What made it all work was that Giz never ate more than he could hold. Many times he walked away, leaving food on his plate. He did like gravy, though, so Gracie added an extra spoonful.

The platter with the sliced turkey was being passed around when Gracie took her seat at the table. "Grace," Moose said. Everyone bowed their heads, even Gizmo, since he knew what grace was. The words were soft, soothing, and comforting. Just the way they were supposed to be on this particular day. When he was finished, Moose held up his hand, and intoned, "Okay, let's eat!"

"Oh, wow, everything is so hot and delicious," Jim Mack said.

"I can't get over how hot everything is. I think it's a miracle that everything is the same temperature," John said, tongue-in-cheek.

They all had a good laugh at Moose's expense. Giz stopped eating long enough to offer up a bark of agreement.

"To say dinner is delicious would be an understatement," Beth said. Gracie agreed, just as someone's cell phone rang. Moose reared back. "No phone calls at the table!"

John pulled out his phone, looked at the caller ID, then at Moose. "I'm sorry, I have to take this call." He put the phone to his ear and listened. Three times he said, "Okay." And then, at the end of the call, he thanked the caller and shut off the phone.

"Who was that?" Beth asked in a jittery voice.

"Dick Breme. There's a problem in Nashville. For starters, they got twelve inches of snow in that freak storm. The storm drains at each end of the alley where Rootie Tootie's is located froze over, and the pipes in the alley burst. The city closed off the alley, and work is under way. There's no heat, and the water has been turned off at the club. Mr. Stonebridge has generators, but there is no access to the club because the water and sewer department are working near it. Dick said Mr. Stonebridge closed the club and said it won't reopen till either Tuesday or Wednesday of next week and not to hurry back."

Beth looked across the table at John, and said, "I don't know if I'm happy or sad about that. Poor Mr. Stonebridge. What is he going to do?"

"There are generators, so he has heat

and electricity. He just doesn't have water flowing through the pipes, but there is a ton of bottled water in the storage room. He'll be fine. Dick said they closed off the alley, so the soup kitchen is closed down, too."

"Well, there's nothing any of us can do for the time being, so I suggest we move on to dessert and coffee. You have a choice of bourbon pecan pie with maple whipped cream or pumpkin chiffon pie with vanilla almond whipped cream. Name your poison, folks." Moose wasn't the least bit surprised when everyone asked for a slice of each.

Giz barked twice. Moose actually laughed. "Damn, can this dog count, too?" Gracie nodded. "Okay, big boy, two pieces of pumpkin chiffon pie coming right up. Who is in charge of the coffee?"

"Me! Since it's my kitchen," Beth said happily as she bounced out to the kitchen. All she could think of was she was home for at least three more days, four if she was lucky.

Talk was general, even upbeat, while the small group consumed the delectable desserts. There was no mention of Luke Olsen and what tomorrow would bring. When the last smidgen of pie was gone, the conversation turned to the cleanup and a few moans and groans. It was decided that since Moose did the major portion of the cooking, with Beth and Gracie helping, the cleanup fell to Jim Mack and John.

"No football until this kitchen is spick and span," Beth announced. "Gracie and I will be upstairs if you need us, which you shouldn't. We'll just leave Giz here to make sure everything gets done right."

"I think I'll mosey on home then," Moose said. "I want to spend some time with Jake before...well, before tomorrow. I hope you all enjoyed the dinner. Be sure to cover all the leftovers since you're going to be here for a few more days. Don't waste the food, you hear?" They all nodded agreeably as Moose slipped into his down jacket. He tweaked Giz between the ears and left by the kitchen door.

"I like that old guy," Jim said as he looked around for an apron. "He's a bit on the gnarly side, but that's okay. At his age, he's earned the right."

"Yeah, Jake is in good hands with Moose. He's like a real father figure to both Jake and Beth. Okay, let's get started. Since these are Beth's good dishes and glassware, we wash by hand and dry. I'll dry since I know where everything goes."

"Like I have a choice," Jim deadpanned as he filled the sink with hot, soapy water.

Beth and Gracie scooted out before they could be asked to pack up the food, Gizmo hot on their heels. As far as he was concerned, the women were more interesting than the men who were washing dishes.

In her bedroom with the door closed but not locked, Beth bounced on her bed and motioned for Gracie to join her. They sat cross-legged, like two little girls about to share earth-shattering secrets.

"Talk to me, Beth," Gracie said quietly, just as Giz leaped up on the bed and wiggled himself between them. Two women with two hands meant belly rubs and ear tickling.

"You know, Gracie, we've been friends it seems like forever. You're the sister I never had. We've shared everything, commiserated and cried and laughed together. I...wanted to tell you what I was doing, but I was afraid you'd try to talk me out of it. I've made my share of mistakes along the way, but I learned from them. So, I'm apologizing here in advance."

"Apology accepted. Now tell me."

"I can't sing."

"Well, helloooo, Beth Masters. I know that. The whole world knows you can't sing."

"I mean I really can't sing. I've been lying to everyone, especially John, about my vocal teacher. Oh, I am taking lessons and paying for them, but Alfie just charges me a pittance because he feels sorry for me. I'm never going to be a singer, and I am never going to take Nashville by storm."

"But...you said..."

"I lied, Gracie. It was the only way to get John to Nashville. Everything I did was for John, not me. I had to make it sound that way, so he would agree to go along with me. He's that good, Gracie. Really, he is. He deserves this chance. His soul is full of music. He makes it come alive. You should see the audience when he plays and sings. They love him. And the guy doesn't need lessons; he's a natural. Even the bandleader, Dick Breme, says so, and that guy has been on the scene for ages. Mr. Stonebridge has taken him under his wing. That would never have happened if I didn't...um...do what I did.

"I haven't said much about John and what he went through over there. When he left the marines, he was not in good shape. He was with me, but then he'd go off somewhere else in his head. I started to get worried and we talked about it and he went to a shrink. He wasn't sleeping, and he was eating badly. Bad memories. The only time he seemed to come alive was when he was singing or playing his guitar. He couldn't hold a job because he'd zone out, and he'd get fired. I knew I had to do something. So I pretended I was following my dream. I begged him to go with me, and at first he said no. And then he said okay. I have all the paperwork and the studio booked to cut the CD in February, but it isn't for me, it's for John. He just doesn't know it yet. I can make it work, Gracie."

"Oh my God! And you kept all this to yourself and didn't tell me."

"I couldn't, Gracie. I needed you to be surprised, and your reaction had to be genuine or John would have seen right through it all. Jake was the hardest part. But I pulled that off, too. He's going for his surgery, and right there it is win-win. In the end, because of what was going on with Jake and then me turning over the matchmaking business to him was what convinced John to follow me. I knew once he made that decision, the rest would play out just the way it was supposed to play out. I'd do it all over again if I had to," Beth said fiercely.

"What I didn't count on was the fly in the ointment, as they say, by the name of Luke Olsen. I have to admit that threw me for a loop, but I was working on it."

"Well, damn, Beth Masters, you sure did fool me," Gracie said. "I don't know if I should hug you or give you a good swat."

Beth chewed on her bottom lip. "There's more, Gracie. This is the part you aren't going to like. But you said full disclosure, so

I'm going to tell you. I had an ulterior motive where Jake is concerned. I wanted the two of you to...you know...get together. You'd be perfect for each other. Like we say, the perfect match. Okay, say it, go ahead."

Gracie laughed out loud. "Well, guess what, Miss Matchmaker? I figured that all out on day one. Your brother is a nice guy. I actually like him. Right now, though, he is as screwed up as you are. Guess it runs in the family, eh?"

"You aren't mad!" Beth said, surprise ringing in her voice.

"Yeah, I am about the first part, but not about Jake. Like I said, I like him. Like, Beth, not love. Even if that were possible, that is waaayyy down the road."

Beth threw herself into Gracie's arms. Giz yelped, then barked. He listened as the two women he loved most in the world started crying. He didn't know whose face to lick first.

"So, we're good?" Beth said between her tears. "You'll keep the secret?"

"We're good, and your secret is safe with me," Gracie said.

# Chapter Seventeen

Beth woke with a start. What was that noise? Was she dreaming? She squinted to look at the little onyx travel clock on her night stand: 4:55. She groaned and rolled over and wiggled, trying to get next to John, who radiated warmth like a big papa bear. Only John wasn't there. She squinted again, trying to identify the noise that seemed to be engulfing the room. She groaned again when she realized it was rainy sleet slashing at the windows. It had probably woken John, and he couldn't go back to sleep. Right now he was probably down in the kitchen, where it was nice and warm, drinking his first of the seven cups of coffee that he consumed every day.

Should she get up or should she try to go back to sleep? It wasn't like she had anything to do. She'd never gone out on Black Friday to get a head start on her Christmas shopping, and even if she were the kind of person who did, she wasn't about to bundle up and get soaking wet trying to save five dollars on something or other. Those days were long gone. These days, she shopped online.

Beth snuggled deeper into the covers and let her mind race. She was wide awake now but reluctant to leave the warmth of her bed. Her thoughts took her to Jake and Luke Olsen in that order. Another quick look at the clock told her Jake was probably up, a bundle of nerves as he got ready for his workup day. More than likely, he hadn't gone to bed at all. A part of her wanted to call her big brother to wish him well, but the smaller part of her cautioned against it. She'd taken a stand, and she couldn't back down. After the operation would be time enough to mend fences if that was even possible. In the meantime, she could say some prayers for Jake's successful recovery. She thought then about going back to church. Maybe they'd let her sing in the choir. She nixed that idea right away when she recalled Alfie's words when, tongue-incheek, he'd told her she should only sing in the shower if the house was empty. They'd both had a good laugh over that.

Her gut told her Jake was going to be okay.

Beth squirmed some more, punched her pillow to fluff it up, and squeezed her eyes shut. Luke Olsen. In a million years she never thought she'd be in the position she was in now. Wild, crazy thoughts flew through her head at the speed of light. Maybe she or Jim Mack should get in touch with Luke's parents. Maybe she should confront Luke and set him straight once and for all. She wondered if hiring a hit man was out of the question. Of course it was. The thought was too stupid even to contemplate. Okay then, sic Gizmo on him. She could take him prisoner, Giz could guard him, and she and Gracie could pretend they were Dolly Parton and Jane Fonda in that movie **Nine to Five**. Or she could hire someone to kidnap him, put him on a steamer, and send him to Bora Bora with no money and no ID.

Beth buried her face in her pillow so she wouldn't cry. How dare that bastard invade her life like this when things were just starting to come together for her. How dare he!

In a fit of something she couldn't define, Beth crawled out from under the covers, swung her legs over the side of the bed, and stomped her way to the bathroom, where she brushed her teeth, showered, and washed her hair. Twenty minutes later, dressed in warm sweats and heavy socks, she made her way downstairs to the kitchen. The first thing she did was to turn on the outside lights to see the weather. Her little terrace was covered in ice, and it was still sleeting.

She turned around. There was no coffee. Where was John? She walked through the house and found him sleeping by the fireplace on a pile of big lush cushions and covered with a messy stitched afghan that she'd made when she was sixteen. The fire was low, almost out, just a pile of glowing red embers. She poked at it and added more logs, careful not to disturb John. She knew why he was here. Another bad dream, where he tossed and turned all night and kept her awake. When that happened, he got up and moved to the spare room. How she wished she could do more for him. The shrinks had told her they saw vast improvement, and he had to work it out himself. And he was, slowly but surely. All she could do was be there for him.

Back in the kitchen, she made coffee and settled herself at the table, where she waited for the last plopping sound that announced her coffee was ready. Her gaze kept going to the old-fashioned wall phone. Should she or shouldn't she call Jake? She wanted to. She wanted to offer encouragement and wanted to...not apologize but to say she wished things were different right now. Twice, her hand snaked out to pick up the receiver, but she managed to pull it back both times. Okay, then, if she couldn't call Jake, she could call Moose. He'd tell her how Jake's morning was going. Jake's pickup by the medical van was scheduled for seven o'clock. Twenty minutes from now.

Maybe she should make something to eat. The problem with that was she wasn't the least bit hungry, so there was no point in messing up the kitchen. She was a coffee-only kind of gal and didn't require food until around noon. She wished she had a cigarette. She'd quit smoking a year and a half ago after a bad bout of bronchitis. She hadn't been a real die-hard smoker, just one or two a day, and sometimes she'd go days or weeks without a cigarette. A crutch. For when things got too out of hand with Jake or John.

Beth was up and off her chair in a heartbeat and in the pantry, where she'd hidden some cigarettes for a time such as this. Many times she'd gone to the pantry, reached for her stash, then put it back. This time, she found a pack of cigarettes behind a box of macaroni. She ripped at the packaging right there and stuck the ugly cylinder in her mouth. She ran to the kitchen, poured coffee and cream, and sat down. She coughed and sputtered, but she kept at it until the wooziness cleared in her head. What did people see in these things? Whatever it was, it didn't stop her from puffing away.

Smoking was a sign of weakness on her part. A sign that she needed a crutch because she couldn't handle her emotions. Jake would smack her upside the head if he caught her smoking. Her eyes filled with tears just as the digital clock on the range clicked over to a big red seven, with two zeros next to it.

Beth blew out a cloud of smoke. She watched it circle upward before she took the pack of cigarettes over to the sink and dropped them in the garbage disposal. If she didn't want to smell like a chimney stack, she was going to have to take another shower and wash her hair and put on clean clothes. John would pitch a fit that she'd smoked. "So, okay, I gave in to a bad moment. It won't happen again," she muttered.

The phone was in her hands before Beth realized it. She punched in Moose's cell phone number and waited. She grinned when Moose said, "The medical van got here an hour early because of the bad weather. They left forty-five minutes ago. Jake didn't even bother going to bed, so he was ready to go when the service called about picking him up early. His surgeon called late last night. It seems he was going on a family trip of some sort and was to leave late today but had to cancel because of the bad weather all across the country. He asked Jake if he was up for surgery over the weekend if today went well. Jake was shocked out of his wits, Beezer, but he said yes. So, it could happen as early as tomorrow. I don't know why, and this is just my opinion, but I think the surgeon cooked up that story just for Jake. Quick and fast before he changes his mind like he's done so many other times. The good thing is, Jake has kept all his appointments and has done everything they've wanted him to do. I think it's a go."

Beth swallowed hard. "Tomorrow! Wow! If it is a go, let me know. I'll pick you up, and we'll both go to MUSC and wait while he's in surgery. Okay, Moose?"

"Yeah, okay, Beezer. I'll call you as soon as I hear from Jake. He hugged me. Do you believe that guy?" Moose said in a choked voice.

"Yeah. Yeah. I believe it, Moose."

Beth went back to staring at the photos and mementos on the refrigerator. A picture of her and Jake at Disney a lifetime ago. They were both wearing the Mickey Mouse ears and laughing into the camera. One of the happiest days of her life. A picture of Jake in a football pose, all virile and handsome as he grinned into the camera. A stunning picture of Gizmo in the Rose Garden at the White House. A picture of her and some of her friends in their caps and gowns the day they'd graduated from Clemson. Jake had taken the picture and then took a bunch of them to some bar and grill where they served baked potatoes that were as big as melons. Funny how she remembered that.

The pictures were curling at the edges, and the magnets weren't doing the job of holding them flush with the stainless-steel fridge. Happier days. She could feel her eyes start to burn, so she got up, rinsed her coffee cup, and poured fresh just as she heard the ping of the front door.

Alarmed, she stood still, hardly daring to

breathe. A break-in? Luke Olsen? Panic ripped through her as she looked around wildly for the knife block. She grabbed the carving knife Moose had used to carve the turkey and held it tight with both hands, the point sticking straight out. She watched, petrified, as the swinging door leading to the dining room inched open. "Don't come one step closer!" Beth shrilled. "John!" she screamed at the top of her lungs.

"Whoa! Whoa there, Beth," Jim Mack said, holding his hands high in the air, palms out. "It's just me, Jim."

"Oh my God! I thought you were...I didn't expect...I'm sorry," Beth said as she slid the carving knife back into the slot of the knife rack. "I didn't know you had left the house. I didn't hear the ping when the door opens. I must have been sound asleep. When did you go out?"

"Around two. Mind if I have some coffee? Actually, I never went to sleep. Guys like Olsen like to be out and about in the middle of the night, when all the decent people in the world are asleep. I've been driving around looking for strange cars. Once a stalker is what we call made, then they switch up. By that, I mean he probably ditched the Jeep Wrangler he was driving yesterday and got a different vehicle. Guys like Olsen love it when the weather turns ugly like it is now. No one goes out, and they're free to observe, to plot, and to scheme.

"I drove around looking for empty houses that are for sale to see if there were any cars parked in the driveways. Most people do not leave outside lights on past midnight, and there aren't that many streetlights on the streets around here, so it was hard to see. I got out a few times to walk around but didn't see anything out of the ordinary. I'll go out again in a little while. Thanks for the coffee, it's good. Where's John?"

Beth threw her hands in the air. He should have been here now the way she'd screamed. "The thing with John is either he doesn't sleep, like you, or when he does, he is in such a dead sleep the building could fall down around him. The shrinks say it's residual effects of his time in Iraq. He's a lot better now than he was when he first got back." Jim just nodded.

Her breathing back to normal, Beth stared across the table at Jim, and said, "I was sitting here thinking about going to Luke's parents and talking to them. I need to do something, Jim."

"No, you do not need to do anything. Do you think for one second that Luke's parents would give him up? Parents protect their young no matter how old they are. He's their son. If you were to do that, they'd immediately warn Luke. That could tip him over the edge. Not a good idea, Beth. Let's just go on the way we have been.

"Did you and John talk about when you're going back to Nashville?"

"No, we didn't. I planned on discussing that today. I think it might be better if we leave tomorrow, once the weather clears. Mr. Stonebridge told John that he has some really good security people he can let you use if you need them. Is that something that would work for you, Jim?"

"John did tell me that. We talked about it. But to answer your question, yes. I do need to sleep from time to time. With stalkers, you have to be on your game twentyfour/seven. They try to do the unexpected. You won't see them for days, sometimes weeks, then they can't stand it and surface, and when that happens, they've moved up a notch or two in their own game plan. As I just explained with the car. He's using a different one now."

Beth nodded. "Would you like some breakfast?"

"I would if you don't mind. But first I want to go upstairs and shower and put on some clean warm clothes. Will half an hour be okay?"

"Sure. Pancakes or eggs?"

"How about both?" Jim quipped.

"You got it." Beth grinned. Suddenly, she felt hungry herself. She watched as Jim gathered up his gear and headed upstairs to the guest room. She risked a peek into the family room, where John was stirring restlessly. He'd be up shortly.

Back in the kitchen, her thoughts everywhere but on cooking, Beth went about her business by rote. A different car. She would never have thought about that. It made sense. Moved now to a different level. That couldn't be good, she thought as she cracked eggs into a bright yellow bowl. As she laid out strips of bacon on the center grill, her thoughts took her to Luke's parents. Jim was right about that, too. What parents would give up their son even when they knew he was in the wrong? She rightly figured some would, but the majority wouldn't. Especially mothers. Luke had to know he was safe where they were concerned.

While the bacon sizzled, Beth pulled out her big six-slice toaster and popped in three sliced English muffins. Next came the pancake batter, which she whipped up in minutes. She let a drop of water hit the griddle to see if it would spurt. It did, which meant that the griddle was ready for the pancakes.

Beth looked around. Gracie was right; she wasn't much of a cook, but she had mastered breakfast because it was John's favorite meal of the day, and now it was hers, too. Unlike Jake, who liked a big, robust dinner. Jake was a juice-and-coffee kind of guy early in the morning.

A smile found its way to Beth's troubled expression when she heard the shower running in the downstairs bathroom. It meant John was up and ready for a new day and whatever it would bring. Wait, she thought, till he saw the ugly weather outside. John liked warm weather and bright sunshine, the same way she did. The truth was they both liked almost the same thing about everything in their lives.

A while later, just as she was about to flip the pancakes, Beth felt John come up behind her and nuzzle her neck. She laughed out loud. "Hmmmm, you smell good."

"Not as good as this breakfast you're making. I could eat a horse, that's how hungry I am. I'll take six of those," he said, pointing to the pancakes on the griddle.

"Coming right up. Jim is upstairs showering. He spent the night outside looking for Luke Olsen. He said Luke has now moved to the next step, which is to switch up cars because you guys made him yesterday."

"Giz is the one who spotted him. You gotta give credit where credit is due. I figured as much. Jim said that's probably what he would do. You're still worried, aren't you?"

"Well, yeah," Beth drawled as she slid the beaten eggs into a huge, oval-shaped skillet she'd bought from a Rachael Ray cooking show. It was perfect for scrambling a dozen eggs at one time.

"Don't be," Jim said, sitting down across from John. "We got your back. You guys planning on doing any Black Friday shopping?" he teased.

"Oh, you wicked man, bite your tongue. You couldn't pay me enough to go out there today to look for a bargain. My day is dedicated to reading up on profilers" —she smirked at Jim—"and looking up recipes for leftover turkey. And to help Gracie if she needs any extra help. And I need to stay in touch with Moose to see what's going on with Jake. So, what are you two planning?"

Jim looked down at his heaping plate and smiled. Now this was a breakfast fit for a king. He said so. Beth beamed. "I don't know about John, but I'm going to do another drive around to check on empty properties and see if there are any cars in the driveways. Or if the houses are empty, Luke might have broken in and stashed his car. I could certainly see him doing something like that."

"I'll go with you. Two sets of eyes are better than one. Beth can lock up tight, and we won't have to worry about her, or I can stay here. Your call, Jim."

"Stay with Beth. I can handle this. Tell me more about that one-of-a-kind dog."

"Giz...well, Giz is..."

# Chapter Eighteen

Mack and John steered clear of Beth all morning long, but they watched her out of the corners of their eyes. She would sit behind her desk for twenty minutes or so, then get up to go to the huge bay window at the front of the house and just stand there, looking out at the weather, which was worsening by the minute. Then she'd go to the kitchen for a soft drink, coffee, or a snack. After which she'd make several phone calls, then go back to the front window. At one point she announced she was going out for a walk. Both men were on her like white on rice.

At one o'clock, Beth started to pace as she gnawed at her acrylic nails. By two thirty, she had the artificial nails off and her real nails chewed to the nub. Mack looked at John and asked if he had any Xanax or Valium.

"I do, but I'm not giving it to her," John said. "I think you or I should go out there and cruise around to see if there is anything to see. You said you wanted to check on those empty houses to see if possibly Olsen is holed up in one of them."

"I'll go. If the guy is that stupid, then he's freezing his buns off. It's in the low thirties, according to the thermometer outside the kitchen door. He can't risk turning on any lights or the heat. People will notice smoke coming out the chimney. Besides, people tend to keep their eye on their neighbors' empty properties. That's what good neighbors do. If he is in one of those empty houses, he broke in in the dead of night, when everyone was sleeping. The thing that bothers me is that there are so few streetlights in this development. It's pitch black out there at night."

"Okay, okay, but keep your cell phone on. Beth is wired pretty tight right now. I'll do my best to talk her down. I wish Gracie were here, Giz, too. I heard Beth tell her to stay home because the weatherman said the roads were treacherous. Gracie agreed and said she was going to stay in her pajamas all day and bake a cake. Plus she said Giz is not good on ice. We're on our own."

Jim rooted around in the hall closet for his protective gear and slipped into it. "I'm going to hoof it. I have some cleats in my trunk. You just strap them over your boots, and they dig into the ice. I shouldn't be too long." He looked down at his watch. "If I'm not back by three-thirty, send out the cavalry."

John's eyes popped wide. "God, I hope that was a joke!"

"It was. Relax. Do you want Beth to see how wired up **you** are? While I'm gone, start thinking about what you're going to do with all those leftovers for tonight's dinner."

"Yeah, yeah. Okay. Be careful." The minute Jim was out the door, John locked it and shot the dead bolt home. He felt better the moment he heard the solid **thunk** that locked Beth and himself indoors. **Safe** was the only word that came to his mind.

Just who the hell was that guy who was reducing them all to this fear? Somewhere, he'd heard the expression "there's nothing to fear but fear itself." A crock if he ever heard one. He put on his game face and walked out to the kitchen. He shouted for Beth to come help him. She appeared in the doorway shouting, "What? What? What's wrong?"

"Nothing is wrong. I called you out here so we can decide what we're making for dinner with all these leftovers. Jim bundled up and is out there checking on things. Enough, Beth. You're safe. I'm here. Jim will be back shortly."

"Easy for you to say, John. But I think you need to give some thought to that screwball taking you out because you're standing in his way. He might be delusional about him and me as a couple, but he sees you as a threat. You need to think about that. You also need to park the Jeep inside the garage. He might get it into his head to monkey around with it during the night. If he's watching, he knows Giz isn't here. Think about it. How would we know if he was out there in the drive-way screwing around with our vehicle? We're either listening to music or watching television and talking in between."

"You have a point, Beth. I'll move the car right now and come back in through the garage, so lock up after I go out."

John was back within minutes, shivering and stomping his feet. "It is really cold out there. Okay, love of my life, we are buttoned down and as safe as we can be. About dinner..."

"Look, what's up suddenly with all this dinner stuff? We're warming up the leftovers. Period. End of story. What? You think I can magically create some kind of gourmet dinner with everything that's left! Well, I can't. So we warm it up or we eat scrambled eggs again."

"Warmed up is good," John said cheerfully. Maybe a Valium or Xanax wasn't out of the question after all. He couldn't remember ever seeing Beth this antsy.

"I haven't heard from Moose," Beth blurted.

Aha. "Well, that works two ways, Beth. Why don't you call Moose. I seriously doubt he's out and about in that bucket of bolts he drives around in, particularly in this weather. He's probably sitting there waiting for Jake or you to call him. Go on, call him, and put your mind at ease. While you're doing that, I'll be in the living room watching for Jim. I'll build up the fire in the den first. Make us some coffee, okay, honey?" Beth nodded as she fiddled with her cell phone.

John could feel the tightness between his shoulder blades. He likened it to going out on patrol when he was in the marines. He hated the feeling because walking or running into the unknown prepared or unprepared was a scary feeling. He peered through the front window, wishing Beth had installed blinds of some kind, but she liked sunshine pouring in through the windows. She never worried about anyone's peering in because she basically lived in the back of the house and not the living room, which was, as she put it, for company.

There was no sign of Jim Mack. Where was he?

As though he could read John's thoughts, Jim pulled his cell phone out of his pocket and called John. "I'm making a second go-round. Something is bothering me about the house at Four-thirty-four Laurel Court. It's a sprawling brick ranch. Do you know it?"

"Yeah. Don and Sally English. Don got transferred to Silicon Valley. The house has been for sale for about six months. A tad overpriced in my opinion. Sally and Beth are good friends. I met the Englishes through Beth. Why?"

"I thought I saw a shadow pass the window. It's probably my imagination, and it is hard to see in this weather. The place looks deserted. The other two empty houses are a wash. It's just this one that has my nerve endings going bonkers. It's a gut thing."

"Yeah, well, I am still alive because of my gut instincts," John said sharply. "What's your game plan, and why did you zero in on this house and cancel out the other two?"

"The main reason is the location of the English house. From the front window, if the guy has some good binoculars, he has a clear shot at your front door. The other two have hindrances. One has a big oak tree in the front yard that pretty much destroys any kind of view, and the other is around the corner, and no matter which window you would be at, you wouldn't be able to see anything other than the top of your chimney. Ergo, the English house. I really think he's in there."

"Okay, what next? Do we call the cops to come check it out? You planning on going up and knocking on the door? What?"

"I don't know. I need to think. We don't want to tip our hand. If I call the cops, it will take them hours to get here, and it is not an emergency. I imagine they have their hands full with all kinds of calls that are serious as opposed to something like this. If I knock on the door, and he can see from some vantage point inside, he will almost certainly recognize me. I'm coming back. I'm passing the house right now. Can't see much. See you in a few."

John swallowed hard. If Mack thought Luke Olsen was in the empty house, then he probably was. Bastard. Tell Beth? Not tell Beth? He shrugged. Better to leave it up to Mack. He walked into the den, where Beth, cell phone to her ear, was multitasking. She had a small card table set up near the fire with a carafe of coffee and a plate of pumpkin spice cookies that no one had eaten yesterday. She held her finger up to show she'd be off the phone in seconds.

A minute later, Beth broke the connection and jammed the phone into the pocket of her sweatpants. "Moose sounds so jittery. Kind of like me, I guess. Well, here is the news. All the tests are a go. And the reason Jake is in such good shape is he never slacked on his daily therapy. He's in great shape. Dr. Frey scheduled Jake for surgery tomorrow. They admitted Jake an hour or so ago. Surgery is at seven o'clock tomorrow morning. Dr. Frey is staying overnight at the hospital. Moose said Jake didn't put up any kind of argument. He's good with it, or so he says. He said he just got off the phone with Jake, and in his opinion, Jake was upbeat. That's a good thing if it's true. Don't you agree, John?"

"I do agree. Jake has made up his mind.

You always said once he decided on something, nothing could change his mind. Kudos to him. There goes the doorbell— Mack must be back. Stay here, Beth."

A moment later both Mack and John stomped their way into the den, with Mack running to the fireplace and thrusting out his cold, red hands. "Oh, man, this feels so good. I about froze out there. I cannot believe this weather. John, can you wrestle me up some warm socks? My feet are so cold they're numb, and I can't feel a thing in my toes."

"Sure thing," John said, sprinting off toward the laundry room. He returned with a pair of bright red wool socks that Gracie had knitted for him years ago. They were his favorite socks for some reason.

Beth watched Mack struggling with his shoes and socks as she pummeled him with questions. "Did you see or hear anything? What do you think? Is he still stalking me? I am so sorry you're freezing cold. I just made this hot coffee, and in a minute I'm going to get you some aspirin for you to take to ward off anything you might be coming down with. Maybe you should take a really hot shower."

"I will, but first I need to thaw out. Oh, Beth, this is like nectar for the gods," Mack said as he gulped the hot coffee. He swallowed the four aspirin Beth held out, and sighed. "This is just my gut feeling, but I think Luke Olsen is holed up in your friend's house, Don and Sally English's. On my first walk by, I thought I saw a shadow by the front window. It could have been my imagination, but I do not think so. And that particular house is perfect for his spying. If he is in there, he can see the front door of this house just perfectly. I really think he's in there." Mack held out his cup for a refill. Beth filled it almost to the brim.

"Shouldn't we call the police?" Beth asked.

"We need to talk about that," Mack said as he wiggled his feet as close as he could to the fire. "If I'm right, and he is in there, then he was watching and saw me walking by not once but twice. If he is in there, he's probably got a sleeping bag, some protein bars, some soft drinks, and maybe a heating pad or two. If I spooked him, he could be out of there in two minutes flat. All he has to do is roll up his sleeping bag and scurry out the back door. I don't know if he's gotten a second car yet or not. He could have one stashed in the garage—there's no way of knowing. He could be leaving by the back door as the police are knocking on the front door. If that happens, he goes to ground."

Beth's expression turned stubborn. "Well, we can't just sit here and do nothing." She turned to look at John, and said, "I think we should go back to Nashville as soon as the weather breaks. We're too open here. He'll have a harder time of it in Nashville."

Mack shook his head. "It's six of one and half a dozen of the other, Beth. The guy is determined, so it doesn't matter much which town you're in. He's already scoped out Nashville, knows where you live, knows where John works. If you stay here, you're pretty much a prisoner in your own house. I thought you wanted to be at the hospital tomorrow when your brother is operated on."

Beth's eyes filled up. "I did say that, and I do want to be there for Jake. The minute I know he's all right, that's when we'll leave. The roads should be sanded and salted by morning tomorrow. John?"

"Whatever you want, Beth, is okay with me. How about if Jim and I go out tonight after dark and sneak up on the house. Jim can take the back, and I can take the front. You can call Don and Sally and tell them we might be busting in their door, but we'll pay for it. Let's think about that, and talk later, okay?"

But they didn't talk. Instead, they hunkered down into themselves and let their minds race with different scenarios.

Within minutes, Beth and John could see Mack's eyes start to droop. When he was finally asleep, Beth covered him with an afghan. She motioned to John to head for the kitchen, where they could talk without waking the detective.

"I hope he doesn't get sick," Beth said fretfully. "I like him. He has the saddest eyes of anyone I've ever met. Even when he smiles, which isn't often, his eyes are still sad."

"There's a reason for that," John said quietly. "His wife was in the North Tower when...you know when. He was working out of the New York office that year on a special assignment. His wife, Carol, was working at an investment firm in the tower."

Beth's eyes filled, and as hard as she fought to keep her tears in check, she failed. "I had no idea."

"Well, don't say anything unless he tells you. He has this...this...this thing about keeping women safe. It's a mission, an obsession. I think in some ways, he must feel like he failed his wife, which on the face of it is ridiculous. He had no way of knowing, and there was nothing he could do. And yet he blames himself. I could see it even though he says that's not true. Let's talk about something else, Beth. Are you sure you want to go back to Nashville tomorrow?"

"Yes, I'm sure. But not until we see how Jake comes through his surgery. Maybe we can help Mr. Stonebridge in the soup kitchen if they open the alley for the people who depend on him for their meals."

"Okay. I don't have a problem with that at all."

Beth got up and walked over to the back door. She cupped her hands around her face and peered out at the oncoming darkness. "There's so much ice on the willow tree, I think it's going to split in two."

"What's the temperature?" John asked.

"A nice thirty-five degrees," Beth said, stretching her neck so she could read the numbers on the big red-andwhite outdoor thermometer. "One degree higher than it was at two o'clock. Maybe it will warm up. It looks like the sleet is turning to rain."

John watched Beth and hated how brittle she looked and sounded. This was something he'd never seen in her before. She was always in charge, always had just the right answer, always upbeat. And now this. Damn, how he hated Luke Olsen, and right now he wasn't too fond of Jake Masters, either, for what he had put Beth through.

When Beth couldn't stand the silence

any longer she blurted out the words she had no intention of ever saying. "Where is this all going to end, John?"

"I honest to God do not know, Beth. I've never come across anything like this before. I think Jim Mack is the best man for the job. I really do. I'm sorry to say we can't count on the police because their hands are tied. They are bound by rules and regulations, unlike Jim Mack, who is independent. I'm not saying Jim can or would do anything against the law, but there are ways for people like him to get the job done. Everything with the authorities has to be transparent, so there can be plausible deniability. How else do you think the CIA operates with all their clandestine operations? Don't forget for one minute Jim's background at the FBI. He knows how to skirt the edges to make things work for him. The bottom line is, we have to trust him."

Beth sat back down at the table and reached for John's hands. "John, do you think Luke's parents know about...about him?"

John sighed. He wondered the same thing. "Part of me says yes, and they won't give him up or cooperate. The other part of me says no, that Luke would cover his butt six ways to Sunday, and if by some slim chance they did have an inkling, he'd make it that you're the one chasing him, blah-blah-blah. Like you said, the guy is extremely good-looking and virile, and as parents, they'd be ready to believe every girl in the world would want their son. The guy is what, thirty-three or thirty-four? You'd think they'd be wondering why he hasn't found a girl to marry so they could have grandchildren. Again, this is one of those sixof-one, half-a-dozen-of-the-other scenarios. If you absolutely need a top-of-my-head answer, then I would go with they know. What do you think?"

"I think they know, too. I wonder what I would do if I were in their place and confronted with a situation like this. I want to think I'd do the right thing. Right is right. Wrong just doesn't work. If you cover up something like that, how do you live with yourself? What would you do,

John, if you were the father?"

The words exploded out of John's mouth bullet fast. "If I were his father, I'd drag his sorry ass to the nearest police station and turn him in. I would, Beth. If they don't do that, then they are just as guilty as he is. Like you said, right is right and wrong is wrong."

"Then why can't we go to them and talk openly? If they come down on his side, at least we know what we're dealing with. Well, not us personally, but Jim could do it. And if we succeed, that would make them complicit. Let them worry how they're going to come out in one piece."

"We can run it up the flagpole when Jim wakes up. I wonder how long he's going to sleep. The other night, he said he's not a sleeper and gets by on two or three hours a night. Said he used to sleep deeply for eight hours every night, but that changed when...well, that changed for him."

Beth looked at the clock. "We should start warming up this food. We won't wake him, but I'll fix a plate and keep it in the warmer."

"That sounds like a plan. I am getting hungry. Hey, look at me, Beth. We're going to beat this thing. I don't want you to have any doubts on that score. Right is might. Remember that,"

Beth giggled. "Gotcha. Okay, you set the table. Use the good dishes. I like the mistletoe and holly pattern on them. My gosh, Christmas is only five weeks away. So what are you getting me this year?" She giggled again as she started to whack slices of white meat off what was left of their Thanksgiving turkey.

"Only if you tell me first."

"Oh, you're no fun! Guess what I'm getting Jake! A skateboard!"

"No!"

"Yep!"

# Chapter Nineteen

Mack shuffled into the kitchen. He smoothed down his hair and looked around, grinned, and said, "Something smells good. Can't remember when I last slept that soundly. What time is it?" His voice was raspy, his eyes unfocused.

"Seven-thirty. You look rested. That's a good thing, Mack. I have a plate warming for you," Beth said, taking in the detective's disheveled appearance.

Beth and John mumbled and muttered as they watched Mack wolf down a platter of food that would have been three meals for either one of them. For sure, the detective didn't suffer from a lack of appetite.

Mack sighed. "That was just as good as it was yesterday. Thanks." He sighed again as he leaned back in his chair. "And you make good coffee, too." He drained his cup and looked at the two of them. When neither one said anything, Mack took the initiative. "Want to go for a walk, John?"

"Sure. Beth, you okay staying alone for a half hour or so?"

"I'm good. We need to move along here. It stopped sleeting, and it's just misting out now. The temperature is now thirtyseven degrees, so at least it's warming a little. It's going to be a mess when it all thaws out, but there's nothing we can do about it. Go ahead, I'll lock up behind you. Make sure you put your boots on."

"Yes, Mother," John drawled.

"I have an extra set of cleats in my trunk, John. I doubt there's been much car traffic on the road to break up the ice. We'll do better if we walk on the lawns since the grass acts as a cushion on the ice. Don't know if it's a fool's walk or not, but at this point, we have nothing to lose."

Beth poured the rest of the coffee into Jim's and John's cups. She sat back down, her nerves twanging like a banjo strung too tight.

"I called Don and Sally and explained that we might be breaking down their door, and they are okay with it, but they did ask why we don't use the key they left with me." John looked across the table at Beth, who laughed out loud.

"I'll get it," she said, getting up and opening the cabinet over the sink. Inside was a small basket that she dumped things into when she didn't know where else to put them. She fumbled around until she found a bright purple ribbon with a key on the end. "It opens the front door. The code to her alarm system is zero-zero-zero-nine. I don't know if the alarm is on or off. I suppose there is a possibility that one of the Realtors might not have turned it back on once they showed the house. I guess you'll find that out when you get there." Her voice was so flat, so devoid of emotion, both men simply stared at her.

Mack nodded as he pocketed the key. "John can enter by the front door, and I will be waiting by the back door in case he's in there and opts for the back way out."

"What about the garage?" John asked in a voice that was just as flat as Beth's.

"I happen to know you can't open the garage door without the remote control. I have that, too," Beth said. "Mine works the same way. In fact, I'm the one who turned Sally on to the company I use." She went back to the cabinet and the little basket. She rooted around till she found the small black square. She handed it to John, who stuck it in his jacket pocket.

"Okay, let's go. Bundle up, John. It's ugly out there." Mack grinned.

Beth walked both men to the front door and burst out laughing when she saw the two side windows that had allowed her to see the delivery girl from Edible Treasures. Now two colorful beach towels covered both windows and were held in place with ugly gray duct tape.

"I told you, Luke had a clear view of the entire front of your house, and that includes those two windows. He can see right into this hallway if he has a pair of high-end binoculars, which I am willing to bet he has. The beach towels might not be designer decor, but they're doing the job I want done. I'm not worried about your living room and the bay window since you really don't use that room and are rarely in it. If there are no lights on, he can't see in. You do, however, crisscross this foyer and come in here from time to time. All that guy needs is one sighting, and he's good for days. That's how these guys operate, how Olsen is wired," Mack said matter-of-factly.

"I wasn't complaining about the towels, Jim. Actually, I'm kind of miffed at myself that I didn't think of it. I just think that this is November, almost Christmas, and here I am decorating my foyer with beach towels. Makes me long for summer."

"Okay, okay, lock up behind us. We'll ring the bell when we get back. Make sure that dead bolt is solid in the slot."

John kissed Beth on the cheek before he followed Jim out the door. They both waited to hear the dead bolt slide home. They looked at one another and started off. "We should have told her to put the outside light on," John muttered.

"No, we should not have told her to do that. You do not want to light up the house in any way to make it easy for him. Will you please relax; I really do know what I'm doing. Beth was right, it's less windy, and it's just misting out. Come on, we need to put those cleats on and move out."

The minute the two men walked out the door, Luke Olsen packed up his sleeping bag, along with all his equipment, and slung it over his back like an oversized army backpack. He was out the back door in under two minutes, all traces that he'd ever been in Don and Sally English's house erased. He was confident he hadn't left any fingerprints anywhere in the house because he'd worn surgical gloves the entire time he'd been inside. As he told himself over and over, this wasn't his first rodeo.

Olsen walked between the yards, careful to stay near ice-crusted shrubbery. At one point he almost laughed out loud when he saw two men walking toward the house he'd just vacated. One of them had to be Beth's friend, and the other one was someone he'd seen in Nashville and was now here. He made a mental note to find out who the man was.

Olsen stayed close to the thick shrubbery until he was two doors away from Beth

Masters's house. He stepped out onto the lawn, crossed both driveways, and in a minute he was standing under the overhang of Beth's front door in total darkness.

Luke Olsen rang the bell and waited.

Inside, Beth was poking at the fire in preparation for laying down fresh logs. She looked at the small clock on the mantel. **They're back already?** was her first thought as she tossed the logs on the fire. She shrugged. Obviously, they hadn't found anything to indicate Olsen had been in the English house.

Beth turned on the outside light. Her hand was on the dead bolt to slide it back when she heard a voice from the other side of the door.

"Beth, honey, let me in. It's cold out here. Come on, sweetie, let's kiss and make up. Did you love the fruit basket I sent you for Thanksgiving? I missed having dinner with you. I hope you have a nice fire going so we can cuddle. I really missed you, honey. We need to make up. This isn't fun anymore, honey. Whatever I did, I'm sorry. Please, open the door."

All the air left Beth's lungs. Suddenly, she couldn't breathe. Her hand shot back away from the lock as her eyes went to the two beach towels. She was going to black out any second. **Breathe, Beth! Breathe, Beth!** She reached out to grab hold of the small foyer table, where she always tossed her car keys if she came in by the front door. Oh, God, where was her cell phone? Where did she leave it? She couldn't remember. The den? The kitchen counter? Where?

**Breathe, Beth!** And magically, air started to seep into her lungs. Her head cleared, and she let go of the table. The spy hole! Olsen was tall, he could see in the little magnified glass. She fumbled in her pocket for a tissue, ripped off a part of it, spit on it, and stuck it up to the round circle. **Breathe deep, Beth! You can do this. The guys will be back any minute. Think! Where did you leave the phone? Focus! Focus! Take deep breaths.**

"Now, why did you go and do that, honey? I know you're in there all alone. I saw those two guys leave. Such pests. You need to get them out of your life. I don't like that they are in your house. I don't like that one little bit. Are you listening to me, sweetie?"

Beth was shaking so badly she could barely stand. Talk to him or not. If she responded, he'd just keep talking. Jim said if he saw her or spoke to her, and if she responded, that would sustain him till he made his next move. **Do nothing,** she cautioned herself. **God, where are you, John?** A horrible thought crossed her mind. What if that nut job outside her door did something to Mack or John? No, no, that would never happen. Mack was too good an investigator to let someone like Olsen get a bead on him.

Her best bet was to keep him talking, but would he continue to talk when she didn't respond to him? He had to know that, sooner or later, both men would be back. Her mind raced as her body trembled. She needed her phone. God, where had she left it? If she could make a mad dash for it, she could throw open the door and take the creep's picture. **Only if you have a weapon,** her brain shrieked. A weapon. She looked around the foyer, her eyes wild. Nothing...

Poker. Jam the poker into the fire until the end was red hot, then throw open the door and jab him. Good, that was good. **How are you going to take a picture if you're jabbing the creep with the poker?**

Where was the damn phone? **The kitchen, it must be on the counter in the kitchen.** Thirty seconds back and forth. Maybe a minute to fire up the poker. Too much time. Ninety seconds was too much time. Crap, what was he saying now?

"I don't understand you, Beth. Why are you punishing me like this? You know we're meant for each other. We're a perfect match. That's what you call your company because you named it after us. I'm starting to get angry here, Beth."

Beth's mind raced. She made gagging, sobbing sounds as she sprinted for the den, where she jammed the poker into the hot flames. Then she raced to the kitchen to look for her phone. Seven, eight, nine, ten seconds. Where's the phone? She couldn't see it. Eleven, twelve, thirteen, fourteen seconds passed as she swept dishes and pots off the counter into the sink. Nothing. Fifteen, sixteen, seventeen, not on the table. **Think! Breathe deep. Run back to the door. Make more sounds to keep him talking.** She got there in time to hear Olsen say, "I'm fast losing my patience, Beth. I need you to open the door right now! Do you hear me, right now!"

"In your dreams, you bastard," Beth said under her breath as she made more garbled sounds. Thirty, thirty-one, thirty-two, thirty-three. How long would it take the poker to glow red? Crap, what was he saying now? Maybe the phone had fallen out of her pocket when she was in the den earlier and it was down between the cushions. How long would it take her to ransack the couch? She made more garbled sounds.

"I hear you crying. I'm sorry, I didn't mean to make you cry. I am upset, Beth. We should have spent Thanksgiving together, so we could make plans for our spring wedding. But first I want you to get rid of those two guys. If you don't, then I'll take matters into my own hands. You're too much of a softie, honey."

Beth felt her jaw drop and her eyes pop wide. She lost it then and screamed at the top of her lungs. "There isn't going to be any wedding, you stupid jerk! I hate your guts! I love John! John is the man I'm going to marry, not you, you creep! I'm calling the police right now!" She ran to the den, grabbed the poker, whose end glowed a bright red. Holding the poker straight out in front of her, she sprinted back for the door, her lips pulled back in a snarl. The bell rang just as she threw open the door. She jabbed blindly, screaming every dirty word her brother had ever taught her when they were kids.

"Whoa! Whoa!" both men shouted as they quickly backed up.

"Oh, God, it's you," Beth said, dropping the poker on the ground. Jim Mack picked it up as Beth fell into John's arms. She started to babble incoherently as the men led her back into the house.

"What the hell happened?" John asked. "Calm down, take a deep breath. You're okay, we're here. We're all safe. Deep breaths, Beth."

When Beth finally got her breathing under control, and her eyes could actually focus, she related what had happened. "I'm sorry, Jim. I did exactly what you told me not to do, but I lost it when he said he wanted to come in to talk about our spring wedding. I was good until I heard that. His tone changed. It was bitter and spiteful. He thinks you two are standing in his way."

John looked at Mack, who was chewing on his lower lip. "Stalker, casebook one-oh-one. I told you this would happen. I'm certain he was in the English house, because I could smell aftershave lotion. If the house has been closed up for over six months that smell wouldn't be there. I can guarantee no Realtor showed the house because there were no business cards on the kitchen counter, and that's where they always leave them, to prove the house was shown. Anyway, we could see the outside light was on here. As we got closer, we could see someone standing outside the door. At that point, we picked up our feet and ran like hell, but I guess he was watching. He had the advantage, and we were on ice, and even the cleats didn't help us all that much. By the time we got here, he was gone."

"Bold-ass bastard," John snarled as he tightened his arm around Beth's shoulders. "Should we call the police now? Beth saw him. Talked to him."

"She can file a report in the morning, but it's a she said, he said. But you're right, at least it will be on file. Now, let's do something for us, like finishing up that pie from yesterday. I think if it's warmed up just a tad, we'll be in gourmet heaven. I have a few ideas I want to run by you for tomorrow. I always find eating sweets when I'm in plan mode makes it all the more palatable."

In spite of themselves, John and Beth laughed out loud.

The clock in the waiting room glared at Beth and John. Both hands were straight up when a tall, gray-haired man in hospital garb approached them, a wide smile spilling across his face. Seeing the smile caused Beth, John, and Moose to sigh in relief. They waited, hardly daring to breathe, for the surgeon's report.

"Sit, sit! You two look like you should be my next patients. It went well. We'll know for certain in twenty-four hours, but I feel confident enough to say Jake will walk again. He's in recovery now and doing better than I expected. He's babbling like a runaway train. He's out of it to a certain extent, but that isn't stopping him from talking. I tried to understand what he was talking about and the only thing I came up with was he is involved in some matchmaking service and saying he had to memorize a four-hundred-word questionnaire or his ass was going to be handed to him on a silver platter. He mumbled a lot about some killer dog and someone named Gracie, who has beautiful eyes. He kept saying over and over how sorry he was that he let you down, Miss Masters. In his ramblings, he said he was going to take the bull by the horns and wrestle it to the ground and make you proud of him. Then he went off on another topic about someone he called a whiny puke, a lazy laggard, and a king-sized pain in the ass. We had to talk him down and soothe him, as he was getting agitated. He was still muttering when I left him in the recovery room. I hope it makes sense to you all."

Beth started to cry, then she burst out laughing. "You're sure he's going to walk again?"

"Unless he falls out of bed and breaks both his legs, then, yes, I feel confident in saying he will walk again. He's going to need a ton of therapy, but I know he's up to it. When he came in for the pre-op, he asked me to check into him doing his rehab at the veteran's center. He said he'd pay his own way and bring his own therapist and trainer, but that he wanted to do his therapy there if possible. He also said he might be able to help some of the veterans— football stuff, you know. I promised him I'd do what I can, and I really don't think it will be a problem. So, that's it for now, unless you have more questions."

"No, we're good. Thank you so much. I hope Jake realizes that he's very lucky to have someone like you on his side." Beth threw her arms around the surgeon, who seemed a bit taken aback. But he hugged her in return.

The surgeon chuckled. "I think he knows it. In fact, he thanked me profusely for putting up with him these past few years."

"When can we see him?" Moose asked.

"In about an hour. Well, that's it for now. I have to scrub now. I have a ten-year-old who's waiting for me to do the same operation. Do me a favor and stop by the chapel to say a little prayer for this boy. I am very much afraid that this one is going to be tricky."

The trio looked at one another. They all had tears in their eyes.

"Moose, we have to leave now. Take good care of him, okay?"

Moose nodded. "I wish you'd at least stay long enough to—"

"No." Beth said. She hugged the old man, tears rolling down her cheeks.

John shook Moose's hand. "You know our plans. Call us if you need us for anything."

"Go on, get out of here; you have a long drive ahead of you. Be careful," Moose said gruffly. "Shoot me a text when you get to Nashville so I don't go out of my mind worrying about you."

Another hug. "Will do," Beth said.

John looked at his ladylove, and asked, "You ready? You got your bag?"

"I am soooo ready, and yes, I have my bag," Beth said, pointing to a flowered satchel at her feet. "Five minutes, and I'll meet you at the elevator. You call Jim and tell him we're on our way."

Beth entered the women's bathroom looking like a stylish thirtysomething young woman. She exited looking like an elderly gray-haired woman supporting herself on a cane.

John entered the men's room looking like a studly jock and exited looking like Beth's counterpart, doing a slow shuffle. When they met up they held hands and entered the elevator and took it to the basement garage, where they then walked up to the next level to meet Jim Mack, who was waiting for them in a black 1995 Buick Regal. He climbed out, handed the keys to John, and said, "Good luck. I'll catch up to you, so don't worry about it.

I'm going to give that jerkoff a run for his money. By the way, the roads are all clear."

"Did you see him lurking around here, Jim?" Beth asked.

"No eyes on him, but he's out here somewhere. I'm going to drive your Cherokee back to the house and park it. In the garage. I'll sneak out the back way and pick up a rental. I'll e-mail you along the way. I'll be sure to set the timers and call Gracie to stop by. Business as usual. Drive carefully. Hey, hold on. What's the news on your brother?"

"He's going to be walking me down the aisle," Beth said happily. "Thanks for asking, Jim."

"Okay, you heard it here first," John quipped.

"That I did, that I did. Congratulations! Be careful now; make sure you don't speed."

"You be careful, too, Jim," Beth said before she rolled the window back up.

"Next stop, Nashville!" John said, excitement ringing in his voice.

"Amen to that, brother." Beth giggled.

# Chapter Twenty

By the end of the first week in December Beth and John had settled in to a new pattern of living in Nashville that Jim Mack set up for them. They moved into a bigger apartment, a furnished one closer to Rootie Tootie's. This meant that they could walk to the club with Jim acting as a bodyguard. He had been escorting Beth back and forth for her singing lessons, but they were now on hold due to Alfie's being in the hospital with a severe case of gout. With time on her hands, Beth volunteered to help Arnold Stonebridge in his soup kitchen and loved every minute of working with the little man.

Arnold tightened up the security at Rootie Tootie's, and all employees were shown pictures of Luke Olsen as he presently looked. Arnold had his people take it one step further and used facial-recognition software to show what the architect could look like if he tried to change his appearance. He hired two extra bouncers to drive home his point about how serious the situation was. Because his staff loved and adored the little man, there was no doubt his orders would be carried out to the letter.

John continued with his job at the café and had no clue he had a bodyguard tailing him every minute of the day. That's how good Arnold's people were.

Nashville had recovered from the freak ice storm, and the Christmas season had gone into full swing. Beth said over and over that she'd never seen a happier place, and she just loved, loved, loved Nashville. John agreed.

Late at night, curled up against each other, the two of them talked about their wedding, which they were planning for April. A spring wedding in Nashville was exactly what Beth wanted. She'd yet to speak to her brother, but she knew in her heart, her mind, her gut, that Jake would be walking her down the aisle even if he limped or used a cane.

With no outward sign that Luke Olsen

was anywhere near, both John and Beth fell into an it-was-all-a-baddream-and-now-it's-over attitude. That bothered Jim Mack because he knew this downtime, this quiet time, was just the lull before the storm.

As the days wore on, John's popularity increased, and most nights it was standing room only at Rootie Tootie's. Every night Beth sat ringside with Arnold Stonebridge, cheering John on. But the best part, as Beth had said to John, was they had both made a wonderful new friend in Arnold. Then she had whispered something in John's ear that made him grin from ear to ear. "Can you really do that?"

"I put Gracie on it, and it's in the works. It's a long shot, but like I said, she's working on it, and so are the other girls. I told them all it's a top priority. I'm kind of hoping something will break around Christmas. Now wouldn't that make the most smashing present of all time?" John kept grinning and complimented his soon-to-be bride by saying if anyone could do it, it was she and Gracie.

While Beth and John continued living

their lives, Luke Olsen was scouring the dregs of Nashville, with no success, hoping to find someone crazy enough to, as he put it, take out John Rossmon. He felt like he was at the end of his rope. He was sick and tired of living on the fly, sleeping in his stolen brown van, washing up in gas station washrooms to conserve his money, which was dwindling at the speed of light. He'd already dipped into what he referred to as his wedding money, something he swore he wouldn't do.

Olsen was running out of time and resources, and he knew it. And to make matters worse, he was no closer to Beth than he had been back in Garden Grove. How stupid that was. They were gone almost a week before he even had a clue they were no longer in the house. He was losing his edge, and he knew it. He needed some kind of plan but couldn't think of anything that would bring him closer to Beth. Why was she doing this? How much longer was she going to punish him? What had he done that was so awful she refused to forgive him? If she would just tell him whatever it was, he would fix it in a heartbeat.

Olsen's eyes narrowed as his fist pummeled the armrest separating the driver's seat from the passenger seat. She said she was marrying that...that...guitar player. He knew they were just words to hurt him because she was angry. And now this text from his parents telling him the police had gone to their office asking for him and saying all kinds of hateful things about him. They wanted him to come home to straighten things out. Like that was going to happen. Not. He'd fix them; he wouldn't invite them to his wedding. Where was their loyalty? He pushed that thought as far back in his mind as he could.

Olsen peered out the side window of the van. He blinked several times when he noticed how all the shops and street lamps were decorated for Christmas. Christmas! He shook his head to try to clear away his thoughts. Christmas! He'd just sent a cornucopia to Beth for Thanksgiving. It couldn't be Christmas already. He blinked again. Just the thought of Beth's spending Christmas with that...that... guitar player sent him into a blind rage. Maybe that's why Beth was so upset with him. He hadn't told her what he was going to get her for Christmas. Women were like that. Just last month, he'd spent over an hour in Victoria's Secret staring at all the sexy lacy lingerie. He'd settled on a black-and-red see-through teddy and was about to buy it when the manager had come up to him and asked him to leave because several women complained about how he'd walked around touching the garments. He'd left in a huff. Maybe Beth had heard about that.

He realized what a crazy thought that was. How could she possibly have heard about that?

Olsen went back to watching the door to the café. It was now two-thirty, and the lunch hour was over. The guitar player would be leaving just the way he left every day at this time. He'd go straight to Rootie Tootie's, where he himself couldn't get past the entrance to the alley that led to the club. The bastard owner had it so buttoned down, wind couldn't get through that alley. So...that meant he had to make his move sometime between when the guitar player left the café and got to the club, which meant he had to trail him on foot or do a hit-and-run. But then the guy tailing the guitar player would jump into the fray. Somehow, he'd have to dispose of him first. They probably thought he wasn't aware of the man, some kind of bodyguard no doubt, but he wasn't stupid—he'd spotted him the first day back.

Olsen's heart started to beat in wild anticipation of what he was about to do. Then a thought hit him. If he was successful, how was he going to get away? Damn, he hadn't thought that far ahead. Stupid, stupid, stupid. The streets were busy; some fool would try playing the hero, that was for sure, if he was on foot. While he knew the streets by now, given the layout of the town, he'd have to make almost a straight run as he hadn't seen any alleys or cutouts that would allow for a hasty exit. The van then. Do the hit-and-run and barrel ahead, ditch the van at some point, and take off on foot. Which in itself presented a whole host of other problems. While he'd worn the surgical gloves the entire time, he knew his DNA was all over the van. He'd have to set it on fire, and even then, those damn CSI guys could find a stray hair that would link him to the van.

Olsen watched John's tail. He watched the traffic light, the congestion, the crowds of shoppers with gaily colored shopping bags. Not good. He realized he needed to go back to the drawing board and come up with a better plan. All in all, he had to chalk today up as an exercise in futility. Now he needed to park the van someplace where no one would spot it and call in the cops. The mall was the logical choice, with all the Christmas shoppers, but it was too far. He needed to be close to the club. Close to where Beth was even though he wouldn't be able to see her. Just knowing where she was made him feel better.

Twenty minutes later, Olsen pulled into a truck stop and parked in the rear. He knew this place, as he'd been here before.

For five bucks he could take a hot shower, shave, and change his clothes. For another ten bucks, he could rent a cot and sleep under blankets for twelve hours. He nixed the latter part, preferring to sleep in the van. Maybe he'd change his mind after he ate. He might be sluggish and need a good few hours of solid sleep. He liked this particular stop because they served home-cooked food, pretty much all you could eat. Good food. It beat the fastfood junk he'd been existing on these past days. Good hot coffee, as much as you could drink, and one to go. In his wildest dreams, he never thought he'd live to see the day he would think this place was a five-star establishment. He was used to fine things, not this rough-and-tumble life he'd been forced to lead. And it was all Beth's fault. He was going to tell her so, too. But then he'd forgive her because he loved her.

A burly trucker held the door for Olsen. The inside of the place smelled good and it was warm. Spaghetti, if he wasn't mistaken. He could smell the garlic. He

almost swooned with happiness. He
headed straight for the back of the truck
stop, carrying his canvas bag with a clean
set of clothes and his bag of toiletries. He
was back in the restaurant in forty minutes,
feeling like he'd scaled a mountain. He
sat in a booth in the back by himself and
ordered the special, which was spaghetti
and meatballs. The coffee came first, and
he drank it in two long gulps. He held it
out to the waitress for a refill. He winked at
her, and she winked back as she filled his
cup to the brim before she left to place his
order.

The last occupant of the booth had left
a copy of the **Nashville Ledger** on the
seat. Olsen picked it up and turned to the
event page to see what was going on in
Nashville for the different clubs. He ran his
finger down the list of clubs till he came
to the **R**s. A very festive month for sure.
A lot of good that was going to do him,
but at least he knew what was going on.
He looked around to see if anyone was
watching before he ripped the schedule
out of the paper, folded it, and stuck it in

his hip pocket. His food arrived a moment later, a steaming platter of spaghetti and four huge meatballs along with half a loaf of crusty bread. He held out his cup again, and the waitress refilled it. There was no winking this time. It was time to eat and time to think.

Jim Mack and two of Arnold Stonebridge's security, Mike and Dave, patrolled the streets surrounding Rootie Tootie's, looking for something that shouldn't be there. A car, a person, something in plain sight that shouldn't be obvious but was for some strange reason. One of the security men had an "in" that allowed him to run license plates on cars they deemed suspicious. So far, Mike had run a total of sixteen plates, but there was nothing out of the ordinary. Today, though, Dave, who claimed to have better eyesight, said he'd seen the same brown van every day for the past week, parked near the café where John Rossmon worked. It belonged to a carpet installer who lived in Forest Hills. The map they had indicated Forest Hills was eleven and a half miles from Nashville.

Jim Mack supposed the owner could be installing carpeting someplace close to the café. People tended to lay down new carpeting before the holidays. He made a mental checklist and told Dave to see if he could come up with a phone number for the owner. He came back dry, which was no surprise. People today were discarding their landlines and relying on cell phones. He himself didn't have a landline in his apartment back in Garden Grove. Everything today was wireless.

"Then how come that guy doesn't have some kind of decal on his truck saying he's a carpet installer? What the eye sees is the best advertisement you can get. Think about it. Stop and really think. How many brown vans have you seen lately? Except for the one we saw a short while ago, that's the only one I've personally seen. Well?"

The two security men looked at each other. Both of them shook their heads. Mike spoke first. "To be honest with you, I don't ever remember seeing a brown van, at least not one that registered with me. Vans are usually white or black, so that the lettering or the decals stand out." Dave agreed, as did Jim Mack. Both security men looked at Jim for further directions.

"We might be onto something and we might not be, but the fine hairs on the back of my neck are stirring. When that happens, something is off or not right. I say we split up and cruise around and try to locate the van. John and Beth are safe for now. You guys know this town better than I. Lay out a grid for each of us to cover. If, and I stress the word **if,** any of us decides this is our guy, we do not act alone. If one of us spots him, then notify the other two, and we'll take it from there. You all agree?" Jim asked. Mike and Dave nodded. "And not a word of this to John or Beth." Both men nodded again.

Dave pulled a small, tattered notebook out of his back pocket. He spread out a city map of Nashville, pinpointed their location, then assigned a grid to each man. "We can meet up at a given time at Logan's Steak House and compare notes. What time is good for you all?"

"Six. It's dark by then, so a brown van is going to be pretty hard to pinpoint after that. Six it is," Jim said as he accepted his small, hand-drawn map. "But if you do spot it, call ASAP."

The men split up and went their separate ways.

As Jim said later, traffic was a bitch. He grumbled that he did more starting and stopping than actual driving. He was fast closing in on the time to meet up at Logan's when his cell phone chirped. "Yeah."

"It's Mike. I think I have the brown van pinned down. I stopped at a truck stop to get gas and had to wait in line, so I drove around the back of the place, and there, big as life, was a brown van. I'm still here. This is one of those places where truck drivers can shower and rent a cot for ten dollars if they want. I think he's here. What do you want me to do?"

"Do nothing. Give me directions, and I'm on my way. Did you call Dave? No? Well, call him, and we'll all meet up. Do not, I repeat, do not go inside until we get there. Don't even go near that van."

Jim felt an adrenaline rush, then he cursed. He, literally, had to go across in rush-hour traffic. He actually debated parking his car and running the distance, but the idea was so ridiculous he didn't give it a second thought. Instead, he lay on his horn and cursed some more as he inched his way forward.

It was two minutes shy of six o'clock when he pulled into Donovan's Truck Stop under a sign that said GOOD EATS in blazing neon. He drove slowly past the gas pumps, his gaze taking in everything. The place was lit up like a stadium during football season. He spotted Mike parked next to an eighteen-wheeler Peterbilt. He parked, got out, and joined Mike and Dave, who had arrived just moments after he did. Jim climbed into Mike's car.

"What's the plan, Jim?"

**Yeah,** Jim thought, **what is the plan?**

"One of you will go inside. It can't be me because I'm positive he's seen me at the kids' apartment and back in Garden Grove. Cozy up to one of the staff. Waitresses love to talk if they see a big tip in the offing.

Don't be chintzy now. Cook up some story—you were supposed to meet your buddy here but there was an accident on the highway, yada yada yada. Find out if the guy is doing the sleep thing. While you're doing that, Dave and I will take a crack at the van. Unless you guys can think of something better." He waited.

When neither man had a better idea, Jim said, "Okay, let's do it."

"I can jimmy the lock. It's an old van with nothing fancy to secure it. You watch the door, okay, Dave?"

Jim had the van door open within seconds. He climbed inside and started to breathe through his nose. Sweat, body odor, rancid food containers, and stale cigarette smoke assailed his nostrils. Five minutes into his search, he knew that the guy who inhabited this van was no carpet installer. He knew in an instant that he'd hit the mother lode when he smelled the same aftershave lotion he'd smelled back in the English house in Garden Grove. But it was the sleeping bag that convinced him Luke Olsen was living in this brown van.

Unfortunately, he didn't find anything to prove that. There were no telltale signs he'd left behind. Just the smells and the sleeping bag. He perked up a second later. The sleeping bag would be full of DNA.

Still, the man hadn't done anything to warrant calling the cops. Unless he'd stolen the van. Which was more than likely. **More than likely my ass,** the detective thought. **The miserable cretin stole this van sure as I'm sitting here.**

Jim climbed out of the van and walked over to Dave. "I am ninety-nine percent certain Luke Olsen is living in that van and that he stole it from the guy in Forest Hills. He's got a sleeping bag in there, which I'm sure is full of DNA. Our problem right now is that if we turn him in or call the cops, he'll probably make bail thanks to his wealthy parents. That will put us back to square one. If we don't call the cops and start tailing him, we might be able to nail him as the stalker. I need to think about this a little more. Right now, you go into that truck stop and get Mike out here."

Dave sprinted off to the entrance. Jim

climbed back into Mike's car and waited. Damn, it was cold. He didn't give the cold a second thought when he let his thoughts take over. They'd found him. By God, they'd really found him. From here on out, the trick would be not to lose him.

More security. As much as Mr. Stonebridge could supply. When the door closed behind Mike and Dave, Mike leaned across, and said, "It's him. He got there around three and ate a big dinner of spaghetti and meatballs. Drank five cups of coffee. He was offered one to go but he said he changed his mind and was going to rent a cot for a few hours. He signed up for shower privileges when he arrived."

"Is the waitress going to squeal on you?"

"I hope not. I gave her fifty bucks, and she said she goes off duty at six. It's almost that, so I think we're safe, at least for now," Mike said.

"Okay, let's hit that steak house and map out a plan. One of you call Mr. Stonebridge and have him send out a few guys to stake this place out."

Mike laughed. "Mr. Mack, this isn't our

first rodeo. Mr. Stonebridge is my boss, and I report to him. I already called him. He said two men would be here by six-ten. And since he said six-ten, he means six-ten. Not sixeleven. You want to make a bet?"

Dave looked at Jim and burst out laughing. "Don't bite."

"Nope. I'll take your word for it. By the way, dinner is on me tonight."

"And the beer? We are off duty now."

"Yep, and the beer, too."

## Chapter Twenty-one

Alow rumbling sound found its way into Luke Olsen's subconscious. He stirred, stretched, then rolled over on the narrow cot. His eyes popped open. Where the hell was he? Not in his sleeping bag, that was for sure. Plus he was warm, sweaty actually. Bright lights, red, blue, green, permeated the room. Damn! The rumbling noise grew louder, followed by another loud rumble. And then he remembered he was at the truck stop, and he'd rented a cot. The rumbling sounds were the eighteen-wheelers pulling in or leaving. The colored lights were the neon lights advertising the truck stop and could be seen for miles from the highway.

Olsen kicked off the light blanket and swung his legs over the side of his rental bed. He looked around to see if he had any bedmates in the dormitory style room. As far as he could tell, he was alone. He was fully awake now and wondering what his next move should be. He headed for the men's room. No sense paying five dollars for another shower. He washed the sleep from his face, brushed his teeth, and combed his hair. Now he was ready for a cup of hot coffee and maybe a slice of apple pie with two scoops of vanilla ice cream. He could ponder his next move while he ate.

He trotted down a long hall to the main part of the truck stop. It still smelled like garlic. The dinner had been good, and it had been hot. He slid into a booth and waited for a tired-looking waitress to take his order. At first he thought the night waitress was the same one who'd served him his dinner, but it wasn't. The only similarity was both women were blondes, and this one was older. Maybe they were mother and daughter, not that he cared.

"What will it be, sweetie?"

Sweetie? Beth was the one who should be calling him sweetie, not this tired, over-worked, and underpaid waitress. Olsen forced a smile. "Coffee, apple pie, and two scoops of vanilla ice cream."

"Coming right up. By the way, since you're the only trucker who rented a bed, you must be the man some guy was looking for. He came in and said he was supposed to meet you, that he was your buddy. Said there was an accident on the interstate, and he was late and wanted to know if you'd arrived, waited around, or left. Showed the afternoon manager your picture. Darren, that's the manager, said you were sleeping. Your friend said not to wake you because you'd been on the road for a long time. We said we'd tell you he was here when you woke up. He didn't come back, though. Maybe you should check your phone. He might have sent a text or called while you were asleep."

Olsen watched the waitress, whose name tag said her name was Sheila, walk away. His heart started to pound inside his chest. The urge to get up and run was so strong, he had to stomp his feet on the floor. His gut instinct warned him not to do anything stupid. That same gut instinct was telling him someone was outside waiting for him to come out. That had to mean they had found the van and had gone through it by now. Not that they would find anything. Everything of any importance was in the canvas bag on the floor. Why? How did they get onto him? No way could he go back to the van. He felt a sudden blast of cold air swirl around his feet. A big trucker stomped his way to a table across from the booth Olsen was sitting in. Because he was so big, he wouldn't fit in the booth and needed the table just for leg room.

Olsen watched as the big man ordered the spaghetti and meatballs and two slices of apple pie. He heard him say, "And, Sheila, keep the coffee coming."

"Okay, Herb. The pie today is mighty good," she said as she slid Olsen's pie across the table. He dug right in and looked over at the trucker. "I can attest to that. This is the best apple pie I've ever eaten. I had the spaghetti earlier, and it was just as good. So, where you headed?"

"Memphis. You?"

Olsen shrugged as he ate the pie he no longer had an appetite for. Memphis was three hundred miles away. "Don't know. I was planning on hitching a ride to somewhere. Anywhere, actually. I beat the crap out of a guy who was messing with my girlfriend. They both filed charges, and I lit out. It's not right, what that skank did. I need to get as far away from here as I can get. Can I hitch a ride with you? I don't have much cash on me seeing as how I left in such a hurry. I can spot you a twenty."

"Sure, no sweat. How'd you get here?" the trucker said, shoveling one of the giant meatballs into his mouth.

"Hitched. I rented a cot this afternoon and slept for a while. I'm almost afraid to go out there. Did you see anyone who looked suspicious—you know, like they're looking for someone like me?"

The trucker laughed. "Actually, I did see two dudes on Harleys. Don't know if they were looking for you or not. They should be frozen by now, but you never know. Those bikers know how to dress for this kind of weather. You can't really see outside with all that neon, but it's been snowing for the past hour. Don't think it will amount to much."

Olsen finished his pie at the same time the trucker finished his spaghetti. Sheila had the trucker's pie and fresh coffee on the table in a nanosecond. He took that to mean the guy was a good tipper.

When it was time to settle the bill, the trucker, who said his name was Herb, asked, "How do you want to play this? You march out of here with me, they'll see you if they're the ones looking for you. I suppose you could go out the back way. I'll pull up to the farthest pump, and you hop in. Just stand by the Dumpster. We'll need Sheila's help to get you out the back door and to stand watch."

"Will she squeal on me if they come in here looking for me?"

"Not likely. Sheila and I are...friends. If I ask her to keep quiet, she will. Sheila might look like she's been rode hard and hung up wet, but that gal has a heart as big as a mountain. She's good people. You can give her that twenty you were going to spot me. Make her life a lot easier."

"Yeah, yeah, sure." Olsen almost passed

out now that his immediate problem was
taken care of. He fumbled in his pocket
for the promised twenty and another five
spot for the pie and coffee. He held it out
to Herb, who took it, got up and walked
up to the register, where he had an intense
five-minute conversation with Sheila, who
looked over at him, nodded, winked, and
then stood on her tiptoes to kiss Herb
soundly. Somewhere from the other end
of the room Olsen could hear laughter and
hoots. Obviously, there were others who
knew the two were friends with benefits.
Whatever, it was all working for him.

Sheila motioned to him to follow her into
the back. She led him down a short, grungy
hall, then into an even smaller room to a
door that led to the Dumpster area.

"Just stand out there, next to the second
Dumpster. When Herb swings his rig
around, the passenger side will be facing
you. Just hop right on in. Look, mister, I
don't know what your story is, but Herb
is a really good guy. Don't take advantage
of him."

Olsen smiled one of his most winning

smiles and said, "He said the same thing about you, that you were a nice person. I would never take advantage of someone who is kind to me. Thank you."

"You want a coffee to go? Of course you do. Herb forgot his, so just give me a minute and I'll go fetch it."

Well damn, this was almost too scary-easy. Herb was right—it was cold. Olsen hugged his arms to his chest as he waited for Sheila and the coffee and for the first rumblings of Herb's rig. What if this was all a big mistake? No mistake if some guy had his picture to show around. Now why would Beth go and do something like that? As he stamped his feet to keep warm, he decided it wasn't Beth at all, but the guy who was leeching on to her. The guy he had been going to take out tomorrow. Only now, that wasn't going to happen.

Get to Memphis, get out, head to a mall, heist a car, and head right back to Garden Grove, and from there it was Plan B all the way. Just as soon as he figured out what Plan B was.

The big rig was approaching just as

Sheila opened the door. She thrust a bag at him, and said, "Four coffees and six sticky buns. Herb does love his sweets. Good luck, sweetie."

Olsen didn't know why he did it but it felt right. He hugged Sheila and thanked her. She beamed her pleasure as she closed and locked the door.

"Memphis, here I come," Olsen said as he climbed up into the cab and pulled the door shut.

"Juke down, buddy, those two bikers are still out there. By now their gonads should be rock-solid frozen." Both men laughed as Olsen looked at the digital clock on the dashboard. Two minutes to the witching hour. And then a whole other new day to work toward making all his dreams come true.

Just as Herb and his big rig roared out of the truck stop, the two bikers, employees of Arnold, finally decided it was time to go into the truck stop and get something warm in their bellies. Without knowing it, the two security men settled into the same booth that Luke Olsen had just left. Both men looked around casually. At midnight, customers were few and far between. No one resembling Luke Olsen was dining. They ordered a pot of coffee and the strawberryrhubarb pie. They leaned in close across the table and spoke in virtual whispers. Chat up the waitress or not chat up the waitress? Meander to the men's room, show Olsen's picture to a few of the diners while the other one chatted with the waitress? Both viable options.

Stan, the more seasoned of the duo, looked at his partner, whose name was Keith, and said, "I'm going to hit the men's room, and I'll show the picture around, but you occupy the waitress. Tell her you want to see the room in case we decide to rent a bed. I don't know how this kind of thing works. It's not busy in here, and we saw those people who are eating come in while we were outside. And, Keith, use your charm, okay?"

Keith nodded and walked up to the counter, where Sheila was slicing into a fresh pie. He asked if he could see the rental rooms. She told him to wait a moment, until she put their food and coffee on the table, and she would show him. The minute they were out of sight, Stan was up and out of the booth. He beelined across the room where he immediately pulled out Luke Olsen's picture and flashed it around. All he got for his efforts were a bunch of no's. Until he came to a table where a whippet-thin man with a scraggly beard was finishing off his plate of spaghetti. His head bobbed up and down. "Yeah, I seen the dude. He was sitting right over there, in that there booth, the second one in. He was talking to Herb. I seen the pretty boy heading out to the kitchen when Herb left. Can't think of his last name, but he does a run from here to Memphis every day—that's how I know him. Anyways, I was thinking to myself that pretty boy was hitching a ride with Herb. Now, I don't know why I say that, just an old trucker's sixth sense. Herb's known around here for picking up strays. Talk to Sheila. Her and Herb have a thing going. Doncha go saying I said anything."

"Thanks. Won't say a word."

"You some kind of cop or something?"

"Yeah, something like that," Stan said as he ambled over to his booth just as Sheila and Keith returned to the main part of the truck stop. He slid into the booth, smacked his hands together, and said, "This looks just the way my mama's pie used to look. I hope it's just as tasty."

Sheila waved as she headed back for the counter.

"Well?"

Keith took a big gulp of his coffee, pronounced it fit to drink, and said, "I only saw one mussed cot. All the others were made up, so that tells me just one sleep customer so far today. They have a sign-in book. I signed us in and paid her twenty bucks just so I could see who signed in before us. Phil Parsons was the name. Ring a bell, Stan?"

"Yeah, yeah, that's Olsen's alias according to Jim Mack. Well, see that skinny little guy over there eating by himself? He said he thinks Olsen left through the kitchen and some trucker named Herb gave him a ride. He recognized the picture I showed him. He also said that Sheila, our waitress, and Herb have a thing going on. Herb drives back and forth to Memphis every day. It's a good bet that's where our guy is headed because some way, somehow, he made Mike and Dave earlier."

"So who do we call, Mr. Stonebridge or Jim Mack?" Keith asked. "Ya know, this is really good pie. I might come back here again someday, and the coffee is top notch."

"I don't like waking up Mr. Stonebridge at this hour. Send a text to Mack and tell him we're headed back to town. If he wants to meet, pick a place, or we can meet up in the morning. Let it be his call. Memphis is over three hundred miles away, so nothing is going to happen for the next few hours."

While Keith sent out a text, Stan was counting out money to pay the tab. He left a generous tip for Sheila, who smiled her thanks, and said, "You be careful out there. I heard it's snowing."

Stan nodded and headed for the door.

"I say we take the car Mack left for us. We can pick up the cycles later in the day. The snow is sticking. You okay with that, Keith? You get a reply from Mack?"

"Yeah. That guy must never sleep. He said he'd meet us at the Dog and Duck, that place on Silver Street that's open twenty-four/seven."

The two men drove off in a swirl of snow, each busy with his own thoughts.

# Chapter Twenty-two

To everyone's relief, less than half an inch of snow fell during the night, and the same amount fell sporadically over the following three days. Jim Mack said he was okay with the weather conditions because it made for better surveillance. That was exactly how he put it.

It was early morning, just a minute past five-thirty, four days after the day they had tracked Luke Olsen to the truck stop and lost him, when Mack met up with Arnold Stonebridge's four security men. He'd just gone through the drill for the second time to make sure everyone was on the same page. They were all sitting inside a warm Nashville Public Works van parked across the street from the Cozy Corner Café, where John Rossmon worked. Mack pointed him out as John approached the café to start his morning shift.

"I think we can do without another pep talk, Mr. Mack," Keith said. "We have it down pat. The guy, if he shows up today, won't make a move until Rossmon finishes his shift around two this afternoon. Thanks to Mike and Dave's 'in' with the cops, we run every license plate that parks on this block. We already know the regulars. We discount female drivers, the elderly, along with teenage kids so as not to waste the PD's time. We're looking for a vehicle we haven't seen before and one that is probably registered out of Memphis, which Olsen heisted after he arrived in Memphis, thanks to a trucker who drove him there."

Mack sighed. He hated it when the people he worked with got cocky. Not that these guys had reached that point, but they were close. They were irritated that they were spending hours and hours watching and waiting, but that's what stakeouts were. Boring and mind bending. The one thing working against them, and Mack said so, was the crowds of holiday shoppers as the countdown drew closer to Christmas. Why couldn't this little street that housed the Cozy Corner Café be nestled among body-parts stores, dry cleaners, and the like instead of the quaint one-of-akind boutiques that women so loved to shop in for the holidays.

Crowds just didn't work for those doing the surveillance; it gave an edge to the person or persons being surveyed. In addition to the crowds, clothing, reversible jackets, and colored hats and caps just added to the problem. It was too easy to switch a black watch cap to a bright red or yellow one. All one had to do was duck into a doorway, remove a jacket, turn it inside out, and the wearer went from beige to dark green or plaid. He lost count of the people he'd tailed and lost for those same reasons over the years when he worked for the FBI. For some reason, these guys were just not getting it, so he kept hammering it home every chance he got. In the end, he sighed and climbed out of the van.

Before he closed the door to the van, Mack leaned in and let loose with his daily reminder. "Mr. Stonebridge has taken a strong liking to Mr. Rossmon and for some reason has taken responsibility for him, so please, don't let him down." And his little speech worked. Until the next time or the weather changed.

Mack walked along, his head down against the wind as his thoughts raced. He was parked two blocks over, totally out of eyesight of the Cozy Corner Café. He climbed into his very ordinary silver Honda and turned on the engine and the heater. He looked at the gas gauge and was glad he'd filled it up the night before. He waited till the car warmed up before he drew his file folder out of the pocket on the side of the car. Today was the day. He was sure of it. Olsen was going to make his move. According to all the information he'd gathered on his profile, plus reading up on similar cases, he was convinced that Olsen had moved up two steps. He'd shelved Beth for the moment, thinking that once he got Rossmon out of the way, she would fall into his arms. Pure Stalker 101. For some ungodly reason, the stalkers never thought beyond the point where they eliminated the person they perceived

FERN MICHAELS

as standing in their way. All they could think was that the path was now clear to their real objective, the person they were stalking. They never thought the police would intervene, never gave a thought about going to jail. Never thought there would be witnesses. Luke Olsen fit into that category so perfectly that Dr. Sonja Hill, the person who wrote the book, could have interviewed Luke Olsen personally.

Mack had read the doctor's book word for word, from beginning to end, at least three times. He could practically recite it verbatim. Today was the day. He could feel it in every fiber of his being.

Mack leaned back in his seat, turned the heater to low, then cracked both front windows. He made sure the doors were locked before he closed his eyes. Not to sleep but to think.

While Mack was thinking, John waited tables, as the four security men talked among themselves, and Beth worked in the kitchen alongside Arnold Stonebridge, preparing the daily breakfast. They'd become friends, best friends actually,

PERFECT MATCH**                                   **425**

since her return from Garden Grove. She
adored the little man with the sad eyes. She
wished there was something she could do
to erase that look. Beth, the world's fixer
upper. Which reminded her, she had to call
Moose for a progress report. After breakfast
would be soon enough.

"You have that faraway look, Beth. Are
you thinking about your brother?" Arnold
asked.

"Among other things, you are a mind
reader, are you not, Mr. Stonebridge?"
Beth giggled.

"When are you going to start calling me
Arnold? I'm sorry, but I can't read minds.
You just look far away."

"I think you'll always be Mr. Stonebridge
to me. That's a good thing. You earned
that title. Actually, I was thinking about
Jake. After we clean up here, I'm going
to call Moose and get a progress report,"
Beth said as she poured orange juice from
the juicer into a pitcher. She carried it over
to one of the tables and set it down.

"I am so glad you made the decision to
let me decorate this place for Christmas.

All the trees and evergreens will get here midmorning. I just love Christmas, don't you?"

"Not exactly. My life hasn't been one... oh, let's not go there today."

"Okay, we won't go there today, but we are going to go there one day. Is this the first year that you are going to close Rootie Tootie's for Christmas Eve and Christmas Day?"

Arnold laughed. "It was your idea. You said decorate. I said okay. John said close, and I said okay. You said private Christmas party, and I said okay. It wasn't my idea, but now that I have agreed, I am actually looking forward to it. I'm thinking it's my first real Christmas. With real friends."

Beth laughed as she squeezed more oranges. "I bet Denny's and the Cozy Corner Café loved you when you asked for breakfast and dinner gift vouchers for your...um...flock."

"They did indeed." Arnold laughed. He really liked his new friend. He looked forward to meeting her brother and best friend, Gracie, and the miracle dog. As well as the cranky man called Moose. Beth had assured him they would all travel to Nashville for a big, old-fashioned Christmas. When he was alone in his apartment at night, and he thought about it, he got so excited he could hardly stand it. It was almost like he had a real family. He didn't tell anyone, but he had gone on the Internet and researched family Christmases so he wouldn't make a fool of himself.

"Are we going to string popcorn and cranberries on garlands?"

"You bet. Hope you're handy with a needle," Beth quipped.

Arnold hoped he was, too. How hard could that be? He laughed out loud.

"FedEx should be arriving by ten this morning. I asked Gracie to send me all my mom's Christmas decorations. Jake was never into it, so I claimed them all. All of the junk we made when we were kids goes on the tree. Wait till you see it all. Sometimes it makes me cry, the memories are so vivid. Every ornament, every whatever, has a story or a memory. I hope

Jake remembers. I want this Christmas to be special for him. I ordered a skateboard for him for Christmas."

Arnold laughed so hard, the tears rolled down his cheeks. Yessiree, he really loved this young woman. In a brotherly, avuncular, fatherly kind of way. He felt the same way about John. He wondered if what he felt for these two young people was what a parent felt. He rather thought it was. And now he was beyond excited that he was going to see and help decorate a Christmas tree for the first time in his life.

Life was good. Very good. Super good. Really, really, really good.

By nine-thirty, the kitchen was clean and tidy and everything put back in its place. "Time to call Mr. Moose, Beth."

Beth nodded. "I'll call Moose and put him on speaker so you can hear firsthand how things are going. Okay?" Arnold nodded as he handed Beth a cup of fresh coffee.

"So, Moose, how's it going?" Beth asked.

"Well, it's going, Beezer. He's walking, not much, but he's walking. Gizmo is right there with him. I swear by all that is holy, that dog is the best thing that ever happened to Jake. When he slumps, he's right there to prop him up. Yesterday, he was telling the other soldiers about the last Super Bowl, and he fell asleep. Giz got right up there in his face and barked in his ear to get with the program. No pain no gain, you know how that works. Gracie lets me take him every day. The guys love it, and so does he. Did she ever tell you what goes on there?"

"No, not really. Tell me." She winked at Arnold and wiggled her eyebrows to indicate he should pay attention.

"Well, the dog goes in wearing his protective gear with all his medals and his dog tags. The top dog in the center, meaning the guy that runs the joint, blows a whistle, and yells real loud, 'Officer on deck!' Now they know that's a navy saying, but he does it anyway. The reason being Gizmo was awarded a field promotion to lieutenant, but the paperwork didn't go through until after...well you know, after. So Gizmo doesn't recognize the term **lieutenant** and only responds to **sergeant.**

Everyone stops what they're doing, comes to attention, and salutes Giz. He eats it up. The dog's a big ham. He snaps off a salute himself, barks, and then it's business as usual."

Beth risked a look at Arnold, who was holding his sides and laughing uproariously. She'd never seen this side of the little man.

"So what are the doctors saying, Moose?"

"That Jake is progressing beyond their expectations. When he starts to slack, Giz nips him in the butt. He's good, Beth. Really good. I didn't tell him yet about Christmas. I want it to be a surprise. The doctors say he can't do that long of a road trip, so we're flying. Jake can afford to take us all in a private plane, he just doesn't know it yet. I do not foresee a problem. Oh, one other thing. He's got just about every paper, every file you sent him memorized. He does his cadence to your instructions. Giz cheers him on."

"Has Gracie been to see him?"

"No. She calls, though, to talk to the dog. I swear, he listens and barks an answer, different barks, different tones.

Some sharp, some medium. Whatever, they seem to communicate well even if it is over the phone. Gracie does miss him, though. And the dog misses her. When he's done for the day, he goes by the door and waits. She calls every day, sometimes two or three times."

"Okay, that all sounds good, Moose. Don't say I called."

"I told him you were at the hospital. He didn't believe me. He asked the doctor, and when he said yes, I swear, Beezer, his eyes filled up."

"Well, I have some stuff to do, so I'll hang up now," Beth said with a catch in her voice. "Hug Giz for me. Tell him I miss him, okay?"

"Will do, Beezer, will do."

"I can't wait to meet that dog," Arnold said.

Beth looked at the little man and smiled. "He's as big as you are."

Arnold laughed just as the front door opened. The FedEx driver wheeled in three huge boxes on a dolly. "Delivery for Beth Masters; you gotta sign for it, lady."

Beth scrawled her signature on some kind of black box and looked at Arnold.

"One Christmas, coming up."

"Can we open them now, so I can see it all?" Excitement rang in the little man's voice.

"Absolutely. Oh, oh, I hear a truck out back. You open the boxes, and I'll have the guys bring in the trees and evergreens," Beth said, pure happiness ringing in her voice.

Arnold Stonebridge wasn't sure if he had died and gone to heaven or was dreaming as he slit the tops of the huge boxes with a paring knife from the kitchen. He looked around to see if anyone was watching. Satisfied that he was alone, he did a little hop, skip, and twirl-around jig. Then he clapped his tiny hands like a little kid.

Life was good.

# Chapter Twenty-three

While Beth regaled Arnold with stories of each Christmas ornament Gracie had sent on, two of his handymen were busy setting up the four live balsam firs that had just been delivered. Beth pounded nails and hooks into every place in the vast club that could hold a swag or garland of the delicious-smelling evergreens. She swooned at the scent as she remembered other Christmases when she was young. One in particular was when she was ten years old and woke in the middle of the night, trying to figure out what she was smelling that was so wonderful.

Arnold was holding a Popsicle-stick figure with glued on cotton balls. On the back it said Jake Masters and the date he'd made it. "Oh, it smells so…so…"

"Christmasy!" Beth giggled.

Arnold stood in the center of the club and looked around, the stick figure in his tiny hands. "I didn't know this is what

Christmas was supposed to smell like. I like it. It's...it's..."

"Wonderful?" Beth giggled again. "The most wonderful time of year in my opinion. Okay, I'm going to call you Arnold now because I see you get it. You have finally let your hair down and stopped being so reserved. Now you're Arnold."

"Is that what you thought?" Arnold asked curiously. "That I was reserved?"

"Yes and no," Beth said as she hammered home a nail and hooked one end of a garland around the nail. "I think it was, is, a defense mechanism. I'm just ordinary, Arnold. You can be yourself around me. Today, we are both going to act like little kids and get this place fixed up like a Christmas wonderland. I want to stand with you up in your apartment and look down on the floor when the crowd comes in tonight. No one is expecting to see the magic we are going to perform, starting right now. You get to hang the ornaments on the lower branches, I'll do the middle, and your people can do the top. That big, old, fluffy, ragged-looking angel has seen better days, but it's still going on top of the big center tree. I personally glued every one of those cotton balls on the frame. My mom said it was the most beau tiful angel she'd ever seen."

"And she was right. We shall treat this angel with all the respect she deserves."

"The worst part of all this is untangling the strings of lights and getting them sitting perfect on the tree. These are the old-fashioned kind, where the bulbs burn out. If that doesn't happen at least twice during the Christmas season, then Christmas is a bust. That's what my dad used to say. Your people can do that— the stringing of the lights, I mean. Oh, Arnold, wait till you see these trees when the lights come on. It's like magic."

"Do you think John will be upset that we started without him?"

"Maybe a little, but he'll get over it. He should be here soon unless the café is extra busy today. Usually, by now he's texting me saying he's on his way home."

"Maybe we should wait till he gets here. Let's go into the kitchen, and I'll make us some of my special Kona coffee. I got a gift packet sent to me years ago by one of my favorite singers, and I've been hooked on it ever since. While we wait for John, you can tell me about your childhood Christmases. And John's."

"Only if you tell me about yours," Beth quipped.

"There's nothing to tell, Beth. The people who raised me didn't believe in anything, especially Christmas. It was just another day. I used to cut out pictures from magazines and papers and put them together and try to envision what it was like. Sad to say, I never felt anything. So, this is a first for me, and for that, I thank you."

Beth felt like crying for some reason. "We're going to sing carols," she said inanely.

Arnold laughed. "You can't sing, Beth."

"What was your first clue?" Beth grinned.

"When you fessed up," Arnold chortled. "You just sit there and text John to see how late he's running while I get the coffee ready. You might want to check in with your Mr. Moose, too."

"Sounds like a plan," Beth said as she pulled out her phone.

John was cashing in his tips with the owner of the Cozy Corner Café when he felt his phone vibrate in his pocket.

Probably Beth wanting to know why he was running late. He'd check the message on his way out.

"Good day today," the owner, Tess Glassman, said as she counted out bills and deposited the loose change and bills in the register.

John accepted the bills, folded them, then buried them in his pocket next to his cell phone. "See ya tomorrow, Miss Glassman."

"Have a good day, John."

John stood to the side to let the last few customers leave ahead of him. It was his job to close the blind on the door and turn the sign that read OPEN to CLOSED. He knew Miss Glassman would lock up behind him. It was a good day. He'd made $140 in tips, almost twice what he'd made on other days. But it was, after all, the Christmas season, and people tended to be a little more generous at this time of year.

John stood under the overhang for a moment as he watched the crowds of shoppers hustling along with their bulging shopping bags. He should think about what he was going to get Beth for Christmas....

Something suddenly felt off to him. He likened it to the feeling he had in Iraq, before he would set out on a patrol. He'd learned back then to pay attention to his sixth sense, something up until then he attributed to women only. Now, if he were a spy, like in one of those espionage novels he was addicted to, he'd practice his tradecraft and know instantly something or someone was out there waiting to pounce on him.

He was already running fifty minutes late. Beth was going to pitch a fit to be sure. He'd given her his word he'd be there to help decorate the club. Still, something wasn't feeling right, so he stood rooted in place under the overhang. It was really cold, so he started to stamp his feet and blow on his hands as he let his gaze go up and down the street. Just people. Nothing was jumping out at him. Go? Don't go? He hunched into his down jacket and flew out of the doorway and headed straight for the middle of the road so he could run the distance to the club. No way could he traverse the crowded sidewalks with all the shoppers. While there was traffic on the road, it was minimal, and he could hear a car if it came too close. Crap! He'd forgotten to check his text message. By now Beth must be wild with worry. Ten minutes tops, and he'd be at the club. If he kissed her till her teeth rattled, she'd forgive him. Hopefully.

It all happened so quickly, John was hard-pressed later on to tell the authorities what happened. One minute he was running full tilt trying to get to the side of the road when a car horn blasted his eardrums. The next minute, he felt a searing pain in his left side, and he was lying on the ground with people yelling and screaming as car doors slammed open. He tried to get up but couldn't move. He heard someone shout to call 911. He wondered if the call was for him. He shook his head, trying to clear it. When he opened his eyes, he saw Jim Mack hovering over him. He knew his coat was open because he could feel the cold and someone poking him and pressing at his side. Because...because... something felt warm and wet. Why would his side be warm and wet?

"EMS is on the way, John. That bastard stabbed you, but my guys got him. Well, Mr. Stonebridge's guys got him. The cops are on the way. Hang on, John. You're gonna be okay, but you're losing blood. You hear me, John? Hang on."

John felt so woozy. Someone had stabbed him. Who? Beth was going to be so pissed. He was late, and now he was going to be even later if he had to go to the hospital. "Call Beth," he whispered. "She's going to be mad because I'm so late. She hates it when I'm late."

"I already called her. She'll meet us at the hospital, and no, she isn't mad."

Mack stood and watched the ambulance careen down the street. The EMS guys flew out of the ambulance and took over. Minutes later, John was on a gurney and being loaded into the ambulance. Mack watched until the driver turned on the siren and the ambulance was out of sight before he approached Stan and Keith, who had Luke Olsen handcuffed to the car door. Two police officers were pushing the crowd of lookie-lous back to the sidewalk as their partners took charge of Olsen, who was babbling about teddies, Victoria's Secret, and guys who just didn't belong in his universe.

The moment the crowd thinned out, Jim Mack led the guys back to where they were parked. "You guys did good. Great job. Now if John had stuck to the sidewalk, I think it would have been a different story. Olsen could have gotten away. You know what they say, everything happens for a reason. John's going to be okay. The down jacket's thick padding saved him. In a couple of days, he'll be good as new. I'll follow you guys to the precinct, and from there, after we give our statements, we'll head to the hospital."

● ● ●

It was five-thirty when John opened his eyes to see a sea of concerned faces. He felt a warm hand covering his. Beth. He could smell her shampoo, like coconut and summer breezes. He smiled.

He looked off to the side and saw Arnold Stonebridge. He frowned. "They said you never leave the premises, sir. What are you doing here?" At least that's what he thought he said, but his mouth felt like it was full of sand.

"Well, technically that's true, but when a friend such as yourself ends up here, I had no other choice. I like to see certain things with my own eyes as opposed to having someone tell me what's going on. And Beth needed company." John thought the little man's voice sounded cheerful. That had to mean he was okay.

John's eyelids drooped. He was so tired. He heard someone say he'd lost a lot of blood. "What about dinner? The decorating? The band, the club?" he muttered.

"Oh, that! I shut it down and put a sign on the door. My people are taking care of things. Right now, that isn't important. **You** are what's important."

John wanted to say something complimentary, something important to the little man, but he couldn't get the words past his lips. He wanted to say what he felt, but his eyes closed. He felt Beth's hand squeeze his as he drifted into a restful sleep.

"He really is going to be all right, isn't he, Jim?" Beth asked anxiously.

"Right as rain in a few days. They're keeping him overnight, and they said you have to leave. All of us have to leave. I engaged the services of a private-duty nurse, who will stay with him until he is discharged."

"What about that evil person who did this to him?" Arnold asked.

"He is behind lock and key. The detective I spoke with said he was out of it, babbling nonsense. They have a call in to mental health professionals and, of course, they called his parents. Surprise, surprise, the parents didn't seem one bit concerned and said they would get back to the detectives.

"I clued the police in on what's been going

on. Tomorrow, they want you, Beth, to go down to the precinct and give a statement. I'll take you. They'll talk to John here at the hospital first thing in the morning before he's discharged."

"I think this calls for a celebration of sorts," Arnold said, as he slipped his arms through the sleeves of his overcoat. "By that I mean I think we should all celebrate back at the club by finishing up the decorating and maybe ordering some pizza. I can make us some eggnog. I think that's what you drink during the holidays. Does that work for everyone?" Everyone said it did.

"Really, Jim, it's over? I mean, I don't have to worry about John or myself any longer?"

"Safe as can be. Luke Olsen won't be going anywhere for a very long time. If he gets the help he needs, he might make a full recovery, but there is that attempted murder charge they're leveling at him, unless some smart defense lawyer goes with the insanity plea. Just get on with your life and don't look back. That's my advice."

"And she's going to take it. I'll make sure of that," Arnold said.

"You all go ahead. I'll meet you in the lobby. I want a few minutes with John."

When the door closed behind the gaggle of people who had been in the room, Beth ran to the bed and planted a big kiss on John's lips. "Oh, God, John, I don't know what I would do if something happened to you. You're the reason I get up in the morning. You're the wind beneath my wings. I know that's what you always say to me, but now it's my turn to say it to you. Oh, and another thing. I want us to get married in February, right after we cut the CD. Jake will just have to do overtime on his therapy so he can walk me down the aisle. I'm going to have a regular parade. Gizmo leading, then Arnold, and then me, Jake, and Moose heading down that aisle. Gracie is going to be my maid of honor. I think you should have Jim Mack be your best man. Who cares if it's politically correct or not as far as weddings go. My mind is made up.

I hope you heard all that, John Rossmon, 'cause I'd hate to have to say it all over again in the same order."

"I heard you. Now go home, so I can go to sleep," John muttered, just as Beth clamped her lips over his. This time he responded in kind.

"You big phony!"

"Takes one to know one."

Beth almost swallowed John's tonsils when she drew a deep breath and pulled away. He couldn't know. Could he?

# Chapter Twenty-four

Beth Masters decided she was happier than she'd ever been in her entire life. Her world was what she called just perfect, and she made no bones about saying it over and over to anyone who would listen.

John had healed quickly, and except for a stitch in his side from time to time, his harrowing experience didn't keep him from being as happy as Beth was. If there was a fly in the ointment, as Arnold put it, it was that he couldn't handle his celebrity status. He almost blacked out when he saw his picture on the front page of the local newspaper that reported on his attack. People came into the Cozy Corner Café and left him outrageous tips. Not because of the attack but because of his celebrity status at Rootie Tootie's. These days, it was standing room only, with fire marshals at the ready.

The best part of everything was the new family they had acquired via Arnold

Stonebridge. As Beth said, "This is where we belong and where we are going to stay." John agreed.

They were all counting down the days to Christmas Eve, when Arnold would close up so they could all be together. Beth was so giddy she could hardly stand herself. Everyone she held dear to her heart would be here, and they would all be together. She was so excited about seeing her brother, it was all she could talk about.

Beth and John moved back to their first apartment the day after Luke Olsen was taken into custody. She helped Arnold at the club, then went home to finish up all the last-minute details needed for the February studio date. She didn't know who was more excited, she or Arnold, who promised to attend. John just took it in stride. Little did he know he was going to be the star.

Afternoons were spent looking for a house that could double as a satellite office for Perfect Match. That was her true calling, and she knew it. She was a little antsy about developing what she thought of as her "specialty groups," specific segments of the population who wanted to date each other. Gracie was all for it. The minute they went viral, they had been inundated with requests from prospective clients. The usual trash appeared on sites saying Perfect Match was exploiting various groups. That got Beth's dander up and she dived in full bore. Everyone deserved to be as happy as she was. So what if some guy had a club foot and was shy and afraid to put himself out there. There was someone for him. Beth just had to find that perfect person. And it was working. Now all they had to do was fine tune her plan and arrange a big get-together. Free of charge. Because she wasn't taking money from anyone unless they trusted her and committed to the plan.

Her first big test, which only she and Gracie knew about, were the little people. They sent out the inquiries one right after the other. One tentative response led to another, then another, and now they had a roster of twenty little people who were interested in meeting others like themselves. Beth was on it night and day. As was Gracie.

Moose had called two days after Jake's surgery with a suggestion that he said came from Jake. Jake saw a need for handicapped people to get together, for the same reason the man with the club foot had reached out to them— he was afraid to put himself out there for fear of rejection. Moose went on to say Jake wanted to work on that and felt he would be an asset. Beth's fist shot in the air when she heard that.

It was all coming together. It was all about caring and details.

Beth's arm snaked out to grab her cell phone when it pinged to life. It was Gracie. "Just so you know, we're getting some bad press from the company I used to work for. I want your permission to get down and dirty with those guys. Do I have it?"

"You got it. They're jealous, Gracie. They see us raking in piles of money by specializing. They should only know we're doing it for free. A yearly membership of a hundred dollars divided into twelve payments. Eight dollars and thirty-three cents a month. Yep, we're raking in the bucks. Do what you gotta do, say what you gotta say, and don't look back."

"You okay, Beth?"

"Better than I've ever been. Have you been to see Jake?"

"I go every day and take Gizmo. He really likes Jake."

Beth laughed. "Well, that's as good of an excuse as any, I guess. Are you two getting along?"

"We are. I like him, Beth. He likes me. We're friends. That's it, okay? If something is meant to happen, it will. No matchmaking here. I mean it."

"I hear you. You're on your own. So everything is good, no more blowback from the hacking?"

"Good to go. Artie and Andy have it contained. I can't believe it's almost Christmas. Four more days! I've missed you, girl!"

"Yeah. I'm going to be staying on, Gracie. I love it here. I think I have a lead on a cozy little house not too far from here. John loves it as much as I do, and we both feel like we have this really big family that we have to look out for. I think I was meant to be here. Just took me a while to figure it out."

"I'm glad, Beth. I gotta run. Giz is ready to go, and when he's ready, he's ready, so I'll call you when I get back from the rehab center. You sure you don't want me to tell Jake he's going to Nashville?"

"Not until an hour before. That's the plan, so let's stick to it. Can I hang up knowing February is when we go live? Valentine's Day!"

"Absolutely! I have to be honest, Beth. When you tossed that out to me, I didn't think there was a snowball's chance in hell we could make it work in your time frame. But, things just magically fell into place. So, yeah, it's a go."

Beth trilled with laughter. "See, you just gotta believe. When something is meant to be, then it's meant to be. I'm off now to pick up Jake's Christmas present. I had them engrave his name on the skateboard."

She could hear Gracie laughing as she broke the connection.

"Four more days to Christmas! Four more days to Christmas," Beth sang to herself as she bundled up to go out to finish her Christmas shopping and take one last look at the little house she planned on buying. How alive she felt! How happy! She said a silent little prayer that things would always be this good.

It was four o'clock in the morning when Moose Dennison opened the door to Jake's bedroom. Gizmo was on his feet in a second. He tilted his head as he waited for an explanation. "We're going to Nashville, Sergeant. Gracie, too. She thought Jake might need you this morning. You're getting this, right?" Gizmo yipped.

"Up! Up! Up! C'mon, Jake, we're going places today!" Jake rolled over, grumbled something, then rolled back over.

"Get him up, Sarge!"

Gizmo was on the bed and ripping at the covers as he pushed and shoved Jake to the end of the bed. Moose turned on the shower, all the while yelling "time was of the essence" and "time was money" and anything else he could think of to wake up Jake.

"What the hell! Have you lost your mind, Moose? It's only four o'clock! Go away!"

"If I tell that dog to bite your ass, you know damn well he will. What's it going to be?" Moose bellowed.

"Why? Just tell me why you're getting me up at four o'clock in the morning."

"We're going to Nashville! For Christmas! Beth invited us! I rented a Gulfstream and used your credit card. I didn't think you'd mind. The shower is running, and this here dog has to go out to pee, so are you gonna move, or do I have to drag your sorry ass all the way into the bathroom? Tell me you aren't going to blow this gig!"

Jake was suddenly wide awake. "Are you lying to me, Moose? Did Beth really invite us to Nashville?"

"She did, and she arranged everything except for the Gulfstream. Calvin even arranged for a therapist, so you won't miss a thing. We're staying three days. Move your ass, son!"

Jake reached for his canes and almost ran to the shower.

Moose and Gizmo headed for the stairs. They had all the time in the world because the pilot had told him wheels up would be eight o'clock. Jake did move a tad slow in the mornings. Moose firmly believed the early bird got the worm.

Forty minutes later Moose blinked when he looked up to see Jake standing in the doorway. He was what he called so spruced up it was hard to believe it was Jake Masters. And he smelled mighty damn good. Gizmo barked either at Jake's appearance or as a reminder to Moose that he was waiting for the bacon and sausage sizzling on the stove.

"Lookin' pretty fancy there, son," Moose drawled.

"Yeah," Jake drawled in return. "You want to tell me how this all came about, or are you going to make me pull it out of you?"

"It was all Beth's idea. I think she's ready to forgive you. Now, that's just my opinion.

On the other hand, maybe this up-close-and-personal gig is so she can give you one final kick in the butt."

"Whose idea was it to rent a private plane?"

"Well, twern't hers. That was all my doing. So don't go blaming her."

"Where are we staying?"

"I rented us all rooms at the Best Western. And they said Giz can stay or he can stay with Beth. Guess it's up to the dog. Seems to me that dog makes all the decisions around here. I grant you, they're good ones," Moose said, one eye on Giz and the other on the frying pan.

"Did you know Gracie put him out for stud a while back? She told me that last week. One of the officers at the rehab center said the K-nine leader contacted him. The government paid her a bundle of money, and she got pick of the litter. She said the pup would be ready to be picked up after the New Year."

Moose pretended amazement. "You mean there are going to be **two** of them there killer dogs out there! Well, woo hoo and all that!"

"I'd be careful what you say around Giz. He takes things personally," Jake said, trying not to laugh.

Moose bent over and looked the big dog in the eye. "So then, big fella, what do I call you, Sergeant or Daddy?" Giz dropped to the floor and buried his face in his paws, as much as to say "I can't deal with stupid so early in the morning." Jake laughed till he choked.

"Just toast and yogurt, Moose," Jake said when he got his laughter under control.

Giz was on his feet and nudging Moose's leg. He was ready to eat.

"It has to cool off first, Sarge. The eggs are ready, though." He set the plate on the floor, but Giz didn't go near it.

"You just don't get this dog, Moose. He wants it all on the plate at the same time. If it's too hot, he'll wait till it cools. Gracie said that's how smart he is. And she should know."

"You two are getting kind of...close, I'm thinking."

"I wish. I like her a lot. I still think she

has...I'm not sure she's over Giz's previous owner. I'm patient."

"Sometimes, a man just has to be patient," Moose said dryly, his head bobbing up and down.

Both Moose and Jake watched Gizmo as he sniffed his food. He took a cautious lick and then dived into his human breakfast of six eggs, four links of sausage, and four strips of bacon. "Don't look at me like that, Jake! Gracie said the dog's vet said he was in perfect health, and if that's what his handler fed him, then it works. And when something works, you don't mess around with it. Sometimes he gets dog food, but he won't eat it, so Gracie said he knows she's just messing with him."

When the dog finished, he walked over to the door, and Moose let him out.

"It's just six-thirty. Now what are we going to do, play cards or something till it's time to leave for the airport? You could have let me sleep a little longer."

"I wanted you bright eyed and bushy tailed," Moose grumbled as he cleaned up the dishes and turned on the dishwasher.

"Now that we have this...togetherness thing going on, this might be a good time for you to tell me what else you and Beezer have been keeping from me. Well?"

"Nary a thing, son. Sorry. You might as well read the morning paper online. I have to get my gear ready."

And that was that!

The sleek, silver Gulfstream touched down at Nashville International Airport precisely on time. Travel time—one hour and four minutes. The minute the powerful engines shut down, Giz unbuckled his seat belt and hopped into the aisle. He waited for Gracie and her carry bag before he marched to the front of the plane. The hostess held out a treat that Gracie had slipped to her earlier. She handed it over. The pilot leaned out to see who was first in line. Then he stood up. Gracie winked at him and mouthed the words, "He's waiting for you to salute him. It's the uniform."

The pilot, a tall, handsome, gray-haired man, grinned as he offered up a snappy salute. Gizmo returned one that was just as snappy, along with a sharp bark. "It's been a pleasure having you on board, Sergeant. You can fly with me anytime." Giz barked to show he'd consider the offer, then they were going down the portable stairs, where a long black limousine waited for them.

Jake eyed the limo and turned to Moose. "You really had a good time spending my money, didn't you?"

"I purely did. Wait till you get the bill for all the pres ents I bought."

Jake laughed out loud. He was loving every moment of this last-minute trip he'd been kept in the dark about.

Finally, all on his own, Jake made it to the bottom of the stairs and all the way to the waiting limo. Giz was at his side the whole way. Gracie beamed her pleasure as he also managed with only a little difficulty to get into the back of the limo on his own.

"Jesus! I did it! I did it! I feel like I just ran a ten-mile minimarathon! I did it!"

Gizmo was all over him, licking his face, nudging him everywhere to show his approval. "I want this dog! Do you hear me,

Gracie? I want this dog!"

"It's a package deal, Jake," Gracie said in a tickly kind of voice. **Oh, be still, my heart.**

**Oh, man, did this woman just say what I thought she said?** For a moment, Jake thought he might black out.

"Yeah, I kind of thought that might be the case," he replied. "Okay, I'll take you, too."

They bantered back and forth for the whole hour's drive to Rootie Tootie's.

When they arrived, Jake admitted to the fact that while he got into the limo by literally falling in, he wasn't sure he could get out the same way. The driver and Moose made it happen, with Giz dancing around to make sure nothing went awry.

The door to the club blew open, and Giz raced to Beth, who stood rooted to the spot. She wanted to run to her brother, but she knew it was the wrong thing to do. He had to walk to her. To prove he could do it. She sucked in her breath while she waited. Her eyes on Jake and only Jake, she could feel but not see that John and Arnold were at her side. She could also feel her heart pounding inside her chest as her eyes filled up. She wanted to run to help this giant of a big brother, but she didn't move. She watched as he gritted his teeth and made sure the two canes were secure on his elbows before he crossed the short distance to where she was standing in the doorway. She could see that his eyes were as wet as hers.

"Beezer!"

"Jake!"

Beth's arms shot out. Moose and Gracie moved quickly to get in place behind Jake so he didn't topple backward. For a little girl, Beth was surprisingly strong. She held him so tight Jake thought she might crack his ribs, and he loved every minute of the pain he was enduring.

"Beezer...I'm so sorry. Jake Masters, also known as a lazy laggard, whiny puke, and a king-sized pain in the ass, reporting in," he said, his voice gruff and garbled.

Beth smiled. "Yeah, but that was then. This is now. At this moment in time, you're just Jake Masters, the big brother I love and adore above all else. Brother and sister again, okay?"

"Yeah. But, Beezer, I need to hear you say the words. I really need to hear you tell me you forgive me. If you don't, then I have to turn around and leave."

"Jackass! Of course I forgive you. Do you think I did all this for nothing? Sometimes, you are dumber than dumb." She lowered her voice, and whispered, "Did you hit on Gracie yet? She's ready to be hit on."

"Uh-huh. Sort of. Kind of. Hell, yeah, I did." Beth giggled at the shocked look on her brother's face. "Crap, you set me up. You knew that would happen! I'll be damned!" Beth just continued to giggle.

Then they were inside the club and out of the cold. Jake gulped in air as he looked around at all the trees and garlands and the people standing there waiting to be introduced. He almost lost it and probably would have, but he felt Giz behind him and knew he'd bite his ass if he didn't man up right now. As in right now!

"Hi. I'm Jake Masters. This is my...my other father, Moose. And the lady is my very good friend, Gracie. This," he said, touching Giz's head, "is Gizmo. My mentor. I do not have the words right now to tell you how happy I am to be here."

"Well, damn, man, it's good to see you," John said, wrapping his arms around Jake's shoulders. "This is Mr. Arnold Stonebridge. Beth and I work for him, and he owns the club."

"It's nice to finally meet you, Jake. Call me Arnold. Your sister has told me so much about you, I feel I know you." He held out his tiny hand, and Jake clasped it in both his, and it was difficult, but he knew somehow that the handshake was important to the little man.

"I wish I could say the same thing, but I didn't find out about any of this till four o'clock this morning. I hope we can sit down and talk."

"Absolutely. And who is this beautiful animal? It must be Gizmo! I've heard all about you, too, Sergeant." Arnold held out his hand again, and Giz offered his. A treat found its way to Arnold's hand. He held it out. Giz took it and carried it over to the biggest Christmas tree in the room and lay down.

Jim Mack finished up the introductions, then they all trooped into the kitchen, where a catered lunch was set out. The hours flew by as the small group talked about past Christmases, friends, and families, until Arnold called a halt and said it was time to gather around the tree in the center of the club and sing carols. "I just want you all to know that this is my very first Christmas with a real family. Beth and John have graciously included me, and I want to thank you for the privilege.

"Since this is my first real Christmas, I have to go by what Beth and John have told me, which is, first we eat this big, as in big, dinner, which will be arriving soon, catered, of course. Then we clean up. That means everyone hustles because they want to get to all those exquisite packages underneath the tree. But first we sing all the Christmas carols, and it doesn't matter if you can sing or not." His eyes went to Beth, and everyone laughed out loud.

"Then we all walk around the Christmas tree and look at the ornaments and relive memories. After that, we all go to the window to look outside to see if it's snowing, which the weatherman said wouldn't happen, but we're going to do it anyway.

"And then we gather around the tree again and we all say a silent prayer for peace on earth and wish all men and women goodwill."

"And then we sit down and open all the presents!" Beth squealed at the top of her lungs. "I'm sorry I stole your last line, Arnold."

"That's okay." The little man laughed. "I hear the caterers in the kitchen setting up dinner. We're having candles and everything because I saw that in a picture once. And there is a small, real-live Christmas tree in the center of the table that is all decorated. I can't wait. Welcome to my home, everyone! And Merry Christmas!"

Jim Mack moved and scooped the little man up in his arms, to Arnold's complete surprise. For a moment he wasn't sure what he should do—be embarrassed, be insulted, or be happy. He looked at the happy faces around him, and said, "So this is how it feels to be up here so high! Merry

Christmas!" he bellowed.

Arnold looked at the faces staring up at him. At long last he saw what he had hungered for all his life—acceptance. He really did belong. He was finally just one of the guys, something he never, ever thought he would experience.

"To one and all," Beth and the others said, as tears streamed down their faces.

Not to be outdone, Giz let loose with three sharp barks of approval.

# Epilogue

Beth stared out the car window at the early morning. February was not one of her favorite months. It was that gray, dismal time between what was left of winter and only a memory of what spring was from the year before. Plus it was cold. It shouldn't be cold on Valentine's Day. It should be warm to go with people's smiles. So far, she had yet to see a smile, but then, the only person she'd seen so far was John, and at best, he was grumpy. He'd only had three hours' sleep because the band had played late, and by the time they got home he was too wired up to go to sleep. She crossed her fingers that all would go well at the recording studio. If he wasn't up to his game today, all she'd done would be for nothing.

"You nervous, babe?" he asked.

"Define **nervous**." This was good. He'd initiated a conversation. Maybe he was perking up.

"You know, jittery. You've been wanting this forever, and now it's here. You have a right to be jittery. It's all going to be fine, so just relax. I'm going to be playing, too, and I'm loose as a goose." He laughed at his little joke. Actually, he wasn't loose as a goose, he was wired worse than Beth. Something in his gut told him today was going to be a total disaster for her.

"So you're happy with the producer you hired?" he asked.

"Yes. I've got it down pat. John, we spent the last six days doing the rough tracks for each song with the rhythm section, thanks to your band. We managed to mold the song, we figured out the tempo and the key. Each musician recorded his own individual track, and it will be mixed in later. We've done everything they asked us to do. Today we do the final take on the lead vocal. We've already done three takes and are good to go.

"Our engineer and producer already mixed all the tracks, so this is our final mix. Anything that could go wrong would have gone wrong by now."

"God, Beth, I had no idea it was costing fifty thousand dollars to do all this. That is one boatload of money. And you're going to be spending another fifty thousand on production and distribution."

Beth wanted to say, "John, you are worth every penny because I believe in you." But she didn't. "It is a lot of money, but one has to follow one's dream whenever possible. I'd do it all over again if I had to."

"You sure your distribution and promotion is sterling? If it isn't, then this could be a bust."

"Absolutely I am sure. Arnold helped me with that. You know he has a lot of influence here in Nashville. He assured me he has it covered. We'll get a lot of good play and press. Look, John, whatever happens, happens. Today all you have to do is the one song, then you can head out to the café. An hour tops. I'll catch a ride back with Arnold. You okay with that?"

"Yeah. I'm happy as long as you're happy. So, tonight is the big party. You got that covered, too, I suppose."

Beth laughed. "Let's just say it's covered,

but not by me. Everyone else did all the work. I just got it up and running. Mandy, Callie, and Lily have their divisions in line. By now, all the clients, or guests if you prefer, should either be arriving or they came in last night. I know Gracie, Jake, and Moose got here last night. Arnold arranged for the caterer. You guys are providing the music. Rootie Tootie's is closed tonight. By the way, what do you think of Arnold's decision to buy up the two properties next to the club for expansion?"

"From what I can see, and what he told me, sounds like a tremendous investment to me. He's sharp; nothing gets by him. He's going to be mad as a wet hornet when he finds out you nominated him for Man of the Year here in Nashville. Tess at the café told me she has it on good authority he's going to take the title hands down. She had every customer who came in for the past month vote for Arnold. I'm hoping after tonight, he comes out of his shell."

"Okay, we're here, Beth. This is it, honey. You ready?"

"I am soooo ready, you have no idea,"

Beth trilled. **Oh, John, if you only knew.**

Coats, hats, mufflers, all their gear was stowed before Beth and John hit the studio. They watched as the producer, his assistant, the engineers, and the technicians readied everything. The band was in place. Arnold Stonebridge was standing on a stool behind a huge plate-glass window. His tiny fist shot in the air. Time to get this show on the road!

John was to take the lead and sing their song. He smiled at Beth as she stood to the side and watched him take a deep breath. Then the music started, and it all happened just the way she had dreamed it would.

**"When I gave my heart, you stole my soul.**
**I felt so lost and empty.**
**Your smiling lies,**
**A great disguise,**

**My tears were mighty plenty.**
**"When I look back I do remind**
**That same old saying's true:**
**Love is blind.**

**I thought you were mine.**
**What was I thinking when I was**
**thinking of you?"**

Beth didn't realize she was holding her breath until she heard the last note. It swooshed out of her as she looked up at Arnold, who was grinning from ear to ear.

**DONE!** In her heart, Beth knew John would make the charts. She just knew it. It looked to her like everyone else in the room thought so, too. Except John, who was wrapping up to hurry back to the café. He still believed this was all about Beth and not him.

The minute John waved and was out the door, Beth let loose. "Okay, you guys know what to do. You take out all my caterwauling and fix it. I'll pick it up sometime around six. Everyone clear on what you have to do? No screwups. I want to thank you all for...for going along with all this and keeping it a secret."

The producer, a man named Evan Evers, looked at Beth, and said, "The guy has the talent. From here on in, it's up to him. He doesn't even have to work at it; it all comes natural to him. Good job! Thanks for the gig, Miss Masters."

Beth laughed. "I saw you guys trying not to wince when I was singing."

"You can't sing, that's for sure. But if I recall, that's the first thing you said to me when we met. See ya around."

Beth turned around to see Arnold moving faster than she'd ever seen him move. He was grinning from ear to ear. "My dear, I didn't think it was possible, but you pulled it off. John does not have a clue he was the star of this recording. I guess you are going to have to fess up pretty darn soon. Like maybe tonight?"

Beth felt a twinge of uneasiness. Tonight she was going to have to do a lot of fessing up. She crossed her fingers that nothing backfired.

As they headed out to Arnold's specially equipped van, he chatted the whole way about how great John sounded, how confident he was that he was going to make it in the music world. From there he babbled on about the club's expansion and what it would mean for the music industry here in Nashville. Beth just kept smiling and agreeing with everything he said.

"I'm really looking forward to your get-together this evening," Arnold said as he settled himself on the hydraulic lift that put him behind the wheel. "Tell me again what it's all about. I love hearing about your business."

Beth sucked in a deep breath. This was all part of the "fessing" up that was going to either make or break her. "It's... it's just something Gracie and I do for our clients. We're kind of different in that way from the other matchmaking services, which are pretty much exclusively geared to the very young yuppies. I hate to use the term **specialize,** but in the end, that's what it is. We have divisions that cater to different demographics. I like to use the example of say, Joe Smith, who has a club foot and is shy about going out to meet someone because of his handicap. Doesn't matter if he's got a PhD in economics, and has boo koo money in the bank. People can be cruel, and I hate that. I really hate that. Why shouldn't Joe Smith have the same chances at happiness as anyone else? Why does he have to stay alone at night watching movies by himself or buying takeout because he doesn't want to face ridicule or ignorant stares? That's what I mean by **specialize.** We're working for everyone, but one division specializes in making those with challenges comfortable enough to venture out. I hope I said that right.

"Just so you know, Arnold, this is not about money; we'll be lucky if this division comes even close to breaking even. And it isn't about exploiting people with challenges. It's about giving everyone a chance at happiness. In time, we might make a small profit, but right now that isn't important to Gracie and me.

"Jake, surprisingly, because he was handicapped himself for a while, is on board with all of this, and he's into it. He does his therapy in the mornings at the rehab, and works with Gracie on Perfect Match in the afternoons. Eventually, Jake is going to work full-time with the rehab

center, and it will go back to just Gracie and
me running Perfect Match. It's all coming
full circle, Arnold. Sometimes, I wish I
wasn't such a hopeless romantic. But I am,
and I always will be. It's who I am."

Arnold smiled, and the smile stayed on
his face all the way back to the club. He
was going to say he would be standing in
the wings in case he was needed, but he
was so tuned to his new friends these days
he knew he didn't have to say the words.

Life was so meaningful these days. He
offered up a silent prayer that it would stay
that way.

The grand ballroom at the Nashville Inn was
alive with music, chatter, and laughter
as the guests of Perfect Match met the
owners for the first time. Jake, Gracie,
Gizmo, Mandy, Lily, and Callie had formed
a receiving line, which Beth joined as soon
as she arrived.

The big grand ballroom had been
decorated with fresh flowers, papier-
mâché, and strings of hearts in honor of
Saint Valentine's Day. No one was actually

dancing, but they were talking, and no one was standing around alone or acting like a wallflower. Beth's battle cry at the onset was "Mingle!" So her challenged guests mingled. As Gracie put it, there didn't look to be a shy one among the 150 guests. Because...as Jake put it, those who were challenged somehow had the ability to look beyond whatever deformity was visible to the naked eye.

Gizmo understood that this was a social occasion, and he arrived in civilian mode, not work mode. He played the room, though, going up to a blind man with a service dog named Shasha. He yipped a greeting that was returned with a yip. Then, in dog speak, he yipped again. Translation: "Wanna get together later?" The return yip was a happy sound. Translation: "Seriously, dude. I'm working. Later." Gizmo trotted off to the far wall, where a long, low table was set up for the little people. He walked among them and allowed himself to be petted and crooned to. He went right up to Arnold, who looked so dazed he appeared out of it. He nudged him to the side and yipped and growled and nipped at the little man's leg. When Arnold didn't seem to be getting the message, Jake appeared and leaned over. "When Beth says mingle, she damn well means mingle. She doesn't want you standing around staring off into space. In case you don't know this, Arnold, this whole thing is because of you. She did this all for you, so you would have someone in your life. There's a little lady over there with bright blue eyes named Emily Baker. She's been batting those baby blues at you for the last fifteen minutes. Even Gizmo picked up on it. You just gonna stand here or what?"

Or what indeed. Arnold was in full panic mode now as he looked across at Emily Baker, who was, in fact, batting her eyelashes at him. He'd noticed her before but thought she had something in her eye. Stupid is as stupid does.

Arnold started to stammer. "I don't...I never ...What do I...? I thought she had some-thing in her eye. I'm not...I had no idea..."

"Listen, Arnold. I don't even know if Tennessee has a river or not, but if it did, and I suddenly threw you in it, either you'd drown or you'd swim like hell to get out. Same thing here. March your butt over there and ask her if you can get her a glass of wine. But introduce yourself first."

"You're sure? That's all I have to do?"

"Yeah. It worked for me with Gracie. Look at us now. We're on our way to something. What do you have to lose? Miss Emily Baker is your age. She makes costumes for showgirls in Las Vegas. She is financially independent and isn't looking for someone to take care of her. She can do that all by herself. But she does want friends and a companion to go through life with. Now, are you going to go over there? Or do I have to pick you up and take you there? Which is going to be a problem with this cane, but I **will** do it."

Arnold looked up at the giant standing next to him and knew he meant every word of what he said. Best to do it on his own. "Okay, okay, I'll do it." He trotted off, Giz at his side.

"I heard all that. You're a bully, Jake Masters."

"Better than a whiny puke, right?"

Gracie doubled over laughing.

"When is Beth going to tell John what she did?" Gracie kept on laughing. "She did on the ride over here. He said he knew but let her do her thing. He said he wasn't looking for fame and fortune, and he did not want to be a big Nashville star. He wants to stay right where he is with the band and Arnold and be a help with the expansion. Beth couldn't have found a better guy."

"So everything worked out just the way it was supposed to. Do you think Beth has some kind of...of..."

Jake's head bobbed up and down. "Whatever it is, she's got it. All you have to do is look at Arnold. Damn, he's into it. Look, he's escorting Emily over to a table. He's laughing. Or is that flirting?"

"They're both flirting. Check out Gizmo and Miz Shasha over there. He's such a gentleman."

Beth joined them. "Look! Look! I knew it! I knew it!" She clapped her hands together.

"What?" Jake asked. "You mean Arnold and Emily?"

"The perfect match!"

Dear Readers,

I suspect that a lot of you readers feel depressed or sad as I do when you realize you are about to read the last page of a book, knowing it's the end. I always want more, maybe just a page; two or three would be great. It rarely if ever happens, as we all know. I decided I could give you all a few more pages by adding a delectable pie recipe that the character Moose used in **Perfect Match**.

Having said that, I just wanted you all to know that Moose borrowed (okay, he swiped it) the recipe from a beautiful, charming lady in California, and palmed it off as his own. Of course, as the author, I allowed that to happen with the beautiful, charming lady's permission.

Kudos go to Ms. Maureen Boyd Biro of California for this award-winning bourbon-pecan-pie recipe. Ms. Maureen is the mother of my editor, Martin Biro. How cool is that?

Just so you know, people, I made this pie. And I ate the whole thing all by myself. Not at one time, though. Without a doubt, this is a blow-your-mind, knock-your-socksoff pie. And the maple whipped cream was so good, I don't have the words to describe it.

Please feel free to be as effusive and complimentary as you wish by going to my Web site and posting your glowing reports if you try this recipe. I will make sure that Ms. Maureen gets all of your comments. Maybe if she gets enough of them, she will create another gourmet delight to share with all of us in my next book.

To all of you, happy reading and happy dining.

Fern

# Maureen's Rich Bourbon Pecan Pie

## INGREDIENTS

**For pie crust:**
2 cups cake flour
1/4 cup pecans, toasted, cooled,
   and finely ground
1 teaspoon brown sugar
1/2 teaspoon salt
1/3 cup chilled vegetable shortening
   (like Crisco)
1/3 cup chilled unsalted butter
   (no substitutions), cut up
3-1/2 to 4 tablespoons ice water

**For pecan filling:**
2-1/2 cups pecan halves, divided
3 large eggs, beaten
1 cup firmly packed brown sugar
3/4 cup dark corn syrup
5 tablespoons butter, melted
1-1/2 tablespoons Wild Turkey bourbon

**For maple-cinnamon whipped cream:**
2 teaspoons vanilla extract
2 cups heavy cream
1/2 tablespoon confectioners' sugar
3/4 teaspoon ground cinnamon
1-1/2 tablespoons pure maple syrup

## DIRECTIONS

1. For the pastry, combine flour, ground pecans, brown sugar, and salt in bowl or food processor. Cut in shortening and butter until mixture is crumbly. Add water one tablespoon at a time, tossing with fork, until pastry holds together, or use on/off pulse of food processor. Shape into ball and flatten slightly.

2. For the filling, coarsely chop 1-1/4 cups of the pecan halves and set aside. Beat eggs, brown sugar, corn syrup, melted butter, and bourbon, in mixing bowl at low speed until blended. Stir in chopped pecans.

3. Heat oven to 350 degrees. On lightly floured surface, roll pastry into a 12-inch circle (1/8 inch thickness). Fit into 9-inch pie plate. (If pastry cracks, gently patch by pressing with fingertips.) Trim pastry to edge of pie plate. There will be a lot of excess pastry. Reserve this for decorative border. Pour in filling. Beginning at outer edge of pie shell, arrange the remain ing 1-1/4 cups of pecan halves in concentric circles, working from the outside in to cover filling. Roll remaining pastry into a 10-inch circle. Using a miniature 1-inch leaf- or acorn-shaped cookie cutter, cut pastry into shapes. Brush edge of pastry with cold water and gently press pastry shapes around perimeter of crust, overlapping each shape slightly, to form a decorative border. Reroll scraps as needed.

Bake pie for 35 minutes, then cover pie loosely with sheet of aluminum foil to prevent overbrowning. (Do not tuck foil around pie; just lay sheet of foil loosely

over pie, if it's getting too browned.)
Bake an additional 15 minutes until
filling is set. Cool pie on wire rack.

4. For the maple-cinnamon whipped
   cream, beat cream, vanilla,
   confectioners' sugar, and ground
   cinnamon in large bowl with electric
   mixer until cream begins to thicken.
   Slowly beat in maple syrup until
   cream forms soft peaks.

5. Serve pie with maple-cinnamon
   whipped cream.

Makes 10 servings.

Store pie in refrigerator but serve at
room temperature. Pie is also delicious
slightly warmed up in microwave, then
topped with whipped cream or vanilla
ice cream.

Recipe from: Maureen Boyd Biro